SHADOWBREED

B⬛XTREE

SHADOWBREED

BY

DAVID FERRING

Published in the UK 1993 by
BOXTREE LIMITED
Broadwall House
21 Broadwall
London SE1 9PL

First published in the UK 1990 by GW Books
A Division of Games Workshop Ltd,
Chewton St, Hilltop, Eastwood, Nottingham NG16 3HY.

10 9 8 7 6 5 4 3 2 1

Typeset by DP Photosetting, Aylesbury, Bucks.
Printed in Great Britain by Cox & Wyman Ltd, Reading, Berkshire.

ISBN: 1 85283 855 8

Illustration on cover by Angus Fieldhouse
Illustration on title page by Stephen Tappin

THE OLD WORLD TIMELINE

A brief guide to the history of the Warhammer World

Year	Event
0001	The time of Sigmar - founder of the Empire, and its first Emperor. The Goblin Wars end as the Goblinoid hordes are driven back over the World's Edge Mountains into the Dark Lands.
0050	Sigmar takes his magical Warhammer back to the Dwarves who made it and is never seen again.
1111	Devastating outbreak of Black Plague reduces whole populations throughout the Empire.
1500	Religious war between Tilea/Estalia and Araby.
1547	Grand Duke of Middenland declares himself the rightful Emperor without election, starting the Age of the Three Emperors.
1750	Kislev separated from the Empire.
1839	Birth of Genevieve Dieudonné (future heroine of **Drachenfels**), in Parravon.
1851	Count Drachenfels sacks Parravon.
1855	Genevieve is turned into an immortal vampire by

Chandagnac the Ancient (cf **Drachenfels**).

1937 Drachenfels' poison feast; death of Emperor Carolus.

1979 Empress Magritta becomes last elected Emperor for 400 years.

2150 Sea Elves return to the Old World.

2177 Death of Chandagnac the Ancient - vampiric 'father' of Genevieve Dieudonné.

2262 Birth of Yevgeny Yefimovich, future high priest of Tzeentch - the Chaos God known as The Changer of the Ways.

2302 The Incursions of Chaos begin a new assault on the Old World. Magnus the Pious appears in Nuln to deliver his now legendary rallying call to arms. Under Magnus' leadership, the chaos forces are beaten back. Magnus is crowned Emperor, and goes on to restore the Empire's former glories.

2369 Death of Magnus the Pious, the crown passes to Count Leopold of Stirland.

2370 Birth of Gotrek the Dwarf - future Trollslayer.

2401 Disappearance of Emperor Matthias IV.

2429 The Burgomeisters of Marienburg declare the Wasteland's independence and secede from the Empire. Emperor Dieter IV is deposed.

2446 Birth of Vukotich the mercenary - future retainer of the von Mecklenbergs of Sudenland.

2456 Birth of the mercenary, Wolf - future companion of **Konrad**.

2460 Birth of 'Filthy' Harald Kleindeinst (hero of **Beasts in Velvet**).

2459 Birth of Oswald von Mecklenberg - Imperial Elector, Baron of Sudenland and father of Johann and Wolf (cf **Ignorant Armies**).

2465 Birth of Orfeo (narrator of **Zaragoz**, **Plague Daemon**, and **Storm Warriors**). At 8 months of age he is adopted as a foundling by the Wood Elves of the Loren forest.

2470 Harmis Detz - veteran soldier of the Border Guard of Khypris in the Border Princes - witnesses the first in a new series of attacks by followers of chaos. Against his better judgement, Harmis joins in the hunt for the plague daemon, Ystareth (cf **Plague Daemon**).

Vukotich in the Northern Forests/Chaos Wastes in the service of Tsar Radii Bokha.

2471 Birth of Detlef Sierck, greatest playwright and impressario of the Warhammer world.

2475 Birth of Johann von Mecklenberg, son of Oswald, the Baron Sudenland.

2477 Prince Oswald von Konigswald recruits a band of adventurers - including the vampire Genevieve Dieudonné - and leads them into the Grey Mountains to seek out and destroy the evil enchanter Drachenfels.

2478 Birth of Konrad; Birth of Wolf von Mecklenberg - Johann's younger brother.

2483 Vukotich impressed into the service of the von Mecklenbergs as Johann's tutor.

2490 In a village on the edge of the Forest of Shadows, the young Konrad rescues Elyssa from a Beastman, and their friendship begins (cf **Konrad**).

2491 The Chaos Champion Cicatrice mounts a raid on the summer home of the von Mecklenberg family, in the Southlands. While Johann and Vukotich escape the slaughter, Wolf is captured (cf **Ignorant Armies**).

Emperor Luitpold dies, and is succeeded by his son Karl-Franz. Birth of Prince Luitpold.

2492 On the island of Morien, Herla, King of Plenydd, and his bard Trystan come up against the malevolent influence of a group of strange Elves. Trystan later travels to Great Albion, then on to Bretonnia (cf **Storm Warriors**).

2495 Gotrek the Trollslayer, accompanied by his human companion, Felix, investigate strange goings on in the Reikwald Forest (cf **Ignorant Armies**).

2496 On their way to search for treasure in Carag Eight Peaks,

Felix and Gotrek join up with the followers of Baron Gottfried von Diehl, travelling through the Black Mountains to exile in the Border Princes (cf **Wolf Riders**).

Far beneath Carag Eight Peaks, Felix retrieves the lost sword Karaghûl (cf **Red Thirst**).

Summer solstice - Konrad's village is attacked and razed by Beastmen. Konrad meets up with the mercenary Wolf, and agrees to be his squire for 5 years (cf **Konrad**).

Around this time, the wizard Litzenreich is in Middenheim, experimenting with warpstone.

Trystan Harper meets Orfeo in Bretonnia and tells him the tale of *Storm Warriors*.

2499   Orfeo meets Harmis Detz in the Border Princes and hears the story of *Plague Daemon*.

Konrad and Wolf employed in gold mine near Belyevorota Pass in Kislev. Litzenreich the wizard is in the service of Gustav the Mad of Talabecland.

2500   **Siege of Praag** - this Kislevite city in the far north of the realm is attacked by massed forces including followers of all four of the Great Chaos Powers.

2501   Johann and Vukotich finally catch up with Cicatrice and Johann's brother, Wolf, in the Northern Chaos Wastes (cf **The Ignorant Armies**).

Summer solstice - Konrad and Wolf head north in search of treasure buried in an abandoned Dwarven temple.

Following his escape from a warband dedicated to Khorne - the Chaos Power known as the Blood God - Konrad joins forces with the wizard Litzenreich. Driven out of Middenheim for pursuing forbidden warpstone experiments, they travel to Altdorf (cf **Shadowbreed**).

2502   Under the patronage of Prince Oswald von Konigswald of Ostland, Detlef Sierck attempts to stage his play *Drachenfels* in the Castle Drachenfels itself. The performance nearly ends in disaster when the Great Enchanter returns to claim his revenge... (cf **Drachenfels**).

Konrad uncovers the true enormity of the Skaven scheme

in Middenheim and Altdorf (cf **Warblade**).

In Estalia, Orfeo the Minstrel becomes embroiled in the internal politics of Zaragoz, and barely escapes with his life (cf **Zaragoz**).

2503   Orfeo is captured by the pirate Alkadi Nasreen, and recounts to him the tales of *Zaragoz*, *Plague Daemon* and *Storm Warriors*.

Following the breakdown of Grand Theogonist Yorri, Lector Mikael Hasselstein, the Emperor's confessor, becomes the most powerful individual in the Cult of Sigmar (cf **Beasts in Velvet**).

2506   A vicious murderer stalks the streets of Altdorf. The tough copper Filthy Harald and the scryer Rosanna desperately search for the killer against a backdrop of growing civil unrest and the machinations of Chaos (cf **Beasts in Velvet**).

Johann von Mecklenberg returns to his family's estates in Sudenland as Baron and Elector.

Genevieve leaves Altdorf.

ALBION

SEA OF CLAWS

Wrecker's Point

LAURELORN FOREST

FERLANGEN

Salzenmund

NORDLAND

MIDDENHEIM

THE WASTELAND

Bergsbur

MARIENBURG

DRAK WALD FOREST

River Reik

GISOREUX

T.

Carroberg

GREY MOUNTAINS

ALTDORF

GREA

Bogenhafen

Upper Grismerie

Axe-Bite Pass

Castle Drachenfels

Grunberg

Kemperbad

Ubersreik

NULN

PARRAVON

River Aver

BRETONNIA

LOREN FOREST

Pfeildorf

AV.

River Soll

River Brienne

QUENELLES

ER OLD WORLD
Surrounding Area

NORTHERN CHAOS WASTES

ERENGRAD

PRAAG

Bolgasgrad

River Lynsk

IIDDLE MOUNTAINS

FOREST OF SHADOWS

OSTLAND

KISLEV

Wolfenburg

THE FOOTHILLS

Herzig

Berghafen

River Urskoy

ALABHEIM

STIRLAND

Upper Talabec

T FOREST

Krugenheim

River Stir

Waldenhof

Wurtbad

KARAK KADRIN

The Moot

ZHUFBAR

Averheim

KARAK VARN

Blackwater

ERLAND

Blackfire Pass

SCALE
(Miles)

0 50 100 150 200 250 300

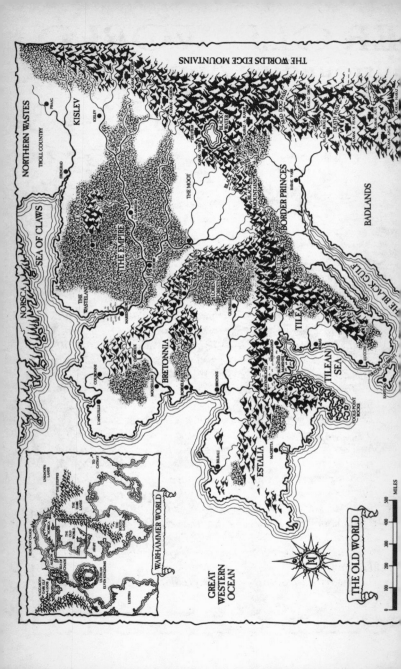

CHAPTER ONE

Sigmar's double-headed warhammer sliced through the air, and with each mighty sweep another of the green horde died, its head smashed to a bloody pulp. But still the goblins came on and on—and each of them became a crushed corpse, victim to the sacred Dwarven weapon.

The dwarfs had named the legendary hammer "Ghalmaraz"— "Skull-splitter"—and today it truly lived up to its reputation. Time after time the heavy hammer swept down, and each time another of the repulsive enemy was no more.

This was destined to be the day that marked a turning point in the tide of history, the day that the greatest of all names entered the annals of legend: when Sigmar, chief of the Unberogens, leader of the eight united human tribes, became known as "Hammer of the Goblins"—Sigmar Heldenhammer. It was the day that the foundations of the Empire were laid. And it was the day that the goblins and orcs and all their unholy allies were banished from the known world.

Dwarf and goblin were ancient enemies. They had

David Ferring

fought long and brutally for supremacy of the lands between the Sea of Claws and the Worlds Edge Mountains, and it seemed that the goblinoids must inevitably triumph through sheer weight of numbers. After centuries of war, the dwarfs were finally driven back to their precipitous homeland, leaving a few hundred valiant volunteers to protect their retreat through Black Fire Pass. This had seemed the last hope of the Dwarven nation, although for the rearguard there was no such hope; it was their destiny to die, surrendering their lives so that their people might survive.

But instead of destroying the heroes left to delay their advance, it was the goblin armies who were annihilated. Trapped between the dwarfs and their new confederates, the burgeoning young race known as humans, the green abominations were slaughtered by the hundred, by the thousand, until the mountain pass was littered with their twisted bodies and the very rocks indelibly stained by their fetid blood.

It was Sigmar who led his troops into triumphant combat against the common enemy, and as he charged through the massed goblinoid ranks, his mighty hammer exacted its deadly toll...

Again and again, the weapon swung, and each sweep left another hideous victim writhing in agony, its brains oozing from its pulverized green skull...

He felt invincible, a new strength surging through his limbs, his spirit infused by some powerful force that seemed as if it had always been a part of him yet was asserting itself from deep within for the first time.

The goblins screamed out their agony and tried to scuttle away from the merciless axe. It was not only the blade that they feared, they were also attempting to escape the sudden burst of light which had illuminated their foul underground lair—from the thunder and lightning that seemed to have invaded their dark domain.

Konrad's lips were drawn back, bared in an atavistic snarl. He could feel the blood lust of his primitive ancestors flood through his body, sensed that he was no longer alone within himself. Countless generations urged him on, became a part of him, and he was almost a spectator to the massacre. It was as if his arms were not his own, that the heavy axe they held was directed by a force which was beyond his control.

This was his moment in time, and slaying the goblin hell-spawn was his mission. He struck out mechanically, his whole body an efficient killing machine unhampered by thought. All he needed was instinct and reaction.

The bodies of countless verminous foe lay sprawled across the floor of the ancient Dwarven temple, their blood flowing as freely as in an abattoir.

And then, almost abruptly, there were no more victims. Every deformed body was dead or dying. Any survivors had crept away into the darkness, and Konrad finally ceased slaying. The wounded he allowed to suffer, letting death claim them slowly and painfully. He rested on the handle of his axe, breathing heavily, and gazed at the charnel house he had created. His expression of murderous violence curled into a contented grin. He wiped at the sticky blood which coated his face. It was not his blood, but the dead no longer had any need for it.

Slowly he emerged from his killing trance, and he gazed up at the source of light that had suddenly illuminated the cavern and which had been his salvation. Before the brilliant sunburst, his foes had begun to overwhelm him in the darkness of their own world.

The transformation as if from night to day must have been the work of Anvila, he realized. The dust was still settling from the rocks which had fallen from above to allow light to reach the temple for the first time in millennia.

Konrad turned towards the distant agonized figure of Wolf.

Konrad and Wolf and Anvila had come to these mountains in search of a lost Dwarven temple, where reputedly a fortune in jewels and gold was hidden. Instead they had found a goblin stronghold—or rather, the goblins had found them...

Wolf had been captured and tortured, and was about to be slowly sacrificed when Konrad had arrived. Now Wolf hung from his wrists, naked, covered in blood. The blood was red, not green; it was his own blood, human blood.

As Konrad made his way towards his comrade, he realized that Wolf looked different somehow. His body seemed deformed, his limbs misshapen. Possibly this was because his whole body was twisted in pain; but his tattooed face had also taken on a strange look, as if his jaw were stretched. And although his flesh was soaked with blood, it also appeared matted with thick hairs. Almost as if he were the primal creature that Konrad had sensed himself becoming...

Wolf was staring at him strangely, as if he did not recognize Konrad, or as though he were still afraid that he was about to be slowly mutilated and finally slain.

"Didn't you hear what I ordered?" he managed to say, his voice weak. "You were supposed to kill me, not him." He spat towards the supine body of the witch-priest. A ball of blood and spit landed on the corpse's ritually lacerated face.

Wolf had issued his command when Konrad first entered the hidden cavern, when they had seen each other from afar by the light of Konrad's burning torch. Instead, Konrad had used his one arrow to shoot the goblin shaman that had been torturing its helpless human victim.

"You can't rely on a bow—it's a peasant weapon," Konrad said, his reply echoing a comment Wolf had made the day that the two of them had first met.

Konrad leaned his gory hammer against the wall and reached for his knife. Then he paused, staring at the weapon which had wrought such deadly destruction amongst his foes. It was an axe that he had used to such devastating effect, not a hammer. Why had he believed otherwise?

His head was still ringing with the sounds of combat and the horrendous death screams of his enemies, with the roar of the explosion and the landslide of falling rocks. He wiped at his face, rubbing away the trickle of blood that kept obscuring his vision. It was his own blood. He had been wounded and was bleeding profusely from several stabs and cuts, but he had hardly noticed. Such injuries had seemed as nothing in the midst of combat.

He used his kris to slice through the ropes that held Wolf bound to the temple wall. As the last strand parted, the blade of the knife suddenly shattered into a hundred pieces. Konrad had owned the wavy-bladed weapon for more than half his life, and it had saved him from death on many an occasion. He gazed at the bone handle, then let it fall to the ground.

"I thought you were going to slit your own throat before you were captured," he said. Wolf had once vowed that he would never be taken alive.

Wolf grimaced as he was helped down, baring his pointed teeth. "Decided I'd rather slit a few of their throats," he gasped.

A moment later they heard the sound of heavy footsteps in the distance, and they both stared towards the opposite side of the cavern—towards the dark tunnels into which the surviving creatures had fled.

Konrad held up Wolf with one arm. His other arm reached for his blood-encrusted axe. Side by side, they watched and waited for their enemies to emerge from the black passages.

The marching sounds came nearer, louder, echoing in the unholy silence. It must have been an army of goblins—and this time Konrad stood no chance.

"Where's all this treasure?" said Anvila.

The dwarf stood at the end of one of the tunnels, and she stared around at the vaulted temple, ignoring the dead and dying goblins as she peered up at the bare walls.

At last there was silence. The screams and moans of the dying had ceased. The green brutes were all dead—or else were too weak to even whimper and soon would be.

Wolf lay unconscious on the floor, and Konrad looked at him. His wounds would eventually heal, although his body would be even more scarred than before. Apart from his superficial wounds, he looked no different from the way he had ever done throughout the time that Konrad had known him. The apparent change in his appearance must have been caused by the suffering he had endured. Either that or Konrad's own senses had been affected by the ferocity of combat. Why else had he been under the delusion that he had wielded a hammer instead of an axe?

He kept gazing at the darkened tunnels, thinking that the loathsome hordes would return any moment. It was the light that kept them away, but how long until they conquered their fear, until they realized how few their enemies were?

When Konrad had ventured into the underground maze in search of Wolf and his captors, Anvila had remained on the surface. Using her engineering skills she had brought daylight to the darkness. The luminescence came from about halfway up one part of the cavern, radiating from what seemed at first to be a broad tunnel—but it was bright instead of dark, covered with a round piece of glass, which gave it the appearance of a window.

"Dwarfs used to illuminate their subterranean temples

by a series of lenses which diverted the light down from the surface, from the sun," Anvila had explained. "I found the lens above, but it was covered in tons of rock—which I blew away with gunpowder."

"Told you she was clever," Wolf had muttered, then he had passed out.

Konrad envied his oblivion and wished that he could also rest; but there could be no rest until they escaped from the temple. He watched as Anvila explored the cavern. She could not have been searching for the treasure that Wolf had hoped for. If there had ever been a forgotten fortune down here, lost when the Dwarven shrine was abandoned during the age of volcanoes and earthquakes, it must have been looted centuries ago.

Anvila inspected the stones and carvings, studying the pillars that surrounded the various passages which led away from the central area. Her finger traced some of the runes, trying to make out what was written by her forefathers who had lived here countless generations ago.

The chamber must have been hewn out of the naked rock, the ground and the walls lined with massive stone blocks. The floor was circular, some two hundred feet across; the walls were curved, arching up to meet one another in a massive dome a hundred feet above the ground.

"This was a Dwarven temple," said Anvila, when she returned, "and now the Goblins use it for their own vile rituals. This must have been some ceremony connected with the last day of spring." She knelt by Wolf and gazed up at where he had been tied, stretched out like a sacrificial offering.

"Tomorrow is the first day of summer?" said Konrad, softly.

That was the day his whole life had changed. Five years ago, on the first day of summer, his native village had been totally annihilated. Konrad had been the only survivor. He shook his head, and squeezed his eyes shut, trying not to remember any of it—but most of all trying not to remember what must have happened to Elyssa on that day.

The blood and gore which stuck to his limbs and torso stank abominably. Now that Anvila was with Wolf, he searched through the rubble of the temple for some water to clean himself.

He had slain many goblins over the last few years, but none so warped and deformed as these. It was living underground that must have so affected their appearance, twisting them into smaller and more hunched shapes, making their skins paler, their eyes larger.

Unlike beastmen, some of whose blood could burn like acid, goblin blood was relatively harmless; but it was always best to get rid of any traces of a slain enemy as soon as possible.

Although unable to find any water within the temple, Konrad retrieved his sword from where it had fallen, then turned back to join Wolf and Anvila. As he did, he glanced up at the huge circle of glass set in the rock wall. It seemed composed of various rings of different sizes and thicknesses.

He began to look away, but caught a glimpse of movement in the lens above and watched as a shape within it became clearer, a figure emerging as if from a fog. He saw a rider, the image of a man on horseback, a man he could not fail to recognize—the bronze warrior!

Konrad stared in disbelief. It was five years to this very day since he and Elyssa had watched the bronze knight ride through their doomed village, a silent figure that had seemed like some supernatural being.

And when Konrad had described the rider who had appeared the day before the village was invaded, Wolf had said that the horseman was his brother, his twin brother...

That was the day that he and Konrad had met, and Wolf had claimed that his twin was dead. Konrad could still remember Wolf's exact words: *Worse than dead...*

Wolf had not mentioned his twin since, and Konrad had hardly considered the bronze warrior. He had never imagined that he would see the rider again.

Had the horseman really returned to haunt him—or was he only the illusion that he appeared?

"Anvila!" Konrad yelled, pointing up at the round glass. "Can you see it?"

"Yes!" she shouted.

"What does it mean?"

"It's a distant image, reflected and magnified by the lenses. The one on the surface must have fragmented, and by some phenomenon it's displaying a stray vision."

"Is it real?"

"Yes."

"Is he real?"

"Yes. He's probably a few miles away, near the edge of the mountains."

But even as she spoke, the ghostly apparition faded into the mists of the lens and was gone.

Konrad continued gazing up at the circle of glass, although there was nothing more to see, then he turned and hurried back to where Anvila and Wolf were.

"I have to follow him," he said.

The dwarf looked at him, but she said nothing.

"I must go. It is—my destiny..."

Anvila shrugged. "If it's that important, go."

"What about Wolf? Can you take care of him, help him out of here?"

"Yes."

"What about the goblins?"

"I'm a dwarf. These are the lands of my ancestors. I know how to deal with goblins."

Konrad stared down at Wolf, and Wolf's eyes flickered open. The pain and agony he still felt were reflected in their ice blue coldness. He gazed at Konrad, his glance going from one of Konrad's eyes to the other. He licked at his lips and opened his mouth to speak.

"Chaos," he whispered. He took a shallow breath, then spoke again, his voice louder. "Chaos!" he warned.

And then his eyes slowly closed and he drifted back into unconsciousness, as though the effort of speaking had been too much for him.

Chaos...

It was a word that Konrad had heard before, a word that was often spoken on the frontier, a word he had even used himself, a word which seemed to mean something different to everyone. Whatever its true meaning, the word sent a cold shiver down Konrad's spine.

Wolf would know; but Wolf was beyond answering.

Konrad also wanted to know about his comrade's twin brother, what had happened to him, how he had become involved with the forces of darkness. He turned to face Anvila. As usual, she showed no reaction and said nothing.

"I must go," he told her.

"You said that. If you have to, then—go!"

Konrad nodded and backed slowly away, heading for the passage through which the dwarf had entered the temple. He was reluctant to abandon Wolf and Anvila, but the dwarf was confident that she could get the wounded human safely away from the mountains and the goblin lair.

Wolf had been the second most important person in Konrad's life, transforming him from a peasant boy into a warrior. But the most important had been Elyssa. It was she, his first love, his only true love, who had given him an identity, even given him his name. And it was five years since she had been murdered when the village was wiped out.

Five years less a day.

Now the bronze knight was nearby, and this was the same date upon which Konrad and Elyssa had originally seen him.

There was no such thing as chance, Wolf had often said—only fate. And Konrad had come to believe that was indeed true.

He must find the horseman. Only then could he begin to find his own true self, to unravel the mystery of his life.

With a final glance at Anvila, at Wolf, Konrad spun around and entered the dark tunnel that would lead him up to the surface.

The passage was too narrow to swing an axe if he were attacked, and he drew his sword. His left hand reached for his knife, forgetting that it was gone. Watching for the glimmer of evil red eyes that would warn him of the deformed enemy waiting in ambush, he stepped into the blackness.

He blinked at the sudden light. The sun was at its zenith, blazing down from a cloudless sky. In winter, Kislev must have been the coldest place in the world—but in summer it seemed the hottest.

He took several deep breaths, filling his lungs with clean air, ridding his nostrils of the nauseating goblin stench which had permeated the underground labyrinth. His skin and clothing were still smeared with green blood, and that would not be as easy to eliminate as the foul odour.

As he discarded most of his stained clothing, Konrad remembered the last time he had been coated with so much gore. That was also the day when the village had been destroyed, when for his own safety he had disguised himself in the hide of a beastman he had killed, joining the berserk raiders who invaded the valley.

He spat, trying to rid his mouth of the taste of death, and trying not to remember the distant past. The latter was much more difficult.

He soon found the huge lens that had once provided the illumination for the underground Dwarven temple. It was circular, at least five yards in diameter. Faceted like a cut gemstone, it lay embedded at an angle in the mountainside. Anvila had blasted away the rocks which for centuries had covered the great glass, and now it was cracked and fractured in numerous places.

Several sections were missing, and this was what must have caused the optical phantasmagoria which had revealed the warrior in bronze. A distant image captured by one of the missing facets had been reflected via the surface lens to its smaller companion in the cavern beneath.

Konrad walked to the furthermost edge of the precipice and tried to see the landscape far below. Despite leaning out as much as he dared, too many of the lower peaks obscured his view. This far away, he had no way of telling where the bronze horseman was, which direction he was riding.

His only hope of discovering the knight's location was to find the correct shard of ancient lens. It must exist, because that was how he had seen the image of the rider. If he traced the missing glass sliver, he hoped to look through it like the eyepiece of a spyglass and thus find his enigmatic quarry.

There were so many shattered fragments of rock from the gunpowder the dwarf had employed, that Konrad realized such a search would almost certainly be futile—but he had to try.

For nearly an hour, he clambered over the boulders and scrambled amongst the dust and debris, hunting for a piece of glass that had become balanced on a vantage point or wedged in a position where it overlooked the ground below. He found many splinters of lens, gleaming in the sunlight like precious jewels, but not the one which he was seeking.

Finally, he was forced to admit that it was hopeless. Every minute that had passed, the further away was the bronze warrior.

He had emerged on the surface via a different crevice in the rocks, although he had taken his bearings at once, and now he headed for the lower slope. He glanced towards the south, along the route Anvila and he had climbed, noticing the familiar landmarks—then he stared into the darkened fissure where he had entered the goblin stronghold.

He was tempted to return, to help the dwarf with Wolf; but he realized there was nothing that he could do. They did not need his assistance. He had come out into the open to find the bronze warrior, and that must be his prime objective.

Following the precarious route by which he had arrived, he began making his way down the mountainside. Going down was no easier than ascending; in some respects it was more difficult. Climbing, he had no fear for himself because he was anxious to locate Wolf, and saving his comrade had been the only thing on his mind.

He had also been facing towards the summit all the time. Returning, he was constantly aware of the altitude, and how very far it would be to fall...

At length, he reached the point where Anvila and Wolf had been ambushed just before dawn. It looked no different from anywhere else on the harsh route—except for the mangled corpses of the goblins that the pair had managed to slay before Wolf was captured and Anvila had fallen down a crevasse. Among the dead lay the body of Midnight, Wolf's horse.

Konrad found a waterskin among the supplies that the white steed had carried up the tortuous slope, and he slaked his dry throat with the welcome liquid. When he had drunk his fill, he allowed the water to cascade over his face, rinsing away the worst of the blood. He rubbed at the slime with the back of his hand, then sorted through the rest of the provisions for whatever he might need.

He did not take much. Wolf and Anvila would also need food and water. There were more supplies with the other horses further down the mountain—assuming they had not been found by another band of goblins, or some different creatures that dwelled in this rocky realm.

Although he was still exhausted, Konrad did not remain for long. He had to keep moving, and he continued down the rugged slope, collecting the items he had discarded on his upward race—his fur leggings, the pieces of armour that had slowed his climb—until finally he reached the place when he had spent the previous night.

Everything seemed as he had left it when he had suddenly *seen* what would happen to his two companions, when he had rushed to their aid, racing hopelessly against the rising sun. The horses were still tethered, but Konrad approached cautiously, drawing his sword, his eyes flickering across the rocks and boulders. The area was deserted.

Konrad finished cleaning himself, before bandaging his wounds. Ever since he had almost lost it, his right arm had always healed more swiftly than the rest of his body. The limb had been severely wounded in combat a few years ago, and it had seemed that amputation would be necessary; but the wound was tended by an elf who possessed healing skills which had saved the arm.

After dressing in whatever he could find and hurriedly eating a few rations, Konrad saddled his horse—then wondered what direction to take. To begin with, there was only one route. He had to continue down the mountainside. The track was no longer so steep or as treacherous, but it was still not easy. On the way here, during this part of the journey they had led their animals, whose hooves were tied to muffle the sound of iron on rock, and they had only travelled during the hours of darkness for fear of observation and pursuit.

Now, however, it was Konrad who was the pursuer—and the route was almost as bad in daylight as it had been at night. He had no time to lead his mount. Speed was of the essence. He had to risk the animal tripping and breaking a leg; it was either that or allowing the bronze knight to escape.

Once he was beyond the mountains, he would have to decide in which direction he should be heading. Until then he kept scanning the area below, watching for a distant rider. But there was no sign of anyone—or any *thing*. The same had been true of the journey here; they had seen not a trace of the alien hordes which infested this part of Kislev. That in itself should have been suspicious, but the trio were grateful for the empty miles.

After growing up in the Forest of Shadows, where an enemy could be lurking behind the nearest tree, Konrad was still not used to the open spaces that existed around the mountains. He could see for miles across the plains. If there were any beastmen in the vicinity, he would probably see them before he was spotted. He was continually on the lookout, but it was not the marauders for whom he was searching.

He soon realized which direction he must take. There was only one possible route.

Five years ago today he and Elyssa had first seen the warrior in bronze. The following day an army of beastmen had destroyed the village and slain everyone who dwelled within. Konrad only survived because he had left the valley before the attack began.

And tomorrow it would again be the first day of summer, Sigmar's holy day. Would history be repeated? Was that why the mysterious horseman was here, a harbinger of death and destruction?

Konrad feared so. The bronze rider was the pathfinder, a scout who led the evil swarms of darkness to their target.

Northern Kislev was a barren and inhospitable region, and the area around Belyevorota Pass was relatively uninhabited. There were a few trading posts, some small isolated villages and forts. The only place of any size was the mine—and that must be the target of the raiders.

Konrad urged his horse on, back to the place where he had lived for almost five years. That was how long he and Wolf had protected the gold mine from incursions by the northern aggressors, leading the toughest troop of mercenaries ever to operate on the borderlands. Over the past two years they had even succeeded in pressing back the invaders. No longer on the defensive, they had taken the battle to the enemy.

Then came the Siege of Praag. Despite its ferocity, that had seemed an isolated occurrence: but perhaps the tide of combat had begun to turn...

Konrad had no proof, not yet. He fervently hoped that he was wrong, but deep in his heart he knew his theory must be right.

He rode long and hard that day, retracing the route that he and his two comrades had taken a few short days ago. He rested his horse as briefly as possible before pressing on again. He was in a race against time, and sunset arrived far too soon. But the darkness did not slow Konrad. He sped on long into the night, until finally he and his steed could continue no more.

It had been a long day, a very long day, but it seemed far longer than a single day since he had awoken before dawn and *seen* the danger that Wolf and Anvila were about to encounter. Then had come his battle against the goblins, when his axe had scythed down the repulsive brutes by the score.

As he slipped into slumber, Konrad wondered about the bronze rider. Had he really seen the knight? Or was it some delusion inspired by the heat of combat, like his belief that he had wielded a double-headed hammer instead of a twin-bladed axe? But Anvila had also seen the armoured figure, he realized, as exhaustion finally overwhelmed him and he slept.

He dreamed that he was killing goblins, who were

trying to prevent him reaching the bronze knight. And amongst the deformed creatures, leading them and urging them to kill Konrad was Elyssa...

He awoke abruptly, sweating, his right fist clenched, trying to grip the handle of his nonexistent kris. He sat up, staring at the stars in the black sky, at the two moons, before lying down and falling into another disturbed sleep.

Soon after dawn, he was back in the saddle, riding across the plain once more, on through the silence and the emptiness, and it was as if he were the only person in the whole world.

Half a decade ago, a defenceless village had been annihilated. Surely it was impossible for the events of that long ago day in far off Ostland to be repeated. The mine was heavily fortified, guarded by seasoned troops who were constantly vigilant, who had defeated the benighted legions from the Northern Wastes in countless skirmishes and battles. There was no comparison.

Yet no matter how many of them were slain, there were always many more of the renegades ready to take their place. Over the past two years, however, they had not seemed so numerous. Had they been building up their forces, preparing for a full-scale assault?

Numbers alone, however, were not sufficient. Had that been the case, the raiders could have swept across Kislev years ago—as indeed they had once done. Two centuries earlier the marauders had overrun the country, then been driven back after an alliance was agreed between the Tsar and the Emperor. The united armies of two nations had repulsed the invaders, forcing them back into their own dark domain.

The enemy's only motive seemed to be to kill, as if that were the sole reason for their existence. Their blood lust was fed by death, any death, and it often seemed as if they were as content to slay one another as they were to kill the humans who blocked their route to the heart of Kislev and beyond, to the Empire.

The day that they had wiped out Konrad's village, however, the beastmen had been united in their barbaric mission. And if they had combined their forces today, put aside their own feuds and hatreds until victory was achieved, then the people who lived near the mine were doomed.

When he saw the pall of dark smoke rising on the horizon far ahead of him, Konrad knew that he was too late.

CHAPTER TWO

Konrad rode on and on, spurring his steed ever more furiously, until finally the exhausted horse collapsed beneath him, sending him tumbling to the ground. The animal lay panting, foaming at the mouth, its coat lathered with blood and sweat. Its hind legs kicked out frantically, as though it were still trying to gallop. Then all movement suddenly ceased; the horse was dead.

Pausing only to collect his sword and axe, his helmet and shield, Konrad ran on, pushing himself as hard as he had his mount.

By now he was only two or three miles away, could smell the smoke, could see the flames. Although he was downwind, he heard nothing. No sounds of combat, the clash of steel on steel, the battle cries of the warriors—nor the death cries of the wounded...

Although many miles from the mountain range that marked the boundary of the Old World, the chain of peaks which ran from Kislev in the far north, down to the

Badlands and beyond in the south, the mine workings were also located in a highland area. Lying in a valley between three towering crags, each of which was linked by a solid line of fortifications, the township was in an ideal position both strategically and defensively. It could never have existed in such a hostile zone for so long and would not have developed into a trading centre for the entire region, had it been otherwise.

The three peaks each had their own watchtowers, overlooking the plains below—and now all of them were ablaze, consumed by tongues of red and yellow flames. Smoke spiralled up from each crag, but it was as nothing compared to the dense black clouds that rose from the encampment.

Konrad recalled the first blaze the marauders had lit when they had ravaged his native village. The temple to Sigmar had been set alight, immolating all those who had been worshipping within, a funeral pyre for the living. It was not the burning temple that he remembered most, however: it was the fire which had consumed the manor house—and what had been within...

He had raced up the hill, hoping that he might somehow find Elyssa still there, still alive. Instead he had seen the most terrifying sight of his ordeal. Despite all the murders and mutilations he had witnessed when he had been caught up in the assault, despite all the hideous creatures that had invaded the village, the image which remained paramount in his mind was that of a man walking unharmed through the inferno that had been the manor house, the man he had called Skullface.

Despite his appearance, he could not have been a man. He was like all the other travesties of life who had rampaged through the helpless village, a subhuman.

Yet Konrad had been able to kill many of those with his arrows. Every one he shot had died. Not so Skullface. The black shaft had penetrated deep into his chest, but been plucked out easily, leaving not a trace of blood, not a sign of a wound.

The preternaturally thin figure of Skullface had been the first creature Konrad had encountered which was unaffected by a mortal wound. In the five years since, there had been so many more impossible beasts that refused to die until they had been killed in a dozen ways.

Slaying goblins was easy, but they were amongst humanity's lesser enemies. Goblins were a part of the Old World, like dwarfs, like mankind. They were not the abhorrent spawn of the Northern Wastes, the *Chaos* Wastes...

It seemed that was where all the creatures known as beastmen had originally come from. As if the frozen wastelands were another world, nothing natural could exist there. It was a land where only evil was born.

The beings Konrad had encountered in his youth had been degenerate specimens, the descendants of those who had invaded the Empire two centuries earlier. When the incursion had been repulsed, the survivors had fled into the dense forests. Compared with those Konrad had seen since arriving at the frontier, they had been weak and slow—and easy to kill.

Almost every beastman seemed different, and each had to be dispatched in a different way. Skullface had survived an arrow in the heart—or where a human heart should have been. But some of the creatures from the wasteland had a score of hearts, each of which must be savagely stilled before the being surrendered its life, whilst others seemed to have no hearts at all...

What would have been a fatal wound to a human was nothing more than a scratch to some of the hellbeasts. Limbs severed in combat could take on their own life, a detached leg becoming a lethal serpent, an arm holding a weapon becoming another deadly enemy. Some of the monsters could even split themselves in twain deliberately, a two-headed foe dividing itself into two one-headed antagonists.

When Konrad slept, he never had nightmares—because no matter what his imagination could conjure, he had dealt with far worse in reality.

He had slowed his earlier headlong pace to conserve his strength, and now he loped forward in an easy run. He could feel the heat from the inferno for the first time. As he gazed at the flames, he wondered what else he would find beyond the blazing wooden stockade apart from the dead.

His nostrils twitched as he scented burning flesh, human flesh. He slowed for a moment, wondering why he was continuing. There was nothing he could do to save anyone within the mine area, he was too late for that. The only things alive would be beastmen—if such abominations could ever truly be called alive.

There was no reason to go on, but this was not a matter for reason. Like the village where he had grown up, the area around the mine had become his home. He belonged here, the invaders did not.

He resumed his previous speed, running into the valley of death.

He reached the first bodies, beastmen that had been slain by the arrows of the defenders. The nearer he came to the fortifications, the more bodies lay sprawled in the dirt, wallowing in their own blood.

It was noon, and they had been dead for hours, but Konrad slowed his pace, picking his way warily amongst the corpses. He was well versed in the tactics of mankind's treacherous enemies. Most of the creatures were brainless, often literally, but others could be feigning death in the hope of snaring an unwary victim.

The very word "death" had no meaning to some of the unholy beings. He had slain creatures in the past, only to see them rise up again a while later, like a human refreshed by a few hours' slumber.

The very fact of a living being passing by could trigger a reflex in some of the corpses, reanimating them for one last frenzied attack. They could sense the warm red blood of a man, although the liquid that flowed within their own veins, even when they had been the bestial equivalent of alive, might be as cold as a lizard's—and could be any colour.

The shapes of those he moved amongst were as disgusting as ever, travesties of both the animal and human, of the insect and reptilian and avian forms, cobbled together as if at random from pieces of other creatures. It must have been so difficult for such unlikely beings even to have survived that it was no surprise that they were hard to slay. They were tough.

But the ones out here had been mown down by flight after flight of arrows aimed from the ramparts, just as Konrad himself had been able to slay a handful of attackers five years ago...

He closed his mind to the thought. The past was gone, as dead as the monsters he had killed so long ago. He must concentrate on the present—and upon surviving through it.

Cautiously, Konrad advanced through the dead, his eyes focused on what lay ahead of him. He blinked as the astringent smoke stung his eyes, and held his shield in front of his face as protection from the raging heat. He kept the heavy axe in his right hand, while his sword remained sheathed.

The triple peaks were linked by a solid wooden palisade, three times the height of a man. Forward of that lay a deep ditch lined with sharpened stakes, jutting upward at a sharp angle. It would take a determined army to breach these lines of defence—and the beastmen had been determined indeed.

The tree trunks that composed the wall were afire, but

the main gate was still barred and firmly closed, further barricaded by the raised drawbridge. The malignant invaders had not entered by that route. Instead, a ramp had been constructed across the ditch, over the stakes and into the fortress—a ramp of corpses...

In the past, Konrad had noticed how the beastmen would often attack in swarms, not caring how many of their number died, in the hope that a few of them might endure long enough to slay one of their human foe. Ten dead, twenty, a hundred, such numbers were as nothing in their insane frenzy. They had no thought for themselves, no instinct for self-preservation, and this was what made them so dangerous.

And now hundreds and hundreds of the crazed beings must have sacrificed themselves, piling their bodies one on top of another, wedged so tight that they had suffocated to death in order that their comrades might penetrate the outer ring of defences.

Konrad tried to avoid the hideous route, to enter by scaling the wall, but the intensity of the fire drove him back. The only way in was via the same bridge of flesh over which the assault had taken place. He began to climb the slippery slope, his feet sinking as he trod upon impossible limbs and torsos, squashing repulsive faces beneath his boots. His feet came up slowly with every step, squelching and sticking in the alien slime.

He was almost at the top when a scaled fist reached from the mound of corpses and seized his ankle. His response was instant, his axe slicing down and cleaving through the warped arm that had grabbed his leg. But the severed hand gripped ever more tightly, and he had to knock it free with the blade. It dropped onto the stack of bodies, its taloned fingers clenching. He kicked it aside and leapt forward.

Then he was over the palisade, peering through the smoke and gazing down into the area beyond. As an unwilling spectator to the attack on his village, he had seen many barbaric sights; and in his five years on the frontier he had witnessed far worse—but as the scene below became clear, he tasted bile at the back of his throat. He swayed, feeling dizzy; he closed his eyes, fighting back the urge to vomit; he opened his mouth, trying to breath in fresh air. Yet there was none. The atmosphere was befouled by the stench of carnage, the odours of burning flesh and spilled blood.

The ladders had all been burned, and Konrad leapt down into the compound. He swung his shield over his shoulder, drew his sword, and advanced into the killing ground.

There was not a square yard that was untouched by blood, that did not have a body lying there—human or inhuman. Or if not a body, then the parts of one. The victims had not merely been slain. That was only the beginning—or the end...

The murdered and mutilated, the maimed and massacred, were everywhere: nailed to walls, hanging from posts, pinned to the ground. They had been ripped apart, half eaten, flayed, set ablaze—and the lucky ones had been dead when that happened.

Some had been strangled with their own entrails, others choked with their innards. Heads cut off, limbs ripped from their sockets, eyes gouged out, fingers sliced off, faces peeled away... the list of barbarities seemed endless.

The anatomies of many corpses had been rearranged, as if in some macabre joke. The head of a dwarf had been embedded in a woman's body, resting in the cavity where her belly had been. A miner's severed legs were replaced with a pair of arms torn from a child. A foot protruded from the chest of a mercenary. Another had his slit throat stuffed with eyeballs, like a necklace of giant pearls. Each corpse had been desecrated in a more obscene fashion than the next. This was more than simple killing, more than vengeance, more than blood lust: it was evil, absolute and total evil.

The essence of Chaos, Konrad realized.

The troops who had defended the mine, the convicted prisoners who dug out the ore, the overseers who guarded them, the dwarfs who worked as engineers, the women who lived here, their children—dead, all dead.

Despite the unspeakable atrocities inflicted upon them, Konrad recognized many of the mercenaries. They were warriors from every corner of the Old World and from even further away. Soldiers of fortune who had died countless hundreds, thousands of miles away from home—and who would never find the fortune of which they had all dreamed.

Natives of Kislev defending their own land, fighting men from every province in the Empire, every city, others from the Estalian Kingdoms and Bretonnia, from the Tilean City States and the Border Princes, from the mythical lands beyond the ocean, Araby and Afric, Cathay and Nippon, all had been welded together into Wolf's crack military force. They had become allies against the common foe. They had fought together, and now they had died together. Died very slowly, most of them, and in great pain.

Konrad bit his lower lip, feeling the warm coppery taste of blood in his mouth where he broke the skin. He clenched his fists around the hilts of his axe and his sword. He wanted to fight, to kill, to throw himself into the fray, to vent his rage and anger against the despicable foes—but there was no one to fight, nothing to kill.

Except for the fires, all was still, all was silent, and even the flames were slowly diminishing. Flies buzzed around the corpses and fed on the blood. A few crows and vultures circled above, waiting for Konrad to disappear. A rat ventured out from the debris of the collapsed stables, then scuttled back inside. Soon the wolves and another predators would arrive, drawn by the scent of death to the feast that awaited them.

For every dead human there were several ugly corpses of the attackers, and they came in every form imaginable. As with their assault on the village, they had put aside their rivalries, uniting in a single assault. Whether they had turned upon each other after victory, as they had done before, Konrad neither knew nor cared.

The bodies of the beastmen were of the type he had fought and slain on many an occasion, the mutated offspring that slithered and crawled down from the Northern Wastes. Impossible beings that had no right to exist, that could not have existed, that stole human lives in order to survive because they had no true life of their own.

Creatures that were feathered and furred, spined and scaled, taloned and fanged, beaked and clawed, winged and tailed, whose limbs were made of weapons, whose bodies were gaudily coloured or cleverly camouflaged, whose faces were upside down or totally featureless, whose eyes were on stalks or without pupils and could mesmerize a man with their apparent charms—but who had none.

Konrad had seen them all, killed them all.

And then there were the others, those whose mutations were far more subtle and could almost pass for human. Sometimes they did—because that was what they had once been...

Just as beastmen appeared to aspire to humanity, it seemed some humans wished to become beasts, to sacrifice their birthright, preferring to worship the dark gods and mutate into creatures which were far less than human. Many of these also lay amongst the dead, the effects of their foul metamorphosis hidden beneath the armour in which they were clad.

Konrad stepped amongst the corpses, his weapons poised, wishing that just one of the enemy would show a sign of life so that he could allow his frustration some release. But there was nothing, and even the carrion eaters would not settle while he prowled the death zone.

For the second time, Konrad realized, he had survived such a total attack. Once again, he had been away when the battle had commenced; once again, he had lived.

The village had been erased from the face of the world. When he had returned a few days later, there had hardly been any trace of habitation. Every building had gone, only their faint outlines remaining. If such a cataclysm were about to overtake the mine, he ought to leave while he still had a chance, but there was something he must do first—something he had tried not to consider ever since he had seen the first trace of smoke on the horizon.

The entrance to the mineshaft itself seemed to have caved in, the massive wooden supports were torn away, leaving a huge pile of rock and mangled bodies—human and not human. Every building within the compound had been ransacked. Bodies hung from every window, were stacked up at every doorway. Most of the wooden fabrications had been burned down or otherwise demolished. The inn was nothing more than charred beams and blackened bones.

There was only one place that concerned Konrad now, which was the gallery above the mercenary barracks, and the room where Krysten had lived. He had avoided looking in that direction as long as he could, but at last his gaze was drawn towards the irregular construction that jutted out from the side of the steepest of the three crags.

Although smoke drifted from most of the windows, the central part of the top floor appeared intact. Konrad almost wished that were not the case, that the whole structure had collapsed into ashes and dust. Then he would not have had to venture up the narrow steps to discover what he knew he must inevitably find.

Slowly, reluctantly, he made his way towards the barracks.

The hallway was packed with corpses, human and otherwise; the stairway was awash with blood, red and otherwise.

It was much darker inside, full of pungent smoke, and Konrad removed his helmet. He left it with his axe and shield in the entrance, then proceeded through the debris and fallen timbers, pushing the corpses aside. Human or not, he kicked them away or shoved them back with his sword. The mutilated flesh was no more than raw meat. The essence of humanity had long fled, their spirits taken by the gods they had worshipped.

He recognized almost all the bodies, those that were still distinguishable. They were troops he had commanded and trusted, girls he had known and loved.

But nowhere did he see a trace of the small figure with blonde wavy hair, although the further he pressed through the carnage, the more likely it was that he would find her.

Every step became harder, and his heart was beating faster than it had during his race towards the blazing mine compound. Earlier, he had stopped himself from being sick—but now he was unable to prevent the emotion building up within him, and the sadness overflowed into a single tear that rolled from his left eye and down his face.

A few days ago it had been Krysten's salty tears he had tasted when he leaned across her slumbering shape to kiss her farewell. Because they both knew they would never see each other again, she had pretended to sleep; but she had been betrayed by her tears.

That was when Konrad thought he would not return, when he had left with Wolf and Anvila in search of the lost Dwarven temple and its hoard of treasure. They had discovered the former, but not the latter. He had left Krysten as he had found her, alone. She had managed well enough before Konrad entered her life, and he believed she would do so again; but no one could survive such an unprecedented attack by the combined legions of the damned.

Or almost unprecedented.

It was not only Krysten that he mourned. The memory of Elyssa was forever in his mind, and because of the present circumstances, her memory was once again prominent in his thoughts.

She had also been slain by the beastmen, murdered when the village had been invaded. And, exactly like Krysten, Konrad had abandoned her to die...

With Krysten, he had not known; but with Elyssa, he had *seen* her death—known that she would be destroyed, although he had been unaware when or how.

But he had also foreseen that Elyssa would bring about his own downfall, and in that respect he had been wrong. She had died, while he continued to live.

Elyssa and Krysten, Krysten and Elyssa. They were exact opposites in so many respects. Was that one reason why he had been attracted to the Kislevite, because she was so radically different that she could not remind him of Elyssa? Elyssa had been tall and dark-haired, whereas Krysten was small and fair. Yet now they were identical, Konrad realized. They were both dead.

He pushed aside the blood-stained curtain and stepped into Krysten's room. A corpse lay on the straw mattress: the corpse of a yellow-skinned beastman, its catlike features frozen into a mask of pain, the hilt of a knife sticking out from the centre of its furry chest.

Konrad stood without moving, his eyes scanning the wrecked room. Dead or alive, there was no sign of the girl. He recognized the blade. It was a stiletto he had won at cards, that he had given Krysten for her protection. It seemed to have fulfilled its purpose. She had escaped, or so it appeared, but how far?

He moved further into the room, prodding the supine creature with his sword, its point slicing into the cold dead flesh. He withdrew the blade, wiping it on the corpse's pale fur. Then he tipped up the mattress, rolling the creature onto the floor, not wishing it to desecrate Krysten's bed for one moment longer.

Konrad knew every inch of the small room, and there was nowhere that the girl could be hiding. He bent down and picked up the tiny figurines that she had kept on a shelf by the bed, the handful of ornaments and trinkets that were her only treasures. The shelf was splintered and torn away, and so he held onto Krysten's mementoes. It was as if he held all that remained of her in the palm of his left hand.

As he rose, he noticed the mirror. That had been another of Konrad's gifts. It had been cracked when he gave it to her, but now it hung crookedly from the wall, even more splintered and shattered.

He stared at the fractured glass, and he remembered another mirror, Elyssa's mirror—the mirror in which he had first seen his own image, and in which he had then seemed to observe a different reflection gazing back, a reflection of himself not as he was, but as he *would* be...

Because of its tilted angle, Konrad was unable to see himself in Krysten's mirror, and neither did he wish to. His consciousness had been snared by the past, but suddenly he saw a movement in the fragmented glass—and the glint of light on a blade!

He sprang back, throwing himself down, and a knife embedded itself in the wall laths above his head. Had he moved a fraction of second later, the steel would instead have lodged in his throat.

He was through the door immediately, chasing his would-be assassin. He bellowed out a war cry as he charged after the hunched figure that scurried along the darkened gallery. The creature tripped over a dismembered corpse and fell. It tried to crawl away, but its route was blocked by more dead bodies, human and bestial.

"Die!" snarled Konrad, his sword raised.

"No!" screamed the figure. "No! I'm human, I'm human!"

CHAPTER THREE

"Thought you was one of *them*, sir. Sees you climbing up there and figured it was me only chance to take revenge for what they done to all me mates, didn't I?"

Konrad had dragged his attacker out into the open to take a proper look at him, and now they stood together in a corner that was relatively clear of bodies, where the stench of death was not so overpowering.

He was one of the miners, and he seemed to be the only survivor of the attack. He stood five foot high, but would have been taller had his body not been so curved from all the years working below ground. His small head seemed to be sunk into his shoulders, as if he had no neck. He had aged prematurely and the thick hairs on his limbs and torso, and those of his scalp and chin, were grey; even his skin seemed grey from all the dust that had settled on his flesh during his time underground. His head kept twisting nervously around, as though he were afraid that the marauders were about to return.

"Why are you alive?" asked Konrad. He kept his sword at the ready, not trusting the grey-haired miner.

"Hid, didn't I?" He glanced at the sword. "Honest, sir, I thought you was one of the beast-things."

His long nose twitched at he reached up to scratch it with his left hand. His right hand was missing, Konrad noticed. It ended in a stump. He must have lost it years ago, either in an accident or as punishment.

All the miners were convicted criminals, sent here to serve out their sentences. It was almost always a life term; few left the mine alive. They were never chained, because there was nowhere they could go. Beyond the mine lay hundreds of square miles of wilderness—and of beastmen. The prisoners could escape the compound without much difficulty, but it was not so easy to escape what lay beyond.

Konrad stared around at the devastation and the dead. He was still searching for Krysten, but hoping not to find her. The miner's dark eyes followed his gaze.

Konrad looked away, then at his own left hand. His fist was clenched, still grasping Krysten's worthless souvenirs that he had been holding when the knife was thrown at him. He dug the point of his sword into the ground, making a shallow hole, then dropped the trinkets in and covered them over.

"What happened? he asked.

"It was dawn and we was getting ready to go into the shaft, sir, when the beastmen attacked. There was hundreds of them. Hundreds and hundreds. No way of stopping them. Never seen anything like it, had I? Hope I never will again. The guards, there was nothing they could do. Like I says, there was just too many of them. It was horrible, horrible."

The miner's nose twitched, and he shuddered momentarily as he told his story.

"They come over the wall, more and more of them, screaming and yelling, killing everyone what tried to stop them. The other miners picked up the weapons what the dead guards dropped, but they soon ended up just as dead. Couldn't do much, could I, not without me hand?" He held up his stump.

"You seem to have handled that knife you threw at me," Konrad remarked, thinking how he had been within a moment of dying, of being killed without even defending himself. His extra sight, his eye that warned him of danger, *seeing* what would happen before it occurred, had betrayed him again.

Over the years, Konrad had relied less and less on the future vision of his left eye. He needed no such warnings of danger; here in Kislev there was always danger. But there could be no ambush, no sudden assault, because there were few places that an attacker could hide out in the barren lands.

He had also become a warrior, a trained fighting man, and his combat skills were sufficient to defeat any assailant. He no longer needed to *see* what his opponent would do a split second hence. His reactions and instincts were enough to beat the best that the heathen hordes had to offer; he did not need another edge to his awareness.

"Good with a knife, aren't I? Always have been." The miner grinned, showing his stained teeth.

Konrad wondered what the man had been convicted of, and why he had lost his hand. He was most likely some cutpurse from one of the towns of Kislev.

"Go on," Konrad prompted.

"Wasn't much what I could do." He shrugged. "Either hide or get killed. Lots of others had the same idea, sir. But it never did them no good, did it? They was found and murdered." He sniffed, peering around at the carnage. "Murdered and worse. Me, I squeezed under a few corpses. That's what saved me." He peered at the smears of blood which stained his torn tunic, wiping at them with the thin fingers of his only hand.

"Lay without moving for hours," he continued. "Then when I sees you, I figure you must be one of them. Felt bad about what I done, about hiding, about everyone else being killed—so I come after you. That's about it, sir." He shrugged and studied Konrad. "How come you wasn't killed, sir?"

Konrad stared back at the miner, not sure whether to believe his tale; but somehow he had lived, and that was all that mattered.

He did not know whether the miner recognized him or not. There was no reason why he should have done. To Konrad, all the slave workers looked the same. And to the miner, all the mercenaries were probably identical.

"I was on patrol," Konrad answered. "When I saw the smoke, I came back." There was no need for the truth, a simple lie would suffice. "What's your name?"

"Name?"

"Yes."

"Heinler, sir."

There had been a momentary hesitation. Probably another lie, Konrad realized, but it was of no consequence. They both knew not to trust one another. His new companion was a convicted criminal, but the only difference between him and many of the mercenaries who had guarded the mine was that he had been caught.

"My name is Konrad. We seem to be the only humans for hundreds of miles. There's no need to call me 'sir'."

"Sorry, sir. When you been a prisoner long as what I been, everyone else is 'sir'."

"Let's see if we can find some water, Heinler, maybe some food."

They searched the compound, but the well was polluted, full of bodies, and all the supplies from the quartermaster's stores had been stolen. The horses from the stables were gone, every human weapon was taken, even the stock of gold ore had been carried away. That had never interested the outlaws before. Whenever they had raided a convoy, their only concern had been to slay not to pillage.

Konrad made his way to the southernmost of the three crags, and Heinler followed. They climbed the steps which had been carved out of the rock, up to where the remains of the watchtower still smouldered, and where the burned bodies lay.

"They headed in that direction?" said Konrad, and Heinler nodded.

There was no sign of the marauders on the horizon. By now they had vanished towards Praag. Konrad realized that he and Heinler were trapped between the alien army and the land whence the hellhorde had emerged. Was this to be a re-enactment of the great invasion two centuries ago, just as the attack on the mine had been a repeat of the elimination of Konrad's native village?

"Skullface," said Konrad.

"What?"

"Did you see a tall man amongst the creatures? Bald, very thin? He would have been one of the leaders."

"Er..."

"You'd have recognized him because he was unlike any of the others. He looked human, probably had no weapons. And he may have walked through the flames without being harmed. Did you see him?"

"Yeah, yeah! Saw him, I saw him!"

Konrad looked at Heinler, unsure whether to believe him. The miner had agreed too eagerly.

"Very tall, very thin, bald, looked human?" said Heinler. "Swear it was him!"

Konrad knew he had given too many clues, that Heinler was simply repeating what he had said; but it made no difference, because Konrad wanted to believe.

Yesterday, the bronze knight; today, Skullface.

Konrad turned away, gazing towards the south again, towards the Empire, towards Ostland, towards the valley where he had been brought up.

"Was giving orders, wasn't he?" Heinler continued. "He was the one what stopped some of the killing, what made the others take prisoners."

"Prisoners?" demanded Konrad, spinning around, grabbing hold of Heinler's tunic and pulling him close. "They took prisoners?"

"Yeah." Heinler leaned back. "Honest, sir!"

"Who? How many? What for?"

The miner shook his head rapidly. "Dunno. A lot."

"Men? Women?"

"Yeah. Men. Women. Both. Anyone who was still alive, not too cut up, seemed like."

Konrad let go, and Heinler stepped nervously back.

There was no reason to ask about Krysten, to find out if the miner had seen her. He was bound to reply in the affirmative, knowing that was what Konrad wanted to hear. But it was Heinler who had volunteered the information about prisoners; he had no idea that Konrad had been looking for one particular person. There was no trace of Krysten anywhere within the burned-down walls of the stockade, which could only mean that the beastmen must have taken her.

Konrad wanted to believe that she was still alive, that he had a chance to make up for his betrayal in leaving the girl here. Yet if she were alive, it would not be for long. The creatures had only postponed her death, were saving her for some hideous purpose of their own.

"Looks as if we've got a long walk ahead of us, Heinler," he said.

"What?"

"Unless you want to stay here, that is."

Heinler stared down at all the bodies spread out in the compound below, and he wrinkled his nose.

"Where we going?" he asked.

Konrad gestured towards the south.

"Wherever they are," he answered.

They retrieved their weapons from Krysten's room, because there seemed nothing more they could take. Everything else from the mine that they might have used had been looted.

Heinler's dagger looked as though it had been made by the miner himself. The handle was a roughly carved piece of wood, the blade clumsily fashioned from a shard of metal. But no matter how crude, it was a weapon, it could kill—and it had almost killed Konrad.

The stiletto was slender but square-bladed, an efficient knife for stabbing through tough bestial hides. It had originally belonged to one of Wolf's mercenaries, a silent warrior who would reveal neither his name nor his native land. He had been on patrol with four others, and they did not return. It was Konrad who had found what remained of them: four human bodies, plus the corpses of a score of the deformed invaders who had ambushed them. But of the silent mercenary there was no sign, nothing except his stiletto which lay on the ground a few yards beyond the carnage, its bloodied tip pointing towards the north.

Because Konrad had his own knife, which had served him so well over the years, he had passed the blade on to Krysten. Now it was his once more.

He and Heinler left by the southern entrance to the stockade, which had been completely demolished by the victorious assailants when they took their leave. Already the deserted stockade seemed to be decaying very rapidly. Some of the other walls of the fortress had collapsed while Konrad had been within the compound, and it was not merely because the flames had consumed most of the timbers. It was if they were totally rotten, had aged a century in a matter of hours, that the whole place had been uninhabited and forgotten for countless years. Before long, everything manmade would have crumbled into dust and been dissolved by the elements.

The sun was lower, but burned almost as fiercely as it had done at noon. Konrad had always believed that there was only one girl he had ever cared about. Now he had discovered otherwise, and all that drove him on was Krysten.

There was no sign of the marauders, but it did not need an experienced tracker to follow their trail. The marks of their passing were easy to find. Every now and then, they came across a malformed corpse, one of the assailants which had died of the wounds it had suffered during the assault on the stockade. Many of the bodies looked as though they had been dead for days, even months; they were rotten and bloated, swarming with flies, crawling with worms and maggots.

It was almost as if the northern army were purposefully leaving a spoor in the wake of its passing, discarding unwanted booty, scarring the isolated trees with wagon hubs as though blazing a trail. There were wheel marks by the score, countless footprints, hoofprints, pawprints, and they covered a wide swathe of land. There must indeed have been thousands of the benighted creatures, but their speed was restricted to the slowest of their number.

Yet Konrad still felt as he had done earlier that day, as though he were the only living being left on the face of the world—despite Heinler being so close. It was as if they were simply travellers who happened to be taking the same route. They were not allies, all they had in common was the fact that they were both human.

Konrad kept on steadily marching, and Heinler matched his pace. The miner must have been tough. He only had one hand, so he must have done twice as much work with that limb as the other convicts did with two. Barefoot, his feet were bleeding, and he was limping slightly. Konrad's boots were made for riding, and he was not used to being on foot for so long, but he tried to ignore the pain of his blisters and aching limbs. While the enemy kept on, he had to do the same. Pushing on remorselessly, they closed the gap between themselves and the enemy. By evening, they could see the dust of the alien army on the horizon.

After so many hours, the invading forces must soon stop. Or, not being human, did they need no rest?

The distance between the thousands and the two narrowed. As far as the eye could see, from east to west, the landscape was infested by the plague of dark figures. It took a while for Konrad to realize that the swarm was separating, some of the unholy horde heading to the left, others to the right, the rest venturing straight ahead. They were dividing their forces in order to strike at several different points within Kislev, he supposed.

The country had three main centres of habitation: Praag, Erengrad and the capital city of Kislev itself. The beastmen and their allies would find the fortifications of the cities far more formidable than those of the mine, the defenders far more numerous, so perhaps their primary intention was to attack smaller towns and villages, spreading fear and panic across the land.

Or possibly the outlaw bands ahead were only the vanguard for the greater pestilence that was yet to come, the tens of thousands of malevolent entities who were to follow...

But all that concerned Konrad was to identify which evil echelon had taken Krysten with them.

After several more minutes, he observed that the legions ahead had come to a halt. There was a gap of at least a mile between each of the three main sections, and so it was unlikely that they had only divided to make camp. They must have split their divisions, as he had suspected, ready to go off in different directions at dawn. Until then, like any other battalions, they lit fires and seemed to be settling down for the night.

For the first time in hours, Konrad allowed himself to stop. He sat slowly down, giving his throbbing ankles and knees, his aching calves and thighs, his tortured feet, the rest that they craved. Heinler sank down next to him, breathing heavily. Blood oozed from his feet into the dirt. Konrad did not even want to think about removing his boots. They were damp and sticky inside, and his feet had squelched with every step he had taken.

"We'll wait until it's dark," he said. "Then we'll go on ahead."

"And..?"

The miner still did not know why Konrad had been following the heathen horde, although he must have guessed. He could not have failed to notice Konrad's reaction when he had revealed that the invaders had not slain everyone within the stockade, that they had taken prisoners. But he had followed Konrad without question, and he had said nothing. Neither of them had spoken until now; there was nothing to say.

"And then we'll see if they have some food and water to spare," Konrad answered.

There had been plenty of both on the route from the devastated mine, if one knew where to look—and Konrad had known. The foraging skills which had helped him survive in the past could never be forgotten. But he had not wanted to stop, to lose valuable minutes. Food and drink were of little consequence compared to what he must do. His mission was the only sustenance he needed to keep going.

And it was not food he wanted from his ruthless foes. He intended to scour every camp, from one end of the line to the other, until he found what he was searching for.

He sat and watched the sun go down, impatient for the night.

He did not want Heinler with him: he was not a fighting man; he did not know how to move invisibly through the dark; he could not ambush guards and silently slay them; he was unaware of the subtle techniques involved in creeping through an enemy camp, slitting every throat without waking those who were next about to die.

But the miner was himself asleep, and so Konrad left him where he lay and advanced through the blackened night. Only the stars shone down. It would be several hours until Mannslieb shed its nocturnal glow over the landscape. Morrslieb might rise before then, but the lesser moon would provide little illumination.

Leaving his shield and helmet behind him, and clenching his axe in his right hand, his sword in his left, Konrad made his way cautiously towards the flickering flames of the most westerly campfire. He tried not to think what the barbaric army might be devouring. As he crept on, he inevitably remembered the way that his native village had surrendered every night to the beastmen, and the same must have been true in so many other parts of the world. Daylight was for humans, but in the blackness the same lands became the domain of the deformed forest dwellers.

Here, however, the hour of the clock made no difference. Because the enemy were creatures of darkness, that did not make them creatures of the night. There were enough of the savages to venture forth at any time; they did not need to hide amongst the shadows. They regarded the north of Kislev as theirs—and now, it seemed, they intended to take over the rest of the country. And beyond...

The night was filled with loud noises and strange smells. The alien army was half-beast, half-man, and the sounds and odours that emanated from the camps were a mixture of both animal and human. There was laughter and screams; inhuman laughter, human screams.

Even in summer, the Kislev nights were cold. Konrad was used to them after so long, but he suddenly shivered. He realized it was the screams that had caused the chill which he felt from his neck to his toes. He recalled the victims of the atrocities in the mining compound. They must also have screamed, screamed long and loud in ultimate pain—those who had not had their tongues severed or their throats torn out.

Tonight, Konrad vowed, some small measure of justice would be exacted for the hideous tortures inflicted earlier this very day. He had slain goblins by the score yesterday, and now it would be the turn of the beastmen. The slaughter would be less spectacular than the mass killing he had accomplished previously, yet it would be no less effective.

He wished he still had his kris, the blade with which he had dispatched his first beastman all those years ago. In doing so, he had saved Elyssa's life. Maybe now his other weapons could do the same for Krysten.

He moved closer and closer towards the most westerly fire. He would begin here, then make his way along the hostile ranks until he found the captured girl. Or until the enemy found him.

They were so confident, or maybe so stupid, that they had not posted any guards. Very slowly, Konrad edged closer, then crouched down so that he could keep the nearest group under observation. Half a score of the grotesque creatures sat around the blaze. In the twisting light they looked even more repulsive than they would have done in the daytime, the flames and shadows alternately revealing their deformities and masking them once more.

Some looked almost human for a moment, until the fire exposed their awful aspects, the bestial characteristics that made them even lower than beasts. Then the light would change and their subhuman attributes would be hidden again, and instead their neighbours would be unveiled as foul travesties of humanity.

Konrad gazed in mesmerized horror. What was so awful was not how different they were from the squadrons of mercenaries Konrad had commanded, but how similar.

They were passing around a flagon of ale; they laughed together, probably sharing an obscene joke; they spoke in their heathen tongue, doubtless boasting of their exploits during the day's extermination; they even sang together, their raucous voices totally tuneless.

Konrad hated and loathed each and every one of them. They would all die, he swore; that was how he would begin his vendetta.

He stood up slowly, taking several deep breaths, stretching each shoulder in turn as he prepared to swing both his weapons in his personal war of retribution. He lifted his sword, raised his axe—then froze, *seeing...*

He spun to the left, aware that was the direction from which the danger would emerge, and he backed away deeper into the darkness. As he did so, he saw a pale figure emerge from the gloom, heading towards the fire. A human figure, tall and slender, totally hairless.

Skullface!

Konrad stared in total amazement, unable to move. The figure passed directly ahead of him, twenty feet away. He had to act now or the moment would be lost. He shook himself free from the imaginary bonds that held him tied, and sprang forward at his hated enemy.

Instinctively, he used his sword; it was a much more precise weapon than the double-headed axe blade. Even though he struck with his left hand, Konrad's left was as strong and accurate as his right.

The point of the blade plunged into Skullface's back, between the ribs below his left shoulder blade, to where his heart was—or should have been. Blood spurted immediately, and that was when Konrad knew he was mistaken. There had been no such blood when his arrow first found Skullface's heart.

He wrenched his blade free, and the tall figure toppled twitching to the ground. After a brief spasm of frenetic writhing, it lay without moving. Konrad had killed often enough to know when his victim was dead. He glanced swiftly around, watching for another intruder, but the pale shape had died without a sound.

Using his boot, Konrad rolled the figure onto its back. He already knew it could not be Skullface; the creature had died too easily. Even in the gloom, a quick glance confirmed his suspicions. It was just another of the bestial foe. Tall and thin, pale and bald—bald because no hair would grow on bone. Its head had neither skin nor flesh, muscle nor sinew.

Then Konrad heard another sound, and he twisted on his heel, springing back as an amorphous mass sprang towards him through the blackness. He brought up both weapons as fast as he could, but not fast enough. The thing knocked him to the ground, its hatchet aimed at his unprotected throat, falling on top of him... then rolling aside.

Konrad felt warm wetness on his face. Blood. But not his own blood. He glanced at the beastman. He could not make out the details of its appearance in the gloom, but it was big and dark—and dead.

Another shape loomed through the night.

"Thought you might need a hand, didn't I?" whispered a familiar voice.

Konrad rose to his feet, wiped the blood from his face with his sleeve, and watched as Heinler retrieved his blade. He had underestimated the man. Because he was a miner, his night vision was excellent; but he also seemed to possess other skills. It was no accident that he had survived the attack when everyone else had died or been captured.

Konrad glanced over to the fire and the group of non-humans who sat carousing around it. They were unaware of what had taken place a dozen yards away.

Like the pale figure that he had mistaken for Skullface, his attacker had come from the other direction. Konrad's vengeful bloodlust had been assuaged for the moment. There was no need to kill again, to take unnecessary risks—not yet.

"Want to tell me what you really looking for?" said Heinler.

Konrad told him.

"Let's go find her, shall we?" said the miner.

"You want this?" Konrad asked, offering his sword. It was best to divide the weapons between them.

Heinler stuck his knife into his belt and accepted the blade; Konrad kept the axe in his right hand, drew the stiletto with his left.

There was no need for discussion. Heinler understood what must be done, and for the first time Konrad really wondered about his companion and his previous profession. He had paid little attention to the miner, or to anything else. All that had concerned him was catching up with the legions who must have captured Krysten. They moved on warily through the night, heading for the glare of the next flames, covering each other's back as they approached their target.

Then Heinler's voice broke the silence. "Look out!" he yelled.

Konrad spun swiftly around, but too late. He felt a terrific blow on the side of his head. He managed to take another pace, turning and starting to swing the heavy axe at his unseen assailant, but then he dropped to the ground and the darkness claimed him.

CHAPTER FOUR

When Konrad finally managed to open his eyes, the first thing he saw was Morrslieb, gleaming high above.

His head was tilted back, his neck tightly tied, and his hands were bound behind him. He was upright, lashed to a tree, naked. He was in almost exactly the same hopeless situation as Wolf had been less than two days ago—even more hopeless, because there was no one to rescue Konrad from his inevitable fate.

He kept staring up at the irregularly shaped moon, not wanting to lower his gaze. The horrendous sounds that assailed his ears told him more than he needed to know about what was happening all around him.

Unlike Mannslieb, the smaller moon never offered much illumination even when it was at its nearest or its fullest—and tonight it was both close and also at its maximum dimension. Morrslieb always appeared to cast a strange light, almost an absence of luminescence. It was as if it were a shadow moon, throwing darkness onto the world it encircled, drawing away any brilliance instead of giving it.

As he gazed at the moon, Konrad took stock of himself and his injuries. He was fastened by the neck and wrists, both ropes securely wrapped around a solid tree trunk. His head throbbed incessantly from the blow it had received and he ached in several other places, as though he had been beaten while unconscious, then dragged across the ground. Many of the wounds he had suffered during the assault on the goblin stronghold had opened up again. He was coated in blood, down his face and over his body, although most of it had dried.

He was alive for the moment, but torture and ultimate death seemed his only destiny.

He lowered his eyes and swiftly glanced all around, then squeezed his eyelids shut with even greater rapidity. He did not want his captors to know that he was conscious—and he did not want to see more of what was going on in the moonlit clearing ahead of him than he had briefly witnessed.

He could not exclude the harrowing images from his mind as simply as he could close his eyes. In the centre of the grove of trees stood a small altar. At its focus was an armoured figure. Clad in red and black, it was armed with a mighty axe and bore a familiar emblem emblazoned upon its shield. Konrad had noticed the design many times before, on some of the banners carried by the legions of beastmen: an X-shape, with a horizontal stroke through its centre and one at its base.

Beneath the elaborate brass helmet, there was no face, however, nothing except darkness. The empty suit of armour sat upon a chair. No, not a chair, a carved throne—because the armour comprised an effigy of the perverted god that this clan of outlaws worshipped. At its feet lay a pile of bones and skulls. Human skulls.

And fresh human heads had recently been added to the heap...

Around the shrine the blasphemous acolytes stood reverently, revelling in the fresh blood that flew freely from the latest sacrifices to their gory lord.

Konrad had seen all this in but a moment. He had also seen the victims. And now he kept on hearing them as they endured the unendurable, as they suffered the insufferable. They screamed as they were tortured, screamed as they finally died, and even then their screams seemed to echo on and on and on.

He risked another glance, to left and right, searching for Heinler. But there was no sign of him. He was not tied to another tree, and neither did his hunched corpse seem to be amongst the acephalous mound of death, his head an offering to the hideous deity.

As his eyes swept the barbaric church, Konrad recognized the last victim. His name was Hralvan, a mercenary from Norsca, who was probably the strongest human warrior Konrad had ever known. He used to cut his own flesh for fun, to hold a blazing torch under his limbs to show that he was immune to pain.

But he was no longer immune. He had stood seven feet tall, with a girth to match his height. Now he had no legs and he wept like a beaten child—but it was blood, not tears, that flowed from his eyes as he was slowly sliced to death.

And the ones who were inflicting such unspeakable atrocities on his massive body were two of the most beautiful women Konrad had ever seen. Except that they could not have been women, not quite; both had slender tails, the tips of which were bifurcated.

Apart from spiked metal collars around their necks and wide loops of bone through their earlobes, they were completely nude. Their limbs were long and lithe—and splattered with blood. As their doomed victim's life spurted forth, they became speckled with even more scarlet. They grinned as they danced around him, licking the drops of crimson from the blades that they both wielded with such dexterity. The knives were like the girls, slim and supple.

Konrad was unaware how many worshippers stood around the altar, because most of them were lost in the shadows; but he could hear all the idolators roaring their depraved enthusiasm, chanting their hymns of blood.

Then there was a sudden silence. A total absence of sound: not a scream, not a whimper, not a chant, not a prayer.

Konrad realized why, but he could not prevent himself from confirming that Hralvan was dead. The giant Norscan had been dismembered, and one of the girls was holding his severed head aloft. Blood dribbled into her open mouth, and then Hralvan's head was added to the trophy collection at the feet of the armoured idol.

There was no one else to kill, no more victims to torture to death—except one...

Konrad clamped his eyes tightly shut, hoping they would believe he was still senseless, hoping that it would make a difference even if they believed it.

The silence continued, but he was aware of the two devil dancers moving lightly towards him. They stood next to him, and he felt their warm breath on his face as they leaned close. Then their hands were on his body, stroking him, their fingers sticky and damp with blood. Even had they begun to cut him, he could have continued feigning unconsciousness; but he was unable to ignore their ghoulishly sensual advances.

He opened his eyes and jerked upwards, supporting himself with his arms as he lashed out with both legs. He missed. The blood maidens sprang back, giggling, and Konrad almost strangled himself on the rope around his throat.

That would be a much less painful, much swifter way to die, he realized. But before he could pursue the idea any further, one of the nude girls had moved behind the tree and released his neck. A second later, his arms were free—but only for a second.

A length of rope hung from each of his wrists, and the other ends were caught up by the beautiful executioners. Even though their faces were masks of red, their long hair dripping with gore, they were hypnotically attractive. They appeared identical; it was impossible to tell them apart.

He rushed at the one to his right, but she leapt away from him. As she avoided his lunge, her knife whipped through the night air—and through Konrad's forearm. He grunted in surprise and pain. As the blood oozed from the wound and trickled to the ground, the worshippers sighed in ecstasy, their ritual chants commencing again as their final victim began to play his role in their obscene ceremony.

The girl brandished her knife in triumph and then put the blade to her tongue, licking at Konrad's blood. Her tongue was forked, like her tail.

Konrad yanked on the other piece of rope, hauling the second profane priestess towards him. She simply let go of the rope, and he fell backwards into the dirt. The ground was like mud, saturated after a downpour. But it was a storm of blood that had turned the earth into such a quagmire.

Then both of the girls sprang at him, twin streaks of red—and two streaks of blood flowed from his throat. Konrad regained his feet, and the naked women circled him, taking it in turns to dart forward, to feint, to pull back, then to spring again and really draw blood with their flashing blades.

They were fast, inhumanly fast. Female torturers were probably preferred because they were more subtle than the males; more delicate, they would not slay too soon with unnecessary force. Their victims would die more slowly, bled to death, drop by drop.

Konrad's body was soon as bloody as theirs, but it was his own blood which gave him a red second skin. He was also in great pain, but it was only superficial and he would not have to endure it for long. His tormentors were only playing with him. When they became serious, he was doomed.

Before it was too late, he had to get on even terms. And what he needed to even the odds was a weapon. He immediately thought of the suit of armour on top of the shrine, and the massive axe held in its gauntleted fist. The thought was sufficient impulse.

One of the tailed girls was between him and the throned figure. Konrad ran directly at her, and she nimbly skipped aside as he had known she would. Instead of turning back, he kept going, rushing at the altar, tearing free from the two ropes.

Until now he had not paid much attention to the worshippers who stood around the diabolic temple. He could not see them very well in the gloom, and his priority had been the predatory duo.

But suddenly his route to the weapon he needed was blocked by a group of shadowy figures, making a wall around the sacrifical area. He clenched his fist, slamming it into a darkened face, hearing a rewarding crunch as his knuckles crushed the bone. The shape fell back, creating a gap.

Before Konrad could dive through, a gloved hand grabbed his shoulder. He twisted free, turning back, seeing the gleam of a weapon in the feeble moonlight. The second figure was drawing a sword, but Konrad wrenched the hand from the hilt and seized the blade himself. The handle was fashioned like a coiled snake, and Konrad raised the sword, completing his turn and heading back to his twin torturers. Then the snake writhed, uncoiled—and its fangs bit deep into his wrist...

Konrad yelled out in agony, dropping the blade, and he rubbed at the two punctures in his flesh.

There was absolute silence, and all was still. The rhythmic chanting had ceased, everyone was staring at Konrad. The fiendish pair stood poised behind him, while the worshippers encircled the three naked blood-soaked figures.

The shape whose sword Konrad had taken stepped forward, and another dark form did the same, bending down to retrieve the fallen weapon and hand it to its owner. The sword hilt was a sword hilt again, the serpent tightly coiled once more.

Konrad glanced at the first dark form, almost indistinguishable in the black night. He noticed the shield the figure carried. It contained the same runic device as the one on the altar, but there was also another design on the shield, a crest that Konrad recognized.

"Kastring!" he said.

The figure had begun to sheath his weapon and turn away, but now he froze. He stared at Konrad for a few seconds, then walked slowly up to him.

"No one has called me that for a long time," he said.

Although he was very close, Konrad could not make out his features because they were shadowed by his helmet.

"Kastring," Konrad repeated.

"I was so looking forward to seeing you die." Konrad heard him sigh. "But I believe that we should talk. We do need a last sacrifice, however." He said something quickly, in a heathen tongue.

Konrad did not understand, but he sensed a movement behind him. He spun around in time to see one of the death dancers decapitate her companion with a single stroke of her long knife. The headless corpse stood upright for several seconds, a fountain of blood pumping from the neck, before collapsing into the mud.

Her twin held the gory head up by its hair and whirled it

around, spraying cascades of blood over everyone who was watching and roaring their bestial approval.

Konrad glanced back to the shape who had given the command. Beyond, he noticed the seated figure on the altar. And although it was hard to be certain, because his eyes had been splashed with fresh blood, it seemed for a moment that the armour was not empty, that there was a shadowy face staring back at him...

"Would you care for some refreshment?" said Kastring, who seemed to be the leader of this group of heathens.

Kastring had been Elyssa's family name. That was why Konrad had recognized the heraldic crest on the shield. But which one was he?

It could not be Elyssa's father, Wilhelm Kastring; he had been killed at the same time she had died. It must be one of her three brothers. They were all older than Elyssa; they had all left the valley before the village and its manor house had been destroyed by the beastmen. And now one of the Kastrings was in command of a band of such creatures.

Elyssa had referred to her family only rarely, and Konrad tried in vain to remember the names of her brothers. It made no difference, he supposed.

A fire had been lit, and it was only wood that was burning, not human flesh. Konrad sat in front of the blaze. He was shivering and felt feverish, weak from the blood that he had lost, totally exhausted by the events of the last few days. His body was a web of painful cuts.

"Knowledge of a person's true name gives one power over that person, they say," Kastring remarked, as he sat down a few feet from Konrad. He did not look at Konrad, and instead gazed into the flames. "The very fact that you are still alive proves, I dare say, there may be some substance to the tale. But no purpose would be served by my requesting your name."

Konrad gazed at the man, trying to recognize him. He had often seen the Kastring brothers, but it had been many years ago. Whichever he had been, he looked much different now. His lips were missing, so that he seemed to be grinning all the time—and a pair of curved horns grew from his skull. Even with the glare from the fire, however, it was hard to make Kastring out, to see where his long dark hair became the thick dark furs that he wore over his armour. Konrad was glad that he could not see what else had happened to the man—if he could still be called a man...

A figure walked towards them. Slim and supple and apparently female, it was the surviving torturess. She was carrying a silver tray, on which stood a jewelled flagon and two matching goblets. Kastring spoke to her, and she set down the tray and poured something into each goblet. It was red. She lifted the tray once more, offering it to him. Kastring gestured and said something else in the unknown language, and she held the tray to Konrad instead.

"She knows nothing about etiquette, I regret," Kastring remarked. "Do take it," he added, when Konrad hesitated. He laughed briefly, without humour. "It's not what you think, I assure you. It's wine, red wine."

Konrad accepted the cup, sniffed at it, took a taste, then swallowed the contents in a single gulp.

Kastring watched, then took his own goblet, spoke to the girl once more. She set down the tray and went back the way she had come.

"I was intending to offer a toast to your very good health, but I venture to suggest that such might be less than appropriate under these inauspicious circumstances."

He swirled the goblet and inhaled the bouquet, then put the cup to his teeth—the lower set overlapped the upper—and tilted back his head. Because he had no lips, some of the pink liquid dribbled down his chin, and he dabbed at the drops with a lace kerchief.

"Pray help yourself." He gestured towards the tray.

Konrad filled his cup again, then again.

"There was someone with me," he said. "When I was caught. What happened to him?"

Kastring shrugged, and he said something incomprehensible, in the alien tongue. He must have been speaking to the huge shape who stood a few yards behind Konrad, the one with the beaked face, the taloned hands, the clawed feet. In reply, the creature let out a huge belch, loud and long. Again Kastring shrugged, sipped at his wine, savouring it on his tongue before swallowing, then he mopped at the stray drops.

Konrad had seen no sign of Krysten amongst the dead, but he did not ask. He would not be told the truth, he was certain, and there were so many other mutant cohorts in the vicinity where she could be held.

"How do you know me?" Kastring queried, finally.

The truth was always to be avoided wherever possible, and so Konrad replied: "I'm from Ferlangen."

"Ferlangen! Now there's a name I haven't heard for many a year. By your accent, I suspected you must hail from the same region of Ostland as I. I dwelled in a poxy village near Ferlangen, but I had many a fine time in the town. Otto Kreishmier and I used to go hunting together on many an occasion. How is the fellow, do you know?"

"Dead."

Kastring raised his glass in a silent salute, but Konrad did not drink. It was Kreishmier who had sentenced him to death for poaching a rabbit—and who had been killed by Wolf in a duel. That was how Konrad and Wolf had met.

"How many years since you departed from Ferlangen?"

"Five," Konrad replied. "And you?"

Kastring said nothing for several seconds, and Konrad thought that he would not reply, but then he said: "Before, I believe. I cannot recall precisely. But what is time other than a chain around our lives? I left because I wished to see the world, the great cities, other lands. And I did. Then I fell in with a bad crowd and..."

If he could have smiled, he probably would have done. Instead, he sipped at his wine once more, and wiped his chin again. He was clean-shaven, had made no attempt to cover his missing lips with a beard. Konrad wondered if his lips had rotted away or whether Kastring had deliberately mutilated himself.

"But tell me more of Ferlangen," he continued. "What of Marlena, Otto's sister? She is still alive, I trust."

"She was."

"She and I had such excellent times together. We were intimate friends for a considerable while. Our families were nearly joined through us, but I was somewhat reluctant to bind myself so permanently. Instead, I suggested that Otto should marry my sister. Did they ever wed, do you know? I was never one for writing letters, I admit. And because of my present circumstances, I have rather lost touch." Kastring shrugged and reached for the wine flagon.

Konrad stared at him even more intently. "It was your idea that Elyssa should marry?"

"Indeed." Kastring lowered his goblet without drinking. "You know my sister?"

"I heard the name somewhere," said Konrad, swiftly. "I don't think they married. Otto was killed before. A hunting accident."

"What a shame. Marrying that fat bastard was exactly what Elyssa deserved." He touched the side of his face. An ancient scar marked his cheek, running from his left eye down to his jaw. He became aware of how closely Konrad was watching him.

"My first battle wound," he laughed. "A gift from my sister. Otto and Marlena were very close to one another, and it seemed reasonable that Elyssa and I should enjoy a similar relationship." Kastring shook his head, sipped at his wine, wiped his mouth. "Alas, she had a different opinion." He laughed again, a laugh that betrayed no trace of humour.

Elyssa had never told Konrad anything about how one of her brothers had attempted to assault her; but there was very little that she had told him, he recalled.

"With Otto dead," Kastring continued, "that would make Marlena the baroness. Perhaps I should visit the old place when we reach the Empire. I would rather like to renew my acquaintanceship with Marlena."

"The Empire?" said Konrad, his voice soft. "You're heading for the Empire?" He already suspected that the armies of damnation intended to cross the border, but he had hoped he was wrong.

"Just a fleeting visit, perhaps," Kastring told him. "Burn a few towns, loot some villages, slaughter all the inhabitants." This time, there was no doubt that he was grinning; the last traces of his lips were curled upwards. "They've had it far too easy there for too long. They've grown soft, like fruit over-ripe for the picking."

Konrad shuddered, thinking what the battle-hardened northern troops—the beastmen and their crazed allies—could accomplish amongst the defenceless townships. He clenched his fist tightly around his goblet.

Kastring sipped more of his wine. "I may even call in on my sister. I'm sure she'll be pleased to see me." He noticed Konrad's glaring eyes. "Come now, don't be so old-fashioned. She isn't even my real sister."

"What do you you mean?"

Kastring yawned, leaning back against the fallen tree trunk behind him. "Oh, I'm not too sure. Father never admitted it, but I'm convinced there was something strange about Elyssa. Mother died soon after she was born, although I don't know if she was really Elyssa's mother, or even if father was Elyssa's father. I believe one of my parents had been up to some—how can I put this?—some mischief. Probably both of them."

Konrad said nothing. Elyssa had revealed none of this to him, but there was no reason why she should have done. She might not even have known. Her mother may not have been her mother, Wilhelm Kastring may not have been her father—or maybe neither of them was her parent. Her origins seemed as mysterious as his own...

Konrad wondered if Kastring had heard anything of his unknown past. They had lived in the same village. Kastring's father had been the lord of the manor and should have known of everything that happened there. But if Kastring did not even know the truth about his own sister, it seemed very unlikely that he would be any more aware of the background of a nameless peasant boy.

Kastring's shield was by his side, decorated with the talismanic emblem of his dark deity, and also marked with his own family design. That was not the only heraldic crest which Konrad remembered from his native village. There was also the pattern on the bow and arrows that Elyssa had given him, the weapons she claimed to have found hidden in a forgotten room in the Kastring family home.

A quiver of some strange rippled leather, ten arrows, and a bow—all jet black, all marked with the same golden pattern: a mailed fist between two crossed arrows. It was the last of those arrows which had found Skullface's heart, that the inhuman had contemptuously pulled from his unbloodied chest. Yet Skullface had appeared to recognize the golden crest, as had Wolf when he saw it on the black quiver and demanded to be taken to the annihilated village...

Could the weapons have belonged to Elyssa's real father?

"Back in Ferlangen," Konrad began, "I once saw another family crest. In black and gold. Two crossed arrows, a mailed fist between the arrow heads. Do you know anything about it?"

After a while, Kastring replied: "That does sound somewhat familiar."

"On a bow, a quiver, a set of arrows?"

"Yes." Kastring's eyes were closed, and he ran his fingers across his brow. "An elf? Some connection with an elf, could it be? I confess that nought else comes to mind."

Konrad stared deep into the flames, trying to concentrate, but his exhaustion and weakness conspired to defeat his thoughts.

Elyssa had given him the bow and arrows, and she had also given him his name. Until then he had none. And now her brother, or the person she had believed was her brother, seemed to have denied Konrad a name.

"You said names give power," said Konrad. "Why didn't you want to know mine?"

Kastring's replies had always been slow, but now he said nothing for almost a minute, and Konrad had begun to think that he must have been asleep.

"Because you will not have it for long," he answered slowly. "You will be dead by dawn."

Konrad glanced around anxiously.

"In effect, you are already dead," Kastring added. "You should not have tried to steal my sword."

Konrad held up his right hand, examining it by the light of the fire, staring at the twin holes. His hand felt numb, but so did his other hand and both his feet. He was tired, very tired, that was all. Tired and cold and wounded.

His wrist was not even swollen. It could not be poisoned. He had only felt any pain when the snake had actually bitten—if indeed there had been a snake. It was probably only a trick, a delusion. There had been no serpent, no fangs puncturing his flesh, no venom flowing through his veins...

A minute earlier, all that Konrad had wanted was sleep,

but now the last thing he intended was to close his eyes and
surrender to the night.

CHAPTER FIVE

Konrad sat up abruptly, wincing at the pain that racked his whole being. The sun burned fiercely down upon his naked body. His throat was drier than ever, his lips cracked, he was covered in a crust of blood. The embers of the fire still smouldered, and the wisps of grey smoke were the only sign of movement. Everything else was still and silent; everyone else was gone.

From the angle of the sun, it was at least three hours since dawn. He seldom slept that long, yet there had been plenty of catching up to do. Although he was no longer so totally exhausted, he felt as if he could easily have found some shade, closed his eyes and slept through the rest of the day.

He resisted the temptation and studied his wrist. The two serpent bites had scabbed over, as had the cut in his arm where one of the inhuman girls had sliced the flesh. The elf who had saved Konrad's arm now seemed to have also saved his life.

According to Kastring, Konrad should have been dead. That was why the marauders had left him here; they believed that he was. It could only be the residual effects of the potent healing magic which had saved him.

He stood up and went to examine the creatures' camp. At first glance, there was hardly any sign that they had been here. Even the headless corpses of the sacrificial offerings were gone. The blood had been absorbed into the earth, baked by the early sun. The ground seemed very dry, and Konrad knelt down to touch it. It had no substance, was as lifeless as sand. The few clumps of grass and plants in the vicinity had become brown and brittle, were wilting away. The nearby trees were covered in fungus and rot, decayed like those where the Forest of Shadows was inhabited by beastmen.

Whatever the invaders touched became corrupted, even the ground upon which they trod.

Konrad fingered his lips, remembering the goblet from which he had drunk, remembering Kastring's lips, wondering if that was why his own were now cracked...

But it was the lack of water, he told himself, the raging thirst that consumed him. Drinking wine always made him very thirsty the next day, and he had been parched even before his first taste.

"It transpires that you are as tough as you look."

Konrad whirled around.

Kastring was a few yards away, mounted on a huge beast that must once have been a horse. Its skin was mottled, red and black, and its flanks were protected by armour; instead of hooves, it had taloned claws; its mouth was fanged like a dog's, and a single spiral of dark horn grew from the centre of its skull.

Despite his own grotesque appearance, Kastring did not look as frightening in the daylight as he had at night. The horns on his head seemed to be a part of his helmet, his grinning teeth were like a mask he wore over his face. His hair hung almost to his waist, and he was clad in black fur and red leather, as well as gleaming brass armour. His snake-hilted sword hung at his hip, his two-crested shield hung from his saddle.

Konrad backed away.

"Have no fear," Kastring told him. "I have no intention of killing you, I assure you. Not at present. I merely wish to invite you to join our expedition."

"If I refuse..?"

"That question does not arise. My request was more in the nature of a command. You should be dead. Because that seems not to be the case, you intrigue me. You will join us. You will amuse me with tales of Ferlangen. I was fatigued last night, I must admit, and so my conversation may not have been very spirited. For that I apologize. We will share many hours of discussion in future, until..."

"Until?"

"Until you die. All things must come to a conclusion, even life, especially life. We are born to die. It is not knowing *when* we shall meet our ultimate demise that makes our lives so interesting, I'm sure you agree? And your own life, I promise you, will be extremely interesting."

Konrad sensed another figure behind him, and he turned. It was the surviving death dancer. She was clad now, wearing sandals and a short loose robe, her body cleansed of gore. Her hair was tied back, but was still the colour of blood; so were her eyes and her feral teeth.

Her forehead was marked with the main symbol that was on Kastring's shield; the cross with two bars had been carved into her flesh, leaving a vivid crimson scar. She looked far more gaunt, far less seductive than she had in the haunted moonlight, but no less terrifying. The spiked band was still around her neck, but now she also wore a necklace through which her knife was looped. The necklace seemed to be made from bones, human fingerbones.

"I don't believe you have been formally introduced," said Kastring. "This is Silk. Or maybe Satin. I'm afraid I never could tell them apart. No matter. Like myself, she has no need to know your name. She does not speak Old Worlder, but you will learn to do everything that she commands. From now on, you and she will never be more than a yard apart. Perhaps much closer. She can be very pleasant company, I assure you. And then one day, maybe soon, maybe not, she will kill you."

Kastring spoke to the girl, who nodded solemnly. All the time, her eyes were on Konrad, studying his naked body. When Kastring had finished speaking, she raised the blade of her knife, kissed it, and blew Konrad the kiss. He shuddered, staring at her lips and remembering her forked tongue and the way it had licked his blood last night.

"She appears to like you," Kastring commented.

Konrad remained silent. It would not be him who died, he promised himself. His erstwhile torturer would be the first to meet death. Either her or Kastring...

"The Empire, Ostland, Ferlangen!" called Kastring, as he tugged at his mount's reins. "Our beloved homeland awaits our return!" The horse reared up, caracolled, then galloped off towards the south-west.

"Any chance of some water?" said Konrad to his guard. "Something to eat? Anything to wear?"

He saw her tail twitch. She spoke, a few grunted syllables, and pointed in the direction that Kastring had taken. Konrad kept watching her and remained motionless. The girl withdrew her knife and raised it at a throwing angle. She was too far away for him to reach before she could hurl the blade, but too near for the knife to miss if she threw it.

Konrad turned and followed the rider; his escort followed him.

He had walked from the Empire to Kislev, leading Wolf's packhorse. Now he walked back, this time with a deadly shadow close behind every step of the way.

It was a longer walk, because without any boat journey it was much further—and because there were so many interruptions for fighting battles, sacking villages, sacrificing captives...

Konrad saw very little of this, and he saw very few of Kastring's motley regiment. They were not like a regular army, taking orders, marching together. They split up into smaller units, choosing their own routes, then came together again for a raid or a massacre.

He was allowed to clothe himself with garments taken from the victims. They soon became ripped, sliced when Silk gave him an order that he did not immediately understand or when he did not respond with sufficient alacrity. His body was covered in tiny stab wounds, as if he had been bitten all over.

He had very little chance of escape, and even less chance of success. Every minute, Silk was within a few feet of him. And beyond her were Kastring's warriors and beastmen, each of whom was eager to kill, craving the offering they could make to their foul lord by spilling fresh blood. It was hard to judge how many there were in Kastring's band. The numbers were forever changing, increasing when they appeared to recruit new members from the areas through which they passed, declining after every clash of arms.

Sometimes they travelled by night, other times their journeys took place during the day. Often they would be on the move for a whole day and a night, then they would halt for a few days. Konrad never understood why. He never asked, and no one ever told him.

They carried few supplies with them. There were no baggage wagons, although there was one chariot. It was always well guarded, and Konrad realized that it must have borne the sacred brass armour which composed the altar.

The troops had to forage for food, or plunder from the farmsteads they destroyed. Most of them were on foot, which meant they could carry very little. A handful of warriors rode on horseback—horses that had begun to mutate in a similar fashion to their riders. These were an elite corps, true fighting men with professional weapons and armour.

They seemed oddly out of place amongst the rest of the warband. They were more like disciplined knights than berserk savages. They had their own warped code of chivalry, and it seemed their only destiny was to fight, that they honoured their chosen deity by the shedding of blood upon the field of battle—either their own blood or that of their vanquished foes. But then the opposite would happen: when the lesser moon was full, more blood sacrifices would take place, but on these occasions it would be helpless captives who were ritually tortured and foully murdered to satisfy the obscene cravings of the Chaos cult.

At the other end of the scale from the warrior knights were the brutal subhumans, dressed in rags, bearing whatever weaponry they had been able to steal. Between these two extremes lay the majority of Kastring's renegades, beings that were neither man nor monster, but some hideous combination of the two.

These were the kind that Konrad was most used to fighting on the frontier, fighting and killing: the creatures whose limbs had become weapons, who had extra eyes or ears or mouths, whose faces were set in their chests, who were part insect, with huge pincers for arms, who were part bird, with great wings on their backs, who were part reptile, with their flesh covered in scales, who had the heads of animals on human bodies—or human heads on bestial bodies.

Their bodies were predominantly red and black, the colours of blood and death; and their fur or feathers or fins or pelts or shells or hides would be striped or streaked or spotted with variations of these two hues. Many of them had eyes which were completely white, without any pupils. They seemed blind, but they could see.

And they were united under the same symbol, the same emblem that was on their banners, the same device that was on Kastring's shield, the same pattern that was on Silk's face—the vicious sign of Khorne, the god of blood...

Khorne, one of the four great powers of Chaos.

The runic design was the mark of death, as if it were the Huntsman of Souls' own unholy signature.

Silk proclaimed her allegiance to her dark lord with his rune emblazoned upon her forehead, and others of the creatures were similarly marked. Many of them had horns which were twisted into the design of Khorne's elaborate cross.

His devotees worshipped their lord through slaughter, through combat on the battlefield, through blood sacrifices. Every death was dedicated to the greater glory of Khorne, and it was not only enemies who could become such offerings. When a death was called for, then it could be the death of another cultist—as had happened when Silk slew Satin.

To Khorne's followers, everyone else was a potential sacrifice. They had no friends, no allies, only future victims. Every day that passed, it seemed more likely that Konrad would become the next blood offering.

But until then, every day that he survived was another victory.

And the days went by, the weeks, the months...until the hideous regiment had crossed from Kislev into the Empire, every mile of their route marked by the death of another innocent—or the occasional ally.

Konrad found himself praying that the marauders would find enough victims, that they would slay someone else, anyone else, so long as he survived. He had to survive in order to kill both Silk and Kastring. At first, that was all he cared about, the central idea which kept him going as he took every step.

Krysten had receded to the back of his mind. Already he was beginning to forget the girl. He had known her less than a year, and whenever he tried to picture her it was always Elyssa whose image he saw. He did not want to remember her, because he felt he had betrayed her. Had he not gone off with Wolf and Anvila, then Krysten may have still been alive. She must surely have been dead by now. He hoped for her sake that she was, because the only reason the legions of the damned ever took captives was for torture and degradation and ultimate sacrifice.

He never felt in immediate danger himself. It was almost as if all the carnage and mayhem he witnessed had nothing to do with him, that he was watching from a distance, an uninvolved spectator to the events happening around him. Even his own punishments seemed to have very little to do with him. His body might be in pain, but his mind was elsewhere. He felt that he was simply travelling in the same direction as Khorne's warband. They shared the same route, and that was all they had in common.

Konrad was aware that this state of affairs could not continue, that something must happen—and something would happen. Reality would return when he came face to face with the inevitable death that Kastring had promised. Either that, or he would be awoken from his trance in some other fashion. He could not imagine what might prompt his reawakening, but he would recognize it when it occurred.

He was uncertain why Kastring was keeping him alive. He seemed to derive macabre pleasure from Konrad's long torment. Maybe they would reach Ferlangen, and there he would be finally executed in what Kastring believed was his home town. Kastring knew Konrad was a soldier, but he wanted him to die like some beast on a butcher's block.

"You are a veteran of many battles," he remarked one evening, as he sat opposite Konrad and his tailed captor.

The girl was throwing Konrad scraps of food. His arms were tied behind his back, and he had to eat from the dirt. It was only a minor torture, but Kastring and the blood girl were vastly enjoying themselves.

"You have caused many deaths," Kastring continued, "and so your own death is of greater significance than that of someone who has not themselves taken life, not shed the blood of others. You are too valuable to sacrifice for no good reason. I do believe that I will save your demise as a celebration for some special occasion."

He watched as Silk poured a trickle of water onto the ground, and Konrad thirstily lapped it up. Then he spoke to the girl, and suddenly her foot was pressing Konrad's head into the dirt, her dagger at the main artery in his throat.

"Or maybe I won't," Kastring added. A few seconds later, he issued another command, and Silk released her prisoner.

Kastring delighted in the humiliation that Konrad suffered, that a warrior had become a slave, and that he was commanded by a female. Konrad felt only hatred, and it became deeper with every passing day. It was a cold calculating hatred, not the futile fury of impulse.

Silk and Satin had been too much for him on that very first night, when he had been weak and exhausted. He could have taken them both now, but there was only one.

He knew he could kill the girl; he could even kill Kastring; and often he considered that the price of his own death would be worth the payment. But then he would reason that he had too much else to do with his life, that ultimate revenge upon his enemies was not worth his own death. Not while he knew he would live through another night. And not while he was still awaiting the time he knew must come.

Several nights would pass without any sacrifice, and

David Ferring

during that interval the number of captives held by the
raiders would increase. And then the time of torture would
arrive once more, he would be bound by the throat and
wrists, and once more he would become the only hostage
to witness the dawn.

That was the one time he was left alone, when Silk went
off to play her part in the obscene ceremony. She would
finally return to him, naked and covered in blood, excited
by the pain and terror and final death she had inflicted upon
her helpless victims. Despite her appearance, she was far
more like an animal than a human. Her tail, her forked
tongue, they were the manifestations of her true bestiality.

"Or possibly you should join us," Kastring suggested on
another occasion. He was in a good mood, having
destroyed a small garrison of road wardens during the
afternoon. "We are always eager to recruit a good man.
Although you need not be a man, of course, or even
good..."

The idea was utterly repulsive, but Konrad pretended to
consider it as he watched Kastring across the fire. It might
keep him alive a little longer.

"What would I have to do?" he asked.

"Kill. You have done that before, I believe. But now you
would kill in the sacred name of Khorne. You're a
mercenary, I know, that is why you were in Kislev. You
killed for money. What kind of reason is that? Would you
not prefer to kill for a holy purpose, to glorify the greatest
of the gods?"

It was not true that Konrad had killed for money. He had
received hardly any payment during the years he had
worked with Wolf, but that had not been his motivation. He
did have a purpose in slaying, he had been protecting
mankind's northern frontier against the incursions of the
creatures from the frozen wastes, the realms of Chaos...

And now he was in the midst of those very creatures. He
felt like a traitor to his race for being here, for being alive

when so many others had died.

The heathens had broken through humanity's first line of defence, making their way across hundreds of miles of territory. Yet it had hardly been an infiltration. Kastring's raiders had burned a fiery trail into Ostland, the first province within the borders of the Empire. The savages had made no attempt to disguise their presence, and this had resulted in more and more opposition being directed against them.

At first, Konrad had wondered whether this was part of the master plan. Kastring's marauders were creating a diversion, drawing away the imperial troops while the massed legions of darkness prepared to invade elsewhere, striking at the larger townships. Yet such a scheme was far too organized for the blood clans. Kastring appeared calculating and cunning, but he was no different from the creatures he commanded. All he craved was blood, all he wanted was to kill, to destroy.

That was how he maintained his authority, by providing his followers with enemies and with victims. The more troops lined up against them, the more opportunity there was for slaughter and the more prisoners there were available for sacrifice.

"Who do I have to kill?" Konrad asked, knowing what the inevitable answer would be.

"We have several suitable captives, I believe," Kastring told him. "Perhaps you would care inspect them, to choose the one which you wish to give to our great lord and master."

Kastring was right: Konrad had killed before, many many times. But he had never murdered. Now, it seemed, there was no alternative. If he did not take human life, then he would also become a victim. Even if he refused, that would not save the person he had to slay. The victim would die no matter what. Konrad must kill. But he could kill quick, giving the merciful release of instant death instead of the lingering agony of torture.

"They gonna kill us, mister?" asked the small figure tied up next to him.

He was about fifteen years old, his eyes wide with fear. He had been brought in with a group of other captives, militia from the nearest town. The others were taken elsewhere, but the youth had been dragged away from them and thrown down with Konrad. His clothing was stained with blood; his face was dirty and bruised, streaked with tears.

"No," Konrad lied. "If they wanted to do that, they'd have done it by now."

"What's gonna happen to us?"

"I don't know," he lied again.

Silk was squatting directly opposite the two captives, and she was grinning, humming a tuneless tune to herself, tapping the blade of her knife on her bone necklace.

"Where you from, mister? When they catch you?"

Konrad said nothing. He wanted to avoid any communication, because he knew from the look in the girl's red eyes that the youth had been chosen as the one he was to slaughter.

"They *are* gonna kill us, mister. I know it!"

"No," said Konrad, trying to reassure him. "They caught me a long while ago, and I'm still alive."

"She wants to kill us," the boy said, lowering his voice to a whisper, "I can tell."

Silk stared at him, but he looked at the ground and would not meet her gaze.

"She one of them 'mutants'?" He spoke the word as though it were the first time he had dared use it.

Konrad realized that the youth knew far more of the world than he himself had done at a similar age; he had never heard of mutants until after he had left his native valley. The village had been overrun by them, and he had not even known what they were called.

Chaos mutants. The source of their deformities lay in the corrupted regions north of Kislev.

"I don't wanna die, mister!"

"Neither do I," said Konrad, softly, thinking how the price of his own life was probably the boy's death.

He gazed up at the dark sky, lit only by the stars. Mannslieb would not rise for several hours, that was definite; the lesser moon was far less predictable, both in its hour and its phases, but it seemed that tonight Morrslieb would be full.

The frightened boy kept talking, asking questions. Konrad said as little as was necessary. Meanwhile, Silk watched and waited, then finally the irregularly shaped moon rose above the horizon—and a hideous scream broke the silence, a long ululating scream of absolute agony.

The assembled beastmen, the mutants, the warriors of Khorne had greeted the arrival of Morrslieb by sacrificing their first captive.

The boy gasped, and Silk laughed. Without her partner in torture, she was not always the main executioner, although seldom an evening of death went by without her taking some part in the orgy of mutilation.

From where Konrad sat, he could not see into the area where the altar had been erected. Since the first night, he had always been out of sight of the killing zone; but he had always been close enough to hear the ritual slayings.

Tonight, he was on the outskirts of the marauders' encampment, on the very edge of a wooded slope that led down to a valley beneath. Below him, he could hear the distant rush of water. As the blood ceremonies commenced, he tried to concentrate on the sounds of the river instead of the sounds of painful death.

There was screaming from the sacrifices in the distance, and screaming from the boy next to him.

"Stop it!" Konrad yelled, turning to the youth and shouting directly into his face. "Shut up! Listen to me!"

The boy became silent, his eyes wide with fear. For the moment, he was more terrified of Konrad than the fate which awaited him.

"You'll be all right. We'll both be all right. That's why you're with me. That's why they took you away from the others. You're not to be killed. They haven't killed me. They won't kill you."

The boy stared at him, and his expression hardened.

"You're one of them!" he accused, and he spat in Konrad's face. Then he turned away.

At least he was silent, thought Konrad. But he kept thinking about the boy's words: You're one of them...

In a way, he supposed it was true. He had been with the savages for many weeks. And if he were forced to kill the boy, that would indeed make him one of them—or almost.

Kastring had invited him to become one of Khorne's followers. If he slew before Khorne's effigy, would that serve as an initiation ceremony? No matter his motive, or his intention, would the slaughter be the first stage of his own descent into the abyss of bestial mutation? Kastring had begun as a man, a human. How had he started to change? Had it happened in the Chaos wastes, or could the mutation occur anywhere?

Konrad had considered that he could save his own life by taking that of another, by killing the boy; but did sacrificing before the shrine automatically mean acceptance of Khorne as his deity? In that case, his life would no longer be his own—he was lost forever. It was more than merely his life that was as stake: if he joined the barbarous clan, Khorne would also claim his immortal spirit.

He wished he knew more. Konrad had never been religious. There were so many gods who were worshipped within the Empire and Kislev, but he had never had much contact with any of their followers and rituals. He knew most about Sigmar Heldenhammer, who was venerated as a deity. Wolf had belonged to the cult of Sigmar, and he always offered a prayer to the founder of the Empire before going into combat.

Silk rose to her feet. At the same time, Konrad became aware that there was silence. The last victim had died.

The last but one—or two...

The girl kicked off her sandals, shrugged out of her robe, let her necklace of fingerbones fall, untied her blood-red hair and shook it loose. She stood naked, armed with her knife; she was ready to kill. She spoke a few words. Konrad recognized the command. She was telling him to get up, but he ignored it. She sprang towards him, her blade at his throat. The tip drew blood. She repeated her order.

She would not kill him, he knew, but she was an expert in pain. With a few swift and accurate knife strokes, she could inflict excruciating agony. Instead, she transferred her attentions to the boy, jabbing him in the shoulder. He cried out in agony. She gestured for him to rise, and he obeyed. She swiftly cut away his garments, and he was naked, his hands still tied around his back.

She looked at Konrad, then she slowly drew the point of her blade diagonally down the boy's chest, right to left. He screamed as the blood began to flow. She did it again, left to right, her red eyes watching Konrad. She was carving the mark of Khorne on the boy, he realized, and she would continue unless Konrad obeyed. He did so; he stood up. But Silk did not cease her mutilation. With two rapid strokes, one to the left, one to the right, she completed the pattern. The boy's torso glistened with trickles of blood.

He swayed, as though he were about to faint, but he held himself upright. His screams had ceased, and now he sobbed. He was not badly hurt. Silk had not wanted him dead. Not yet.

Now she stepped towards Konrad, and her knife flashed.

He winced as she sliced his cheek for disobedience. Her blade kept working, and after a few seconds he was also naked. She growled a command, and Konrad began walking slowly towards the shrine. She pushed the boy, and he also began to move.

The worshippers awaited them, dark silhouettes who encircled the armoured effigy of Khorne. One of the shadows stepped forward.

"Delighted that you could accept our invitation," said Kastring. "Is this your guest?"

The boy stood motionless, dazed, his eyes fixed on the shrine, staring at the skulls and fresh heads at the feet of the seated brass figure.

"I'm going to kill you, Kastring," Konrad hissed.

"You seem to misunderstand the situation," Kastring replied. "The only killing you are going to do involves this young gentleman. Neither do I believe this is the most appropriate time for you to threaten me. I'm the one who issues the threats. And, as I once promised, I will have you killed. Eventually."

Silk's knife severed Konrad's bonds, and Kastring held out a dagger to him, hilt first. Konrad accepted the blade, and as he did he felt the tip of the girl's knife at the base of his skull. As Kastring stepped back, so did Silk.

Konrad and the boy were left in the centre of the area, in front of the altar. The ground beneath their feet was wet with blood. The boy turned away from the shrine to look at him, at the knife, then at Konrad's face.

"I knew you was one of them," he said, very quietly, and he lowered his head.

Konrad wanted to deny the accusation, to tell him that he would dispatch him swiftly, whereas any of the others would have slain him slowly and horribly. But there was no point. He would only have been speaking for his own benefit, not the youth's.

The idolators began to chant their hymns of blood.

"Do it!" Kastring commanded, his voice louder than all the sacrilegious prayers.

Konrad gazed at the shadowed shape which had spoken, and he held the knife loosely in his hand, testing its balance, weighing it for its flight through the night—and into Kastring's throat.

Before he could act, the blade was suddenly knocked from his hand. Silk had hurled herself silently at him, and she shouldered him aside. Unbalanced, Konrad fell into the mud. He instantly rolled away, believing that the blood girl was about to dive on him. Instead, her target was the young Ostlander...

Her blade plunged into his chest, and his cry was terrible, long and ear-piercing. He fell, and Silk went down with him, her knife carving deep into his torso. After a few seconds, she sprang up. In one hand she held her knife, in the other was a lump of raw human flesh. It was the boy's heart.

His beating heart!

There was a roar of approval from the worshippers, and she reverently placed the gory organ at the feet of the brass figure.

Konrad had been unable to find the dagger and was back on his feet, and he became aware of a dark shape moving towards him. He heard a sword being drawn from its oiled scabbard, and he knew it was the sword with a coiled serpent as its hilt.

He backed slowly away, glancing quickly over his shoulder for another potential assassin. When he looked back a moment later, there was a slim figure between himself and Kastring. It was Silk, but she was facing her leader, threatening him with the reddened blade she held.

Kastring halted, said something in the heathen language. Silk said nothing, but neither did she move aside.

"She does like you," said Kastring. Then he forced a contemptuous laugh, sheathed his sword and turned away.

Silk looked at Konrad, and their eyes met. For some reason of her own, she had killed the boy when Konrad had refused, and she had defended him from Kastring's wrath. But she had also saved Kastring's life by knocking the dagger from Konrad's hand. Konrad had no idea why she had interfered in the ceremony, protecting him from Kastring. Whatever the reason, it must surely spell doom for both of them.

The dark shapes around them melted away into the deeper darkness, leaving them alone, alone with the body of the young Ostlander and the corpses of all the other victims who lay as gory offerings to Khorne's bronze altar.

As they gazed as each other, Konrad suddenly realized what she must once have been: human.

And he also knew that this was the moment he had been awaiting. It was the time of his awakening.

Konrad walked away and Silk followed. She was a pace behind him when he reached the spur of land above the river. He turned as the girl raised her knife, standing motionless while she thrust the point of the weapon into the trunk of the tree next to him. The blade glinted as it vibrated. Mannslieb had begun to rise, a sliver of brilliance on the horizon, already shedding a radiant light far greater than the dull glow created by Morrslieb. The river lay far below, and on the edge of his vision Konrad noticed another glimmer further down in the valley. It was also the reflection of moonlight on metal.

And he finally became aware of what he must do.

The girl pressed herself hard against him, turning her face up to his. No matter what, he hated her absolutely, but for a moment he remembered what he had thought when he first saw her and Satin: that they were the most beautiful women he had ever seen.

Until now he had always refused the temptations of her body, no matter what torments she inflicted upon him in reprisal. Because of tonight he owed her this one final tribute to her lost humanity, to her forgotten femininity.

Her flesh felt warm and soft, and that surprised him. He tried to ignore the blood on her skin, her feral eyes, her forked tongue and tail. He sank to the ground, allowing her to assume the ascendant role, as if still accepting his subservience to her.

She was at her least animal, he at his most. When she cried out, it was not the rutting call of some bestial mutant but the sounds a woman made at the peak of passion. He was the one who growled primitively, driven by his deepest instinct.

This was the way life was created, the way of Konrad's unknown origins, the way that Silk herself had begun her true existence, before her body had become corrupted by Chaos, her spirit stolen and twisted.

Konrad reached up to her, beyond her, and for the first time he allowed her lips to touch his. Again, so warm, so soft. They kissed—and it was the kiss of death.

Silk sighed as he slipped the dagger into her back and plunged it deep into her heart. Their eyes met for one last time, and the girl's were wet with tears. She leaned back and she smiled and she died as easily as if she were still human.

Konrad caught her as she fell, and he rolled free. He withdrew the blade and stared down into the valley, searching for what he had observed a few minutes ago, the glint of moonlight on armour.

On bronze armour...

CHAPTER SIX

Konrad hurled himself headlong over the edge and down into the darkness, clutching the dagger in one hand. He was finally escaping his barbarous captors, but more importantly he was in pursuit of the mysterious bronze knight.

This was why he had stayed with Kastring's clan for so long. It was almost like *seeing*, but he had been totally unaware of the nature of the vision until now because the event had been so far ahead.

There was no longer any sign of the armoured rider below, but that was because of the conditions. The light was not as good as it had been at the top of the slope, and there were too many trees obstructing his vision.

He had killed Silk; she had allowed herself to die at the moment when she had recaptured the essence of her humanity. Konrad's only regret was that he had not been able to slay Kastring. Although free of his red shadow, there had been no time to creep through the night and take his revenge against the leader of the evil outlaws. It was infinitely more important that he find the bronze figure he had seen at the bottom of the valley. He must reach the knight before he could ride out of range.

He slipped and stumbled, rolled and crashed against one of the trees which grew from the side of the valley. Ignoring the pain, he was back on his feet almost at once and plunged onwards, immediately colliding with a sapling which blocked his route. It splintered, and Konrad's hectic descent continued. As he recklessly threw himself down the steep slope, he again lost his footing and tripped, but this time there was no tree trunk to block his fall. He rolled over and over—and over a precipice.

As he dropped through the air, he saw the rocky ground rushing up at him. But the narrow river was also below, and he plunged into the cold waters, narrowly missing a sharp pinnacle of rock. He sank below the surface, then kicked himself to the top. He trod water for several seconds before taking a long drink from the icy river. He swam to the edge and hauled himself onto the stony bank.

He sat there for a few seconds, regaining his breath and examining his cuts, scrapes and bruises. The dagger was still in his hand. This was almost an exact recreation of how he had kept a tight grip on his kris when he had fled by river from his village; but now a knife was all he had.

How could he confront the bronze rider when naked, armed with only a dagger? He neither knew nor cared, not at the moment. He first had to locate the enigmatic figure.

Five years ago he had escaped from an army of beastmen; now he had made a getaway from a smaller band of the bestial marauders. And, as he thought this, he heard the noise of pursuit from high above...

They were coming after him, yelling out their war cries, howling their animal fury, the savage sounds slicing through the night air just as the blades they carried would slice into Konrad's flesh once they found him.

He glanced around, finding his bearings in the dimness. He had seen the glint of light to the left, and that was the direction he took. He dashed along the river's edge in pursuit of the figure he had first seen half a decade ago. The fast waters raced past him, as he headed upstream, and he leapt the dark roots which fed from the water. He had a few minutes' start on his enemies. They would come down the slope far more cautiously than he had. Others would try to find a different way to the river, attempting to cut him off at either end of the valley. Before he was trapped, he must find his elusive quarry.

Konrad sprinted through the night, all his senses alert: feeling the hard ground beneath his feet, tasting the cold air on his tongue, hearing the river rushing past, watching the twisting valley ahead, sniffing for the pungent scent of the beastmen tracking him—and seeing, *seeing...*

His extra awareness gave him no warning of trouble; he was in no immediate danger. Either that or his future vision was once more betraying him.

Then he came to a sudden halt, and he dodged behind the trunk of a wide tree, because far ahead he had seen the reflection of moonlight on metal. Cautiously, he peered out from the side of the tree. A hundred yards away stood a horse, a horse completely covered in bronze armour. But there was no sign of the rider.

Konrad climbed the slope and used the woods as camouflage while he paralleled the river, closing the gap between himself and the horse. He moved slowly and silently, and it seemed to take forever until he was above the animal.

There was no doubt it was the same mount he had first seen over five years ago. He recognized the elaborate armour in which it was clad, encasing the steed from head to hoof. There was not an inch of horseflesh in view. Its skull was covered by an intricate chamfron from which two horns protruded, horns that matched those on the rider's own helmet, he remembered. The shield still hung from the horse's armoured flank, and the long lance stood vertically next to it, strapped to the back of the saddle. Even the leather of the straps and the saddle were bronze, as if dyed somehow.

The rider must have dismounted, and that meant he was more vulnerable. Weighed down by the bulk of his armour, he could not move as fast. If Konrad could surprise him, he could slip his dagger between the helmet and gorget and into his throat.

But it was not his intention to kill the bronze warrior. He was not sure, however, what he really did want from the knight. He needed to interrogate him, ask all sorts of questions. Was he really Wolf's twin brother?

And where was he this very moment..?

He could not be far away. Konrad kept watching, his eyes scanning the darkened river valley as far as he could see. There was something odd about the horse, he noticed. It had not moved; it was in exactly the same position that it had been when he first saw it. Standing like a statue, a yard from the riverbank, it reminded him of those equestrian monuments to great chieftains he had occasionally observed, except here the rider was missing. It was also like the altar to Khorne, he thought, an empty armoured shape.

Under other circumstances, Konrad could have watched and waited for as long as it took the knight to appear; but time was of the essence. Kastring's marauders would arrive at any moment. He glanced back up the hillside, and thought he could make out the dark silhouette of the spur from which he had noticed the bronze warrior. Judging by the angle, this was exactly the same place from which Mannslieb's light had been reflected. It seemed he had only seen the horse, not the rider.

Could he have fallen into the river? The horse might have thrown him, or stumbled in the dark, and he had rolled into the water. Because of the weight of armour, perhaps he had been unable to rise and thus drowned.

Konrad moved down the slope, towards the horse. And there, by one of the trees that grew from the water, he saw the armour. The knight's helmet and gauntlets, breastplate and backplate, pauldrons and rerebraces, couters and vambraces, cuisses and poleyns, chausses and solerets, sword belt and scabbarded blade, all lay upon on the ground. It seemed that the outfit had been abandoned, cast aside. Where could the knight be? Had he stripped off his heavy suit in order to sleep, or perhaps to bathe?

Stepping warily forward, Konrad knelt to examine the bronze. He glanced at the horse. Wolf had said that the steed was the twin of Midnight, his own mount, and Konrad knew that the white horse had been a killer in its own right. But the animal continued to remain absolutely motionless.

Konrad heard a sound, a shout in the distance. He stood up swiftly and retreated a few paces. If it were the unknown warrior who had called, he was defenceless without his armour and weapons, and Konrad felt confident. Then there came an answering yell, and he realized that it was his pursuers. A handful of the blood beasts were a few hundred yards away, heading towards him.

He glanced down at the sword and began to reach for it, then he paused, studying the armour. During the attack on his village, he had disguised himself in the flayed skin of a beastman. This would be far more than a disguise, he realized.

Dropping the dagger, he began to pull the armour over his naked skin. He should have worn protective clothing beneath the suit, to prevent the metal rubbing his flesh, but there was none. The armour was not cold, as he had expected, perhaps because his skin was chilled by the night.

It was usually very difficult to get into a suit of armour, and assistance was needed to tie the straps and buckles and help with the weight; but Konrad was in a hurry, and his haste seemed to make every item easy to fit. Breastplate and backplate were joined together as a cuirass, complete with taces and tassets. The parts for each arm and leg were similarly linked into whole pieces, simple to pull on and attach.

He buckled the swordbelt around his waist, fastened the gorget to his throat, drew on both gauntlets. Like everything else, they were the ideal size. Because bending down would have been difficult, he had previously placed the spiked helmet on a boulder. He picked it up.

During his years on the frontier, he had usually worn armour of some type during combat, but never the full panoply. He found it too heavy, too restrictive. The bronze armour, however, seemed completely different. Already he felt comfortable, and he could hardly feel any extra weight.

He did not have time to question this, because he heard a howl not far away. He turned in time to see two bulky figures rushing along the riverbank; dog-faced degenerates of Kastring's command, moonlight glinting off their weapons as they charged towards him.

Konrad lowered the helmet over his head, pushed down the visor and started to draw his sword. Then he glanced at the horse. It remained motionless. He noticed there was a sloping rock by its side which he could use to climb into the saddle, but he had only just managed to clamber up the rock and haul himself onto the horse's back when the first of the beastmen attacked.

The sword stroke caught his arm, the power of the blow denting the armour and almost unseating him. He slipped his spurred feet into the stirrups, grabbed the reins, and as he did the horse suddenly moved for the first time. It reared up, bronze hooves flailing, pummelling Konrad's assailant and then trampling the ugly creature underfoot.

Konrad knew this must indeed be the equine twin of Wolf's horse.

The second savage hurtled up the same rock that Konrad had climbed, and launched itself through the air at the rider. Konrad had already drawn his new weapon. His arm and the sword were as one. They flashed through the air, and the dog head was severed from its humanoid body.

Konrad felt a sudden jolt of heat, almost as if he had swallowed a glass of Estalian liqueur. But instead of a warm glow on his tongue and down his throat, this apparent heat affected his whole body, radiating throughout his entire being; its source seemed to be his right arm, his sword arm.

He was pleased that he had slain an enemy; that was what the strange sensation must have been. He had felt fire in his veins again, the thrill of battle. It seemed so long since he had held a sword, ridden a horse, fought in combat. He peered through the eye slits in the visor, eager to find more of the foe to slay. He soon discovered them.

He had hardly tugged the reins, barely begun to move his body to give the horse its commands, before the animal responded. It turned and broke into a canter, heading up river to where more of the benighted marauders had appeared in Mannslieb's light.

In a matter of minutes, Konrad shed as much blood as was spilled during a sacrifice to Khorne—and there were even more fatalities.

His sword swung through the night, slashing and slicing, and the bronze of the blade turned to blood as the beastmen turned to corpses.

Konrad felt invulnerable. Every life he took gave him new energy. With every drop of blood that he spilled, he became more invigorated.

The horse seemed to know exactly what it must do, and he did not have to think about controlling it. Neither did he have to think about killing, that came naturally.

The creatures of Khorne attacked with club and sword, spear and mace, but they all met the same fate. They died.

The bronze armour absorbed every blow that evaded Konrad's shield, and none of the mutants succeeded with a second strike. They all fell to a sword thrust, or their limbs were hacked off as the sharp blade swept down, and they ended their lives as their sacrificial offerings had done, bleeding to death.

They came from both ends of the valley. Despite what had happened to their comrades, none of them retreated. They attacked with insane frenzy, incited by the flow of blood. The floor of the valley was littered with hideous bodies; others were carried downstream by the swirling torrent of the narrow river.

A final stroke, and Konrad stabbed his sword into the forehead of a furred monstrosity—the forehead where its third eye had been. It was his last victim. The creature kicked and writhed, finally dying.

There was silence, total silence. There were no cries and screams and moans from the wounded. There were no wounded.

The Chaos brood had died by the score, but these were only a few of those with whom he had reluctantly travelled so far, from Kislev into the Empire. All the dead had entered the fray on foot. None of them had been the mounted elite, the terror troops.

And none of them had been Kastring.

Konrad went in search of his hated adversary.

Kastring must have known that all those he had sent after Konrad were dead. He would have heard the sounds of combat; the clash of weapons and the inhuman cries of death would have echoed up the slope. He might even have glimpsed the battle through the trees from his vantage point above.

Konrad had to take the long way around in order to climb the hill, via the head of the valley. Even so, his mount was able to carry him up the incline at a very steep angle. He remembered Midnight, the way Wolf's horse had been the only animal able to climb the rugged track to the lost Dwarven temple.

The night was almost over by the time Konrad reached the top of the slope. Morrslieb had vanished from the sky, and Mannslieb would soon be rendered almost invisible by the sun. Already the sky was beginning to lighten towards the east, heralding the dawn. The marauders had left in great haste. They had not had time to dispose of the headless bodies of their victims. One of the dead still had its head, the boy that Silk had slain. There was a gaping hole in his chest, his broken ribs showing through where the tailed girl had ripped out his heart. Like all the others, however, he seemed to have been dead for weeks, not hours.

Even in the half light, Konrad noticed that the ground where the savages had camped was lifeless. Everything had begun to decay and rot. The trees would soon be like fossils, but blackened as though charred by flames; and it was as if tons of salt had been poured upon the ground, not the blood of innocent victims. Nothing would ever grow here again. Chaos had staked its claim to another part of the Empire.

But why had its minions been in such haste to leave? Could they really be so terrified of Konrad? That was the only explanation. They were unaware that they had fled from their fugitive prisoner, however; they believed he was the bronze warrior, because it seemed that was who had slain so many of their number.

Konrad had never fought such a battle. Although he had killed more at one time, when he had slain so many goblins in their foul subterranean lair, the fight against Khorne's evil servants had gone on much longer. Many of his antagonists had been berserkers, with no combat skills, but there had been an equal number of veteran warriors amongst the mutants.

He should have been exhausted, but he felt totally revived. He had been a prisoner for many weeks, had never been fed properly, had always been weary and dispirited. Yet now he was fully fit, completely alert; he did not even feel hungry or thirsty.

He glanced at the ground, inspecting it for wheel tracks. There were plenty of hoofprints, leading in a variety of diverse directions; but whichever way the chariot bearing Khorne's altar had gone, that was the route Kastring would have taken. The wheel ruts led towards the west, deeper into the heart of the Empire. Konrad followed, the dawn sun behind him.

It seemed only a few minutes later when he noticed three mounted figures in the distance, They had halted and were spread out across his path. They were the rearguard, he suspected, making a stand here in order to allow the chariot with its cargo of sacred armour to escape.

Each rider was mounted on a huge animal, a creature which had once been a horse, or whose ancestors had been. Now they were horned and clawed, scaled and armoured, and scale and armour were often fused into one. The same was true of the riders. They were clad in red and black, and it was hard to distinguish where the fur that they wore became their flesh, where their brass armour became metallic bone. The two on the flanks had their heads completely covered by elaborate helmets, wrought into the symbol of Khorne; but the middle one of the trio was Kastring, solemn and brooding.

Fifty yards from the three dark knights, Konrad halted. He fitted his shield over his left arm, gripping the handle with his gauntleted fist, and drew his sword. He had not cleaned away the blood, but the bronze was unstained and gleamed in the scarlet light of dawn.

"Who are you?" Kastring demanded.

He had not wanted to know his name previously, and Konrad considered saying he had none; but he remained silent.

"What do you want?" said Kastring. "Which god do you serve? Why have you chosen a quarrel with us?"

When Konrad maintained his silence, Kastring drew his serpent-hilted sword. The rider to his left was armed with a long-handled axe, the third with a morning-star, a spiked ball on the end of a chain.

And when Kastring swung his sword as a command to attack, it was those two who suddenly charged at Konrad.

Almost before he could instruct his own mount, Konrad's horse sprang forward and began to gallop towards the Chaos warriors. He rode between them, his shield blocking the axe, the quillons of his sword hilt entangling the chain and tearing it from his opponent's grasp. The three combatants were past each other in under a second. Kastring had not moved, and Konrad expected that he would join in the fray. Instead, he stood his ground and watched.

Konrad's horse turned, and so did those of his opponents. They thundered back towards him, one still armed with an axe, the other now bearing a sword. This time, they slowed, as did Konrad. They attacked from both sides, but he did not try to escape. He used the shield to defend himself against the axe. It was a heavier weapon, more unwieldy, and fewer blows could be struck than with a sword.

Konrad's own sword met that of his other enemy, sparks flying. Again, the blades clashed. Then again. But the next time, Konrad drew back at the last moment, and his foe's weapon flashed past him. Konrad lunged forward, and the metal plunged into the soft flesh of his opponent's side, through the gap between breastplate and backplate. The blade passed completely through his body. When Konrad withdrew it, his enemy slumped forward, then dropped from the saddle.

By then Konrad had focused his attention upon his second assailant. He took another axe blow on his shield, then dropped his guard. The knight's arm was raised for a repeated assault, and Konrad simply thrust out his sword, the blade entering the throat immediately below the helmet. He sawed his weapon to left and to right. The helmet toppled to the ground, and the warrior's head was within.

The rider remained upright in the saddle, and for a moment Konrad thought that the duel was not yet over. He had fought apparently dead opponents many a time previously. Then the axe dropped, so did the shield, and finally the headless corpse tumbled to the earth.

Konrad saw Kastring reach for his warlance, its serrated blade decorated with various talismans, bleached bones and plaits of hair. Konrad sheathed his sword and unfastened his own lance.

They rode towards each other, their horses cantering as the riders lowered their weapons, and then the animals broke into a gallop. Watching over the top of his shield, Konrad stared along the length of his lance as the gap between himself and his implacable enemy narrowed.

It was over in a moment. Konrad's bronze shield deflected the spear point, while his own lance penetrated Kastring's chest, impaling him. Kastring flew backwards, skewered on the end of the lance like a sheep upon a spit. He slid off and fell to the ground. Konrad rode towards him and gazed down.

"Who are you?" Kastring gasped, staring up at his conqueror. Blood bubbled from his mouth and flowed from the gaping wound in his chest.

He was still defiant, still proud and arrogant. Even his death was like a victory. He had lived for combat, and this was the way he had chosen to die, his own blood a final offering to Khorne. Konrad wished that he could have humiliated Kastring, awarded him a dishonourable and degrading death.

He remained silent, watching as Kastring reached for his sword, his hand moving with agonizing slowness. But before his fingers could touch the snake hilt, his hand slipped back and he was dead.

Konrad experienced none of the triumph he should have enjoyed with victory and the conquest of his enemy. He had felt a surge of warmth when each of the three knights had fallen victim to his weapons, as had also happened with the death of each mutant, but that was all.

He replaced his shield and lance, then reached up to raise his visor. It would not move; it must have jammed somehow. He struggled to push it up, but to no avail. He used the heel of his gauntlet, hitting the underneath of the visor with his hand. Neither did that succeed.

He needed more force, he realized. The pommel of his sword should serve his purpose. He took hold of the hilt to draw the blade and attempted to pull it from the scabbard. Nothing happened. He must have sheathed it wrongly, at an angle, and it had become wedged. He seized the hilt with both hands and tugged as hard as he could, but he was unable to release it.

Once again, he tried to free his visor, but it was still firmly stuck. When he began to undo his helmet at the shoulder, the fastenings would not come loose.

His endeavours would be less difficult if he were on the ground, he decided. He attempted to climb down from his horse, but discovered that was also impossible...

He could move his leg a fraction, but could not not move the armour itself. It seemed to have become a part of the armour of his mount.

Man, horse, armour, they were as one.

He was the bronze horseman.

He was bronze; he was horse; he was man.

The horse took him where he needed to go, and the armour provided him with all the nourishment he required. The armour fed on life, and the lifeforce fed him.

It was his function to find the lives necessary to sustain his armour, his horse, himself—find the lives and then take them.

He was a prisoner within the bronze suit, but the suit and its mount needed him to achieve the deaths which they required for survival. At such times the sword would be released from its scabbard, so that it might fulfil its function of slaying.

Even yet he possessed some vestigial trace of independence. He did not have to slaughter, to steal lives. But if he did not do so, then the armour would feed off his own life, draining away another piece of his humanity. He could feel the bronze becoming part of him, himself becoming part of the bronze. This was what had happened to the horse; animal and armour were totally as one.

And this was what must have happened to the previous wearer of the suit. The armour had finally sucked him dry, then fallen apart to await the next victim who would step into the panoply.

He was the warrior in bronze.

CHAPTER SEVEN

The bronze knight rode on, killing whenever he must, because that was the only way in which he could survive.

He was a warrior, however, and he only killed in combat. But in a world of war and battle, a land of armies and soldiers, there was never a shortage of victims.

Many a trooper fell to his sword; many a horseman died on the end of his lance.

And then there were all the others who also sacrificed their lives to him, the ones who did not belong to any true military force, the bestial creatures who saw him as no more than another enemy to be slaughtered. Instead, it was they who were slain.

There was no consciousness involved in any of this killing. It was simply his function, what he did, all he did. He was the perfect death-dealing machine.

He saw an enemy. He fought the enemy. That enemy died.

The rider was invincible, invulnerable, and every victory

granted him further power to continue his crusade against life—both human and inhuman.

The days passed by, days and nights without number; and with each of them were the miles, the miles beyond counting.

And on rode the knight in bronze.

Deep within, he was aware of the pain.

He felt no real pain, not as such, because machines were immune to the sufferings that affected living creatures. But he endured a different kind of agony, which meant that the shell which held his inner being captive had decided it was again the time to slay.

He needed to kill soon, or he would lose another part of himself to his captor. If there were no alternative source of nourishment, he would replace the next victim—yet his own death would take almost forever.

He must find relief from that burden. He must kill.

Beyond the narrow slits in his visor, the darkness was fading. It was the beginning of another period of light, the time when men and non-men walked the world, the time for fighting, the time for killing, the time for death.

And there, ahead of him, stood his victim...

This was the way it had been so frequently. He did not need to search for an adversary, because they sought him out, issuing their challenges to arms. He paid no more attention to the silver figure than he did to any of the others, took no heed of his words. After so long, they were all the same.

What was less than usual about this one was that, although armoured like a knight, he was on foot. He stood in a glade between two rows of trees, his sword in one hand, a huge oval shield in the other. The bronze warrior also drew his sword. His horse began to canter forward, picking up speed as it approached his new opponent.

But halfway to the swordsman, the animal suddenly jerked back and slowed its pace. It had never done this previously; something was evidently wrong. The horse soon gathered momentum again, although its legs seemed uncoordinated. The rider was thrown about in the saddle as his mount lurched forward. He gripped the reins firmly, trying to control the steed with his body and his legs. He had never needed to do this before.

The armoured shape ahead stood in exactly the same position as it had. It neither raised its sword in offence nor its shield in defence.

Rider and horse moved ever closer, but the horse was again losing speed, and each of its legs seemed out of step with the others. It kept veering away from the target, before pulling back in the correct direction.

A single blow was all that would be needed to fell the motionless figure, and the warrior raised his sword—or attempted to...

His arm refused to obey his command. He could feel his muscles straining, but the armour in which his arm was trapped would not move. It had locked rigid. Then, abruptly, the horse collapsed beneath him and he was thrown from the animal.

He landed in a heap at the feet of the unmounted knight. He was unable to turn his helmet, and his vision was restricted to a narrow angle which encompassed part of the sky and his fallen horse a few yards away.

Only then did he realize that he was free of the animal. He had been separated from it for the first time since...he could not remember.

There was very little that he could remember. It seemed that he and the horse and their combined armour had been united for all of his life. He was dimly aware of a previous existence, that he had once lived an independent life, but he was unable to recall any of it.

He saw various movements between himself and the

motionless horse, a few small and broad figures examining him and the animal. Men, like he had once been. No, he realized, prompted by a distant memory—dwarfs. The creatures were dwarfs. He could see four of them.

He heard their excited voices and gruff laughter as they congratulated one another. What they said was completely meaningless, until he suddenly recognized a word, and then another. They were speaking in their own tongue, which was why he had not comprehended at first. But he had once understood some Dwarvish, he remembered—or almost remembered.

"Is it not exactly as I predicted?" said another voice.

This he understood completely. It was a human voice, using the language that had once been his own, but he was unable to see who was talking.

"All my contemporaries refuse to move away from their libraries, to get out into the real world. They are content to repeat what has been done for centuries. Where is the future in that? Ha! The future! They are the past, this is the future. I am the future!"

The speaker finally stepped slowly into view. It was the armoured figure.

"Help me off with this ridiculous outfit," he ordered, and two of the dwarfs assisted with the removal of his silver armour.

The outfit was far too large for him and had magnified his height considerably. He could have been no more than average size, yet seemed much taller in the company of the four dwarfs. His hair was black, streaked with silver, and hung almost to his waist; his beard was equally as long.

The dwarfs were also bearded and long-haired, although their colours were ginger and red instead of grey and black. They seemed like squashed versions of the human. Their bodies were stocky, their limbs thick and short, their fingers were stubby, their noses flattened and eyes deep-set. They wore thick garments criss-crossed by belts and straps from which hung their weapons and tools.

Their human leader gazed down at the fallen knight, and all the rider could do was stare helplessly up. He wished his own armour could be shed as easily. The bronze held him trapped. He was locked in the smallest possible prison, one exactly the size of his body, and he still could not move even a fraction of an inch.

"Now let me see what is inside here," the human said, and he turned towards the fallen horse.

"You sure this is safe, boss?" asked one of the dwarfs.

"Safe? What is safe? You want to be safe, you get another job. Everything is a risk, and so we must risk everything."

"We've come this far, Ustnar," said one of the other dwarfs. "There's no going back now."

"Yeah," agreed a third. "What's one more bit of warpstone to us?" He laughed and moved closer to the armoured horse, pulling his heavy gloves on even more securely and reaching for the crowbar that hung from his belt.

The fourth produced a hammer and chisel and also walked up to the fallen beast. They began to work on the bronze, prising between the armour plates. The other two joined them, hacking and probing at the metal.

All the rider could do was watch as the bronze was slowly lifted away from the animal. He could not see too clearly at first, because the dwarfs obstructed his view. Finally they moved aside, and he gazed at what he had been riding.

It was a skeleton. There was nothing left of the horse except its whitened bones. Exposed to the sunlight, the skeleton crumbled in under a minute, the bones turning to dust.

"How long till that happens to us, boss?" asked the one called Ustnar.

"The sooner it happens to you," said another of the

dwarfs, "the better!"

Ustnar raised his hammer angrily, then vented his rage by kicking at the remains of the bones. A cloud of white dust flew up from his boot.

"That's how we'll all end up, I suppose," he said. "It's just that I'm in no particular hurry."

"The rider will be the same," said the human. "Get the armour off the bones, collect all my apparatus, then we can load everything into the wagon and be away from here."

One of the dwarfs came towards him, knelt down and inserted the end of a chisel beneath the edge of the helmet. That was exactly the way to kill an armoured knight, he remembered; he had done it so often. A chisel or a dagger, the effect would be the same. He would die.

Again, he tried to move, tried to speak, tried to make some signal that he was still alive, captured within the bronze. But what difference would that make? Even if they knew he was alive, they would kill him.

The dwarf raised the hammer to strike—then paused. He lowered the tool and leaned close to the visor, his eyes meeting those within the helmet. He frowned, removed the chisel.

"Hey, boss, I think you should take a look."

"At what?"

"I think he's still alive in here. I can see his eyes."

Another head leaned down, that of the human. He was as thickly bearded as the dwarfs, but his nose was aquiline instead of flared. His pale eyes studied those below.

"I think you may be correct," he said, after a few seconds.

"Let's see."

The burly figure of Ustnar shouldered the other dwarf away, and he stared down.

"I can't see anything."

"Eyes," said the human. "There are eyes. If you can understand me, close your eyes."

He shut his eyes.

"Open them."

He did so.

"That proves nothing," said Ustnar. "Whatever is in there, it isn't *alive*. It's a Chaos creature. We should destroy it."

"It cannot do any harm at present," said the human. "I wonder if I can get it out of there?"

"No, boss! We've got to play safe. Whatever it is, kill it!"

Ustnar raised his hammer over the helmet, but the human pushed him away and continued looking into the visor.

"This is interesting," he said, as if to himself, "very interesting. Yes, I think I shall take this specimen back with us." He smiled with satisfaction, although it was almost hidden behind his thick beard. "What a challenge! Put it in the wagon."

"Boss!" protested Ustnar.

"Do it!"

"Won't the suit dissolve him before we get back to Middenheim?" asked the dwarf who had first seen the imprisoned eyes.

"I do not think so. It is inert now. Whatever the circumstances of that unfortunate within, they will not deteriorate before we return. Unless, of course, he dies before then."

"We can't go taking Chaos infection back to Middenheim," Ustnar protested.

"Why not?"

"Er...we'll be caught. We'll never get past the watch."

"Ustnar, we both know that you dwarfs can get in and out of the city any time you wish. If you won't reveal your secret tunnels to me, then at least you can take my new specimen in with you."

"It's the Carnival next week, boss," the other dwarf said,

quickly.

"What is that to do with anything?" said the human.

"The festival is in the autumn this year, boss. Only a few days away. Thousands of people will be arriving. We can easy smuggle this thing in amongst the crowds, could pretend he's already dressed for the masquerade if we want."

The human nodded thoughtfully, then with more emphasis as he came to a decision. "Fetch the wagon. Dismantle all my equipment." He leaned down and stared in through the visor, his eyes only an inch from the metal. "You blinked a minute ago, although that may have been of no significance. It is my intention, however, to try and get you out of there. This not through any altruism on my part, I assure you. I have my own motives for what I plan to do. Do you understand?"

He closed his eyes, then opened them again.

He was still a prisoner within the bronze armour; that much had not changed. For several days and nights he lay at the bottom of a wagon, completely unable to move—and he was in pain.

This was not the kind of pain he had endured for so long, an awareness of being hurt, of being subtly devoured by the armour that enveloped him. The bronze may have become lifeless metal, but now he was in torment, real agony. His skin burned wherever it was in contact with the armour, which was everywhere. He was in total contact, totally aflame. There was no release from the torture, because the armour still held him absolutely immobile, unable to move a muscle, unable even to scream.

There was no cessation, even for sleep. He never slept; his punishment would not permit it. Nor was there any hope of final oblivion, because his captors seemed determined to keep him alive. He was still trapped within the same prison, although he had exchanged one jailer for another—and the result was infinitely worse.

He burned forever in eternal, infernal pain.

While he burned within the armour, he shivered and trembled. It was the only movement he could make.

There was the light, the darkness, the days, the nights, the times when the wagon was moving and the times when it was not. There were the voices of the human and the dwarfs. He tried to concentrate on what was said in order to maintain his sanity, but he was soon distracted by the agony which was his entire being.

After a century, they pulled him upright and sat him at the front of the wagon, next to the dwarf who had first noticed his eyes. Two of the others laughed and joked as they bent his hips and knees to make him sit upright; one did not.

"This isn't going to work, boss."

"Ignore him," the dwarf by his side said. "He's only happy when he's complaining. Give him a purse of gold, a tankard of ale, a beautiful maiden, and Ustnar's the most miserable bastard this side of the World's Edge Mountains!"

He and the dwarf rode in the wagon, the other four were on horseback. For the past aeons, all he had seen was the sky. Now he was sitting up for the last part of the journey to Middenheim.

Ahead, he saw the towering pinnacle of rock upon which the second largest city of the Empire had been built—and he wondered how he knew it was the second largest city, how he knew about the Empire. A lifetime ago someone had spoken to him about Middenheim, he recalled, someone who had visited the city of the white wolf. Wolf? That seemed familiar, but what wolf..?

The peak loomed high above the surrounding forests, and even through the tears which forever burned his eyes he could make out distant buildings carved from the hostile rock. Far ahead, the road twisted and turned as it wound its way up to the looming city, borne upon a series of stone bridges, an elaborate viaduct.

"We built that," said the dwarf. "Well, not *us* exactly. Our ancestors. *My* ancestors. Couldn't get any humans to construct anything that would last as long as that, huh? The humans reckon they found this place; but they would, wouldn't they? The mountain was called Fauschlag— 'Fist-strike'—although of course we had our own name for the pinnacle. I'm not boring you, am I? Just tell me to shut up if you want." He turned his head and grinned, then his smile turned to a frown.

"I hope Litzenreich knows what he's doing," he continued, his voice low. "Or else we'll all be in the shit. And not just us, I suppose. I wish I hadn't mentioned the carnival, but I suppose he'd have persuaded us to get you into the city another way. You know about the Middenheim carnival? You must do, *everyone* in the world knows about the carnival!"

"Can't you ever stop talking, Varsung?" said Ustnar. "If he isn't already dead in there, you'll talk him to death."

"It's nice to have a civilized conversation with someone who doesn't keep complaining."

Ustnar returned to the rear of the wagon, where the other dwarfs rode. The human called Litzenreich led the way, while Varsung drove the vehicle and kept on talking to the silent armoured figure by his side.

The two horses pulled the wagon up the long winding viaduct towards the city. There was plenty of traffic on the road, wagons and coaches, people on horseback, far more on foot, and their pace slowed and finally halted as they neared the gates. Ahead, guards checked everyone who wished to gain admittance to Middenheim.

Finally, Litzenreich reached the head of the queue. Varsung halted the wagon behind him, in the shadow of the high city walls. There were two guards. One was waving traffic out through the massive gates. The other cast his eye idly over the wagon, stared at the armoured figure sitting by the driver, then glanced at the riders surrounding the vehicle.

"Where you all from?" he asked.

"Middenheim. I am Litzenreich. These fellows are in my employ."

The guard nodded. "I recognize all of you," he said. "Except him in the fancy suit. Who's in there? Why's he hiding away?"

"Who?" asked Litzenreich.

"Him. The one in armour."

"There is no one in armour. Only you."

The guard looked puzzled. He closed his eyes for a moment, opened them, shook his head rapidly, and stared at the bronze figure.

"I've been on duty too long," he muttered. He gestured for the group to proceed, and they entered the city of the white wolf.

"Nice one, boss," remarked Varsung.

"It was nothing," said the human. "I hope that no one from the Guild sees what we have here. Pull in as soon as you can find a quiet alley, and then we can hide my guest."

"Home at last," Ustnar said. "I'll be glad to get off this bloody horse. Never thought we'd make it."

"You never do," Varsung replied. "I sometimes think you'd be happier if we didn't get back."

"Watch it, you little—"

"Little! Who's talking, shorty?"

"Stop arguing," commanded Litzenreich. "We all have work to do. This is only the beginning."

The wagon turned into a narrow entrance and halted. The prisoner within the armour felt himself being moved to the back of the vehicle, then everything became dark. The wagon began to move again, its iron-rimmed wheels rattling over the cobbles. After a period of time, all motion

ceased. He was picked up and carried out from the vehicle.
It stayed dark; he remained completely covered, masked
from the view of the people of Middenheim.

He heard boots on steps, much cursing and arguing,
doors being opened, then shut, the echoing of footsteps
along narrow passages and stairways, more doors opening
and closing, and finally there was stillness again. Stillness
and then light, narrow bands of illumination shining in
through the helmet. He was lying on his back, staring at a
distant dirty ceiling.

He was still afire, had not yet been totally consumed by
the flames which seemed to engulf his entire being; and he
was still trembling, frozen by the ice which held him in its
merciless grip.

A face loomed above him, that of Litzenreich. He
peered in through the visor.

"Blink your eyes."

He did so. That was almost the only movement he could
make, opening and closing his eyelids; that and moving his
eyes to either side.

"Anything, boss?"

"I cannot tell. It is too dark. Pass me a lantern and a
mirror."

Bright light was reflected within, and he blinked, and
kept on blinking to let the man know he was still there, still
alive, still a prisoner. He thought he saw his own eyes
gazing back at him from the mirror, and that almost
reminded him of something. He tried to grasp the memory,
but it was too elusive and was gone.

"Yes. He is in there."

"It, boss, that's what you mean." Ustnar leaned over the
helmet. "And if we do get it out of there, then what? We'll
only have to kill it. Might as well do that now, boss, save us
all a lot of trouble later."

"This is going to take a lot of warpstone," said
Litzenreich, ignoring the dwarf. They both moved out of

sight. "I will need all the stuff we brought back with us."

"All of it, boss?"

"Don't worry, Ustnar," said Varsung. "We can always get more from our regular suppliers."

The other dwarfs laughed, but Ustnar did not.

"To work," ordered Litzenreich. "To work!"

He heard the human and the four dwarfs moving around the chamber, heard the sound of metal being sharpened, smelled the charcoal as a fire was lit, listened as they spoke in lower voices, as though afraid of being overheard. He tried hard to concentrate on everything that was happening, to draw his attention away from the eternal agonies which tore him apart.

Some of his senses were still active, he realized, as the time slowly passed by. He had not considered this until now. He could see and hear and smell. The suit of armour had not been able to destroy him totally. And he could think.

A few words were spoken in the Dwarven language, and he wondered why he understood the words. He had known dwarfs in the past, one in particular. But who? What was so significant about mirrors? He had almost seen himself reflected in the glass held above the visor.

Himself..?

"As I said previously, I intend to free you from the Chaos armour in which you are trapped," Litzenreich told him, gazing down.

Chaos? Another word which seemed familiar, yet whose meaning he could not begin to comprehend.

"If there were any way that I could administer some kind of soporific in order to ease your inevitable torment, then I would. But that seems impossible. I should warn you that this experiment will hurt you more than it hurts me." He smiled and then leaned away. "Let us proceed."

A strange odour had been assailing his nostrils, a smell that he did not recognize. He saw shadows on the ceiling, the outlines of the occupants in the room as they moved around him. He heard scraping sounds as something was dragged close to where he lay, and the illumination seemed to decrease slightly. He had been enclosed in some way, but it was beyond the limit of his restricted vision.

There was more noise, and he saw a huge metal device being lowered towards him from the arched roof. It appeared to be some kind of insect, made of metal. It was held by a series of chains and ropes, and various levers jutted out from its lower edges. They looked like metallic claws, and they came to rest a few inches above him.

The dwarfs began inserting a series of rods into the side of the strange device, and with these they were able to make the artificial claws move: the levers bending like arms, the claws opening and closing like fingers. The thing was like a spider, eight-legged, suspended in a web of chains.

When everything appeared to be working to their satisfaction, there was a rattling of chains and the steel spider glided to one side and vanished.

He heard Litzenreich giving his commands to the dwarfs, and after a while the spider returned. In each metal claw it held a glowing instrument; there was a hammer and a saw, a chisel and a knife, a pair of pincers and a turnscrew, and two contraptions he did not recognize. They glowed with heat, but with far more than that. At the very epicentre of each device was a point of absolute blackness, a total darkness which seemed to absorb all light within its immediate vicinity.

They planned to open him up with this equipment. No, not him—the bronze armour.

But he *was* the bronze armour...

He gazed with terror as the spider was lowered even closer towards him, and its metal arms began to move, each of them bearing an implement which was directed at the armour in which he was held captive. They started to work their way into his metal, his flesh, peeling back the bronze, flaying away his skin.

He had believed he was in pain earlier, but that had been as nothing in comparison to what he now experienced. He was overwhelmed with absolute agony, the refined essence of torment. All he could do was squeeze his eyes shut, so that he did not have to witness his own living autopsy. But even with his eyes closed and flooded with tears of poison, he could not dim the brilliance of the mechanical insect ripping its way into his body.

For the first time in ages, he managed to utter a sound, a cry of infinite torture.

And he heard a distant voice say: "He's dead, boss."

CHAPTER EIGHT

He was free of the suit. More: he was free of his body...

He felt himself rising up.

But who was *he?*

What was he?

He was more than a body, because that was the part of himself which he had left behind.

His essence floated away from his physical form. He had no eyes but he could see. And what he saw was himself, the human shape within the armour.

He seemed to be hovering at ceiling height, and the metal spider should have obscured his vision, yet his eyeless gaze could focus through the device.

A few pieces of bronze had been torn away to reveal the flesh beneath—or what had been his flesh...

What lay below was but a corpse, a lifeless corpse. It was still almost entirely covered with armour, but he could see through the bronze, see the emaciated body beneath.

It was covered with a web of red; the arteries were

clearly visible through the translucent skin.

A shield of metal encircled the figure, behind which the four dwarfs and the one human sheltered. The human was clad in silver armour; the dwarfs wore helmets and mailed gauntlets.

It was the dwarfs who operated the levers which controlled the spider's claws, manipulating the implements they held. They could only observe what they were doing indirectly, by looking into a series of mirrors that topped the metal barrier.

The glowing contraptions with the hearts of darkness continued removing the bronze from the figure.

But the figure was dead. *He* was dead. He felt no pain, not any more. He felt nothing, because he no longer had any physical senses.

Instead, his senses were far more than merely physical. He was not restricted to what his human body could perceive.

His body was dead, but he was not. He was more than his body, so much more.

His essence survived, and that was the infinitely greater part of him. It was the part that had existed before he was born, then been trapped at birth—just as his physical body had been trapped by the bronze armour.

Now his body was free, although it was too late: his liberation had finally killed his mortal embodiment.

But it had also freed his soul.

He gazed down at what had been an element of him for so long, the flesh and bones in which he had inhabited the material world. He had abandoned his body without regret, as easily as he had once cast off unwanted clothes.

There was no longer any connection between his temporary human form and his true substance.

He moved on up, higher, passing easily through the arched ceiling, higher, through the solid rock, higher, through the buildings above, higher, through the roofs and attics and rafters and tiles, higher, then out into the air, higher.

Middenheim lay below, a city hewn from the very mountainside. It was like a toy fortress. Roads and villages, rivers and forests, all were laid out like a living map.

Far below, he could see hundreds, thousands of tiny points of movement. They were people, as he had once been.

And, as he had once been, they were of no consequence.

With the escape from his body, his memories had also been released. He remembered. He remembered Wolf.

It was Wolf who had first spoken of Middenheim; and he recalled it was a dwarf who had taught him to fight with an axe, from whom he had learned some of their ancient language.

And he remembered Krysten. That was why he had pursued the malevolent armies which had destroyed the mine and annihilated almost everyone within; he had been searching for the girl.

From his vantage point, with all his restored and heightened senses, he could have effortlessly located Krysten—if she were still alive.

What of it? He had memories of the girl, but they were not his memories, not any more. He had other memories, true memories of the spirit world.

And that was where he belonged now.

Finally free from his earthly bonds, he continued to ascend, rising faster and faster.

He watched the landscape recede below, saw the whole of the Empire far beneath. He could even identify the desolate site of the village where he had spent most of his human life. But it was of no significance, not now.

He saw Kislev, its northern frontier marked by the unnatural hybrid colours where the Chaos wastes began.

The Sea of Claws, the Middle Sea, the Great Western Ocean, the Southern Sea, the blue that bordered the green and brown of the Old World on three sides, he saw it all, all and more, including the lands which did not appear on any map, or which had been inaccurately measured or located by cartographers who relied only on the legends of travellers.

Higher, higher, over the most distant of distant lands, over fabled continents, over islands that had never been named, had never been discovered, over unknown seas and lost oceans.

They were as nothing. The whole world, that lowly sphere, it was a grain of sand.

He arose beyond the planet and its two specks of dust, the tiny moons which revolved about it.

Further than the sun, itself nothing more than a spark of flame.

Further, faster, higher, deeper, past more insignificant points of light, more suns, infinitesimally small, infinite in number.

Into the heart of the universe—and then beyond, beyond all distance, beyond all time, until a billion stars became as one, then faded and vanished.

He was alone in the absolute void, lost in an eternity of solitude.

Without any reference in the ultimate darkness, he allowed himself to float forever, adrift in the endless spectral cosmos.

But he discovered there could be no total nothingness. Beyond forever, further than the infinite, he found himself remorselessly drawn towards his own kind, to his true genesis.

To the ocean of minds, the sea of souls...

A glint of light, coming closer, closer, growing, expanding, resolving into individual stars. Another galaxy, a universe of the dead.

Except they were not stars, not incandescent infernos. They were spirits, the true essences of existence.

Here they dwelled, beings without being.

He had been here previously, he recalled; many times, times without number.

His periods of imprisonment within a material body were as nothing compared to the duration of his inhabitation of a dimension without matter, perpetuity without limit.

Yet this was not a place of peace, of rest. Peace and stasis were impossible. That could only mean entropy and absolute decay, the total absence of anything—of everything.

And there could be no ultimate vacuum. Beyond nothing, there was always more.

Like the physical life where he had been entrapped, here was conflict and conflagration. Some spirits were easily overwhelmed and annihilated, others formed alliances to combat their enemies, and in doing so they created those enemies.

The firmament seethed and bubbled, was forever restless. There were winners and losers, almost as if non-existence were a reflection of the tangible world where life held so many spirits as hostage.

Like sought out like, and became absorbed into a greater whole, powerful and opposing forces of singular determination. Each of these was totally antagonistic to every other such grouping.

He did not belong within any of the greater entities, yet he was not totally independent, not any more. Only with unity came strength to defeat the negative forces.

He found himself being drawn towards one of the smaller essential forms. Feeling the warmth of attraction as he grew nearer the power, he sped towards the true heart of his desire.

Then stopped!

And suddenly he was moving backwards, being pulled away against his will, torn from his true destiny. He fought and struggled, but to no avail. Slowly at first, remorselessly, he was dragged across the infinite, back the way he had come.

His speed increased, accelerating ever faster; and in the blink of an eyeless eye, the omneity which had been his fulfilment had vanished.

He was torn away with far more urgency, across the desolate interstices of the dimensional matrix.

There was speed without distance, without temporal restriction, without illumination.

Until—there was light. The flickering stars rushed towards him, engulfing him, impelling onwards with ever greater speed.

Finally, he noticed that he was focused directly on one star, one world. Then he realized the awful truth which he had been trying to avoid...

It was the world where he had lived so recently.

He had been gone for aeons, an infinity even in cosmic terms, a time during which galaxies had expired, been born again.

He remembered, remembered it all. His life, his death. And everything in between.

Trapped inside the suit of bronze armour, that was how he had suffered his death.

Suffered...

Material life meant suffering. From birth to death, there was only pain and agony.

He remembered. There would be but a few years of life—a mere moment as such matters were measured on the true scale—and yet its endurance would seem eternal.

He remembered. Born in a village amidst a forest, growing up, learning to use a bow as his first weapon. Then the raid on the village. He had departed earlier and thus escaped death, but Evane remained. When he returned, everything had been destroyed by the goblins. He found his first love, or most of her: the invaders had stolen the head from her corpse.

He remembered, remembered.

Down he sped, hauled back by the invisible lifeline that he wished he could sever, but which he could not resist.

Back, back, away from the liberty of the ethereal, back into the prison of flesh.

And like all the newborn, he screamed both in defiance and defeat at his birth.

CHAPTER NINE

Konrad screamed.

"Ah!" said a voice.

He opened his eyes, and he knew instantly that there was something wrong with his vision. He could see, but everything seemed to have changed slightly, although he was not sure how. A figure was leaning over him. It was Litzenreich; he saw him clearly.

"I was about to proclaim the experiment a success, although alas the subject died," said Litzenreich. "It seems I shall have to modify my conclusion."

They were still in the room where the dwarfs had begun to remove the bronze armour. With great effort, Konrad glanced down—the first movement he had been able to make for so long, he realized. The armour was gone but when he saw himself, he gasped.

It hardly seemed his own body; it was so emaciated, little more than a skeleton covered with skin. Or was that skin? His entire torso and limbs were so red, it appeared that his flesh was raw, that his skin had been peeled away with the armour. He opened his mouth to speak, but no words would come; his lips seemed frozen.

"You are in great pain," said Litzenreich. "Or you would be had I not administered an assuaging infusion when I saw that you still lived. Do not try to speak or move. There will be plenty of time for that. Your body must renew itself, and you must recover your strength. That will be the time for talk."

Konrad was aware of the dwarfs moving about in the darkened room, dismantling their equipment, and he could hear the sounds of metal being dismembered. Above, he saw the spider device whose claws had removed the bronze carapace.

A few brief minutes could have passed, that was all, yet he seemed to have been gone from this earth for all eternity.

But time was relative. It could be expanded and compressed, twisted and distorted. During his infinite journey, an aeon had been but a second here in the world of men.

He was back once again in his body—although, he supposed, that body had not been his while he was trapped within the armour. Already, his metaphysical experience was beginning to seem like a dream. This was reality; what had happened while he was unconscious was nothing but the delusions of his tortured mind seeking release from the torment of his body.

Unconscious? Or had he really died for a few seconds? Had his heart stopped—and then begun to beat once more?

He tried to concentrate, to fix in his mind what he could remember of his epic supernatural journey. He needed to discuss it all later, when he found someone able to interpret his memories.

He was certain, however, that the most recent memory would not fade. He had apparently been recalling his early life. Yet his memories had been confused, not totally accurate. It seemed as though he had parents, parents he had known...

He wished that he had concentrated more upon that memory, because it was further back than he had ever been able to recall. If he could remember, it would give him a vital clue to his enigmatic past.

Then he realized that it was not his own past he had recalled, but someone else's. Even at an age when Konrad had no parents, this other person did have them. That early life bore many similarities to the one he had imagined, such as the way the village had been attacked and destroyed. Except, it seemed, it was a nearby village that had been wiped out. Also, it was goblins who had been responsible for the atrocity, not a horde of mutated beastmen.

And it had not been Elyssa who had died, but someone called Evane.

The name was firmly lodged in his mind. He had never heard it before, so who had she been? Why did she seem so important in his memory? Or someone else's memory...

"I will take good care of you," continued Litzenreich. "After all the trouble I have gone to, it would be a pity to lose you now."

He ran his fingers through his long beard, nodding in triumph. Despite the grey in his untamed beard and hair, he was probably only about forty years old. Litzenreich was a wizard, Konrad knew. Only a magician could have freed him from his prison of armour. Indeed, only a magician could have defeated the bronze warrior.

Now Konrad was in his domain, a subterranean lair carved out of the mountain, far below the inhabited parts of Middenheim. What did Litzenreich want with him? There would be a price to pay for his liberty. The magician would expect a reward for what he had accomplished. Even if Konrad were wealthy, he realized that was not the kind of recompense which would be expected. The rewards demanded by spellcasters were more than mere coin.

He had escaped from Kastring only to be captured by the bronze panoply. Had he again exchanged one kind of imprisonment for another? All that could be certain was that for the moment he was totally helpless, either because of his weakened body or because of the potion which Litzenreich had given him, or perhaps from a combination of both.

"First," said Litzenreich, "I must get you away from my experimental chamber." He summoned two of the dwarfs. "Take him to the last room in the eastern corridor, and be very careful."

"Whatever you say, boss," said Varsung.

He and the other dwarf lifted Konrad onto a wheeled table and pushed him out through the doorway, along a series of low narrow passages. Litzenreich walked ahead, finally unlocking a door at the end of the lowest and narrowest of tunnels. Varsung went inside and lit the lantern which hung from the bare rock of the small chamber. Konrad was wheeled through and lowered onto the straw mattress on the floor.

"Fetch Gertraut and Rita," Litzenreich ordered, and the other dwarf retreated. "Light a fire," he added, and Varsung moved towards the fireplace and began to do so.

"It is cold in here," said the wizard, "and you must remain uncovered. That is the only way your wounds will heal. You will require constant attention. Someone will be with you all the time, and she will call me if you require my assistance."

The young women entered the room. They were both slim and fair-haired, and they studied Konrad as Litzenreich spoke to them. He had lowered his voice, and Konrad did not hear what was said. The magician glanced at Konrad briefly, then left the room. Varsung nodded to Konrad, made the ancient Dwarven 'good fortune' sign with his thumb, and followed Litzenreich out of the door.

Shadowbreed

The door was bolted on the outside.

Konrad may have returned to his own body, but he was as helpless as a newborn baby—and he was treated as such. He could do nothing for himself, and so Gertraut and Rita did it all.

The time passed, very slowly. Deep underground, he had no way of measuring the hours or the days. All that changed was who sat with him. He would hear the heavy bolts being drawn back, then the door would open, and the two girls would exchange places. If ever one of them required help, they summoned it by means of a rope which rang a bell along the passage.

They fed him, cleaned him, gave him the various potions to help relieve the pain. Strangely, as his skin re-formed over his tender flesh, the torment increased. It was as though his skin were a new cage, as the bronze armour had been, except it was too tight for his body.

At first, he could not have moved had he wished to. Whenever they relieved one another, the girls would shift his position on the mattress. The one who left would take away the blanket upon which he had lain, freshly stained with the blood from his open sores. As he regained his strength, and his bones no longer protruded through his flesh, he was careful not to move of his own accord. He did not wish Litzenreich to know of his recovery.

Konrad had made one discovery about his senses. Almost his first reaction upon realizing that he had regained his life was to notice that there was something wrong with his eyes.

But that was incorrect: the opposite was true. His vision was now perfect. His eyes had never been in true alignment. His left eye had possessed the talent of future vision. It could warn him of danger; he could frequently see what would happen before it occurred. The power had grown more and more erratic and unreliable over the years. In a way, it had become more of a hindrance than an asset.

127

Now it was no more. He had no proof. How could there be any evidence of a lost skill? Yet he was certain that he no longer had the ability to foresee danger.

When had it gone? During his confinement within the armour, it seemed all that was left to him had been his sight. Perhaps even that had been taken away. Or possibly he had lost his gift when the bronze had been removed. Or maybe it had happened during his apparent flight from his body...

Whatever the circumstances, Konrad was glad. Ever since realizing that others could not foresee danger as he did, he had felt uneasy. No one should possess any such extra skills. Why had such a gift been granted to him? In some respects, it was like a mutation. And the most common mutation in the world was that which afflicted beastmen. They were deformed, evil, and his own talent had seemed similarly tainted.

From now on, he must rely only on his normal five senses and the aptitudes he had developed over the years. And as soon as it was possible, he would use all of these to accomplish the same purpose—escape.

He had no idea what the wizard had planned for him, and he had no intention of finding out. Litzenreich occasionally came to visit him, and so did Varsung. They tried to provoke some reaction, but to no avail. Konrad refused even to admit that he was capable of speech. He simply lay immobile and silent.

All he could do was think. Mostly he thought about the past, his own and the equally mysterious past of his false memories...

A split second, that was all he needed. He knew that he would have to keep totally alert because the right moment must inevitably come—and finally it did.

When Gertraut and Rita changed places, that was the

most likely time to attempt an escape, but they were never alone. One of the dwarfs was always there, guarding the door.

He heard the bolt being drawn back, but Gertraut had entered the room no more than an hour earlier. Varsung came in. Whenever he or Litzenreich appeared, one of the other dwarfs always stood outside in the corridor. This time, the passage was empty. It was only half a chance, but that was more than sufficient. Varsung stood with his back to Konrad, speaking to Gertraut.

Konrad sat up quickly, spinning around and reaching out for the hilt of the dwarf's sword. Once it was in his hand, he used both legs to kick the dwarf away. Then he sprang up, dashed out of the door, turned into the passage. But somehow his legs gave way beneath him, and he fell to the ground.

"I am glad to see you can move," said Litzenreich, who was standing a few yards away.

Konrad was still holding Varsung's sword, but he offered no resistance when the dwarf removed it from his grip. He realized he had been tricked. They knew he was not as weak as he pretended. It appeared, however, that he was far weaker than he himself thought. He picked himself up, his head spinning.

"What do you want with me?" he said.

"What do you want with me?" the wizard repeated. "Is that it? Is that the first thing you have to say? Not *Thank you for rescuing me?* Gratitude. Courtesy. Have you ever heard of those words? Do they exist where you come from?"

Konrad leaned against the wall, and he nodded slowly.

"What is your name?" asked Litzenreich.

"Konrad."

"Where are you from?"

"A village several days from here, but I've been in Kislev for five years."

"Take him back inside," said Litzenreich.

Varsung and Gertraut helped Konrad into the chamber where he had been kept, and sat him down on the mattress. Gertraut filled a beaker of water.

"Haven't you got any beer?" said Konrad. "I'm fed up with water."

"I think he's about recovered, boss," said Varsung, grinning.

"So it appears." Litzenreich stepped into the room. "Leave us. Fetch him some ale."

The other two departed. The door was closed, but it was left unlocked. Litzenreich was a wizard; he did not need bolts to keep Konrad his prisoner. He sat down in the one chair, and they gazed at one another. Konrad glanced away, not wishing to become mesmerized.

"Thank you," he said, finally, in order to break the silence.

As if that were a signal, Gertraut returned, handed Konrad a tankard brimming with beer, then left.

"What do I want with you?" asked Litzenreich, echoing Konrad's earlier question. "Nothing."

Konrad stared at him. He was more suspicious than ever. The wizard must want something. He wiped at his lips with the back of his hand. "Nothing?"

"As soon as you are fully healed, you are free to go."

"Free? Why has the door always been locked if I'm free?"

"I did not wish you to come to any harm, that is all. What happened when you rushed out of here a few minutes ago? You fell over. You are not yet strong enough to leave. When you are, you may do so."

"I can simply walk out of here?"

"Yes, although that may not be such a good idea."

"Why?"

"The good citizens of Middenheim would probably not take kindly to a naked man walking the streets. The watch would arrest you, and their hospitality is far less generous than mine, I assure you."

"You could give me some clothes, or lend me some."

"I do not think so. I have already done enough, do you not think? You are not a beggar, you would not ask me for more. And I am certain that you are not a thief, you would not steal from me, not after all the expenses I have incurred on your behalf."

"You want me to repay you?"

"Not at all. You have no financial resources, I believe."

"You don't want money, but you want something else. What?"

Litzenreich shrugged. "I am not certain, not yet. But I am sure you are an honourable man. I have done you a great service—or at least I presume I have. You did not wish to remain within the bronze armour, did you?"

"No."

"As I was saying, I have done you a great service and I am sure that I will find some service that you may accomplish for me in exchange. I think that is reasonable, do you agree?"

Konrad nodded. He supposed that the magician must already know what he wanted in return, but there was no point in pressing him for the answer which he so clearly did not wish to give.

"How did you unseat me from the bronze horse? How did you get me out of the armour?"

"Two questions, but almost the same answer." Litzenreich stood up. "I feel, however, that you need to rest after your recent exertions. We shall discuss this subject in the near future. Meanwhile, is there anything you wish?"

Konrad thought for a moment before answering. "A book? I'm bored doing nothing. I'd like something to read."

The wizard raised an eyebrow, evidently impressed that Konrad could read. "What kind of book? Poetry? Science?

Geography? Philosophy? History?"

"History."

"I shall choose something from my library." Litzenreich left the room and closed the door. It was left unbolted. For the first time, Konrad was alone.

After a while, Varsung entered. He was carrying some clothes, and also three volumes.

"Thank you," said Konrad. "And thank you for..."

"What?" The dwarf frowned.

"For seeing that I was alive."

"Ah, yes! As soon as I saw your eyes, I knew there was life there." He rubbed at his back where Konrad had kicked him, and he pulled a face. "I'm almost wishing I hadn't noticed."

The dwarf had taken a great risk in allowing Konrad to seize his sword; he did not know that he would not find himself impaled upon his own blade.

Varsung saw Konrad looking at the hilt of his sword, and he grinned. He drew the weapon with his right hand, then thrust it straight into his left palm! But as soon as the tip touched his skin, the whole blade disintegrated, dissolving like broken glass.

"I wish Litzenreich was the armourer for all my opponents!" the dwarf laughed.

It seemed there had been no risk at all. The wizard had devised the sword to trap Konrad. He should have realized: dwarfs were usually armed with axes.

"My eyes," said Konrad, remembering. "What colour are they?"

Varsung looked at him suspiciously.

"This is no trick," Konrad assured him. "I want to know what colour they are."

The dwarf picked up the lantern and moved closer. He held the light in front of Konrad's face, gazing at each of his eyes in turn.

"They're... different," he said. "They seem the same at

first, light green. But the left one is more yellow really, almost gold."

Konrad nodded. His eyes might now both give proper vision, but it seemed they were not identical. They were still different colours.

"I've got to be going," said Varsung. "Anything you need, just open the door and yell."

Konrad watched him go, then picked up the three books and read the embossed lettering on the leather covers. *The Empire Divided* was the title of one, *Years of Despair: the Vampire Empress* was another, and the third was simply called *Sigmar*.

That was the volume he selected, and he pulled the lantern closer. One of the few books available on the frontier had been a battered copy of another biography of Sigmar Heldenhammer. Konrad had read it several times, even though many of the pages were missing.

He opened *Sigmar* near the front and began to turn to the beginning of the saga. But as his eyes idly scanned the open page, one of the first words he saw was a familiar name.

It was Evane...

Konrad read what he never had before.

He was aware of how Sigmar had been born two and a half thousand years ago, the son of Tafal, chief of the Unberogen tribe. He had lived at the southern edge of the Great Forest, in a fortified village.

What Konrad had not previously known was that there was another village nearby. The headman was called Quant, a sub-chief of Tafal's, and it was he who taught Sigmar to use the bow and arrow. Quant had a son named Errol, and also a daughter named Evane. The three children grew up together as close friends; and as the years passed, Sigmar and Evane became even closer. It was accepted that when the two were old enough they would marry. But then the goblins had attacked Quant's village...

Sigmar was the first to reach the village, having seen the ominous pall of smoke while he was out hunting. The whole place had been looted and destroyed, everyone within slaughtered. He found Evane's body, but the ugly marauders had taken her head as a gruesome trophy.

It was this terrible episode, Konrad realized, which had shaped the rest of Sigmar's life. This was why he had become such an enemy of the green hordes and dedicated himself to their destruction. He had waged a one-man war against the hideous creatures, and over the years he built up an army sworn to defeat the goblins and drive them from the known world.

Konrad had not known about Evane, not until his strange vision, when he had seemed to return from his infinite voyage across the universe. But why should he have dreamed of a person he did not know? He must have heard her name somewhere else, perhaps from a storyteller who had narrated the famous tale around the campfire one night on the Kislev border. It was the only explanation, and that was why in his dream he had confused the legend of Sigmar with his own early life. The attack on his native village, when Elyssa had been slain, had been very similar. In Elyssa's case, however, he had not even discovered a headless corpse.

He thought of Krysten, who must certainly be dead by now. Life was short on the frontier, and he had lost so many good men, so many friends. He tried to convince himself that Krysten was no different from his comrades in combat, because that might have made her loss more bearable, but he knew it was untrue.

Konrad read on, trying to lose himself in the epic tale of Sigmar. Allying his human legions with the dwarfs, the goblinoids' ancient enemies, Sigmar finally defeated the goblin swarms at the battle of Black Fire Pass. That was where Sigmar won his name "Heldenhammer" for wreaking ultimate vengeance against so many of the foul beings with the legendary warhammer Ghal-maraz.

In some respects, Konrad realized, his own life paralleled that of Sigmar's. Evane and Elyssa had both been murdered, by goblins or beastmen. They both seemed to have been victims of increases in hostile activity by such inhuman forces. Sigmar had lived during one of the most violent eras in the history of the known world, and now another era of relative peace was ending: for the first time in two centuries the Empire itself was in danger of invasion. Its frontiers had already been infiltrated by Kastring's accursed warband, and there must have been many more such marauding Chaos cults on the rampage.

Chaos. It was a time of Chaos once more.

Like Sigmar, Konrad had become a warrior fighting against the hordes of destruction; and like Sigmar, he had fought his own battle against the goblins when he ventured into the subterranean lair to rescue Wolf. Instead of a battle hammer, however, he had used a double-bladed axe to wreak his vengeance upon the green horde.

But Sigmar, he thought ruefully, had never been imprisoned beneath a fortress city, captured by a mad magician.

Konrad closed his eyes, remembering. He had used the axe because he had dropped his sword when he fired the arrow at the goblin shaman that was torturing Wolf. It had proved a better weapon for the task at hand, like a mighty butcher's cleaver to swing at his enemies, severing heads and arms. Wherever he struck, another of the verminous creatures had screamed and died, and then the huge axe would swing once more, cutting a swathe of destruction through his hated foes.

Yet, at the time, he had believed he was using a warhammer...

He had put this out of his mind since, preferring to

forget what he could not explain; but something of such significance could not be easily forgotten. He recalled how he had seemed possessed as he fought, as if some unknown power governed his actions. Whenever he was in combat, his fighting instincts took command of his body. Often, it seemed, there was no need for thought; fighting was on a different level of existence than thinking. If he had time to consider what he should do, debating all the foolhardy risks he had so frequently taken in the past, then he would have hesitated more often than not—and hesitation would have meant failure. Fortune favoured the brave.

That was not the way it had been during the underground battle, however. It was something greater than mere reaction and skill that dominated his aggression; a feeling that he was not alone against the goblins. At the time, he had imagined that his unknown ancestors were guiding him, a whole ghostly legion which stretched back to the dawn of time.

It was similar to what he had experienced during his phantom flight through the stars, when he had been drawn towards that unimaginably bright entity where he felt he somehow belonged.

Krysten had always been fascinated by dreams. They were humanity's doorway to the spirit world, she claimed. When people slept, their souls were free to wander; dreams were the adventures of the soul and could be interpreted by seers. Konrad did not believe her, and he always teased the girl about her beliefs.

Now, he was no longer so certain. He had never witnessed anything like the visions that came to him when the bronze armour was removed. Unlike other dreams, it had no connection with anything he had ever experienced during his waking times; and unlike many others, it did not return to him.

The following morning, Litzenreich asked: "How did you come to be inside the bronze armour?"

They were in the chamber where Konrad had spent so long recuperating. Now that he did not have to pretend, he paced up and down the room.

He explained briefly what had happened: he had been a prisoner of Kastring's mutated band, escaped, found the armour, climbed inside to defend himself from his ruthless pursuers. What he said was true, but he did not reveal everything.

He did not say that he had first seen the bronze knight five years earlier, when the warrior had ridden into his village; he did not say that he had observed the horseman's image reflected through a lens inside the ancient dwarven temple; he did not say that he had been pursuing the mysterious rider; he did not say that he had finally fled from the Khorne worshippers as soon as he glimpsed moonlight reflected upon the bronze.

The wizard nodded. "As you say, you cannot have been within the armour for very long or else there would have been nothing left of you except bones, as happened to the horse. And there must have been even less of your predecessor; he must have been totally absorbed. The bronze feeds off life, the life that it slays or the life within the armour."

"But—what was it?"

"A creation of Chaos," said Litzenreich simply, as though the answer were evident. "What else? I had heard about this creature previously. It has roamed the known world for many years. When it was reported to be near Middenheim, several Knights Panther were sent to investigate. I heard that they never returned, and I thought it worthy of my attention."

"Why?"

Litzenreich stared through his narrow eyes, and it was almost as though he did not understand the question.

"Why? Why? Because it was there!"

Five years ago, when Konrad had spoken to Wolf about the bronze warrior, Wolf had said that the knight was his twin brother. But how long ago had his twin become the enigmatic knight? Was he the first to wear the armour? How many others had been held hostage by the bronze?

It seemed that there must have been a long series of warriors within the suit of armour. Konrad had merely been the latest—and the last. It was no coincidence that he had found the armour. It appeared that the panoply had been awaiting him. It was as if they were meant for one another, that it had been his destiny to become the bronze knight...

"The warrior seemed invincible," said Konrad. "How did you stop him?"

He realized that he was speaking as though the knight were someone—or something—else, that it had nothing to do with him. But it was true. The knight had been the bronze armour, and Konrad had merely been within the armour. He was like a servant who had simply done his master's bidding.

"The best method to fight a creature of Chaos," replied Litzenreich, "is with Chaos."

Konrad waited for him to continue.

"Warpstone," said Litzenreich, as though the word were a spell. "Warpstone," he repeated, nodding for emphasis, as though the two syllables were the answer to everything.

The word was familiar, but Konrad had even less idea of its full meaning than he did the nature of Chaos.

"It is the effect of warpstone that leads to mutation," Litzenreich explained. "Without warpstone there would be no beastmen. The bronze was Chaos armour, forged with warpstone. The way to combat warpstone is with warpstone. Like repels like, just as two lodestones will push away from one another."

Konrad waited again, hoping that the rest of the explanation made more sense. His incomprehension must have been evident, because Litzenreich said:

"I set myself up as the Chaos rider's next challenger, drawing it into a line of trees, each of which was hung with warpstone so arranged as to resonate and magnify—" He broke off, glanced at Konrad—who had noticed how the wizard described the bronze figure as 'it' and not 'you' then continued: "The warpstone in the trees nullified the effect of the warpstone in the armour. That was the only thing holding the horse up, and so it fell. Because you had not become totally fused, you were unseated. Understand?"

"Yes," replied Konrad, and he almost did.

"When Varsung realized that you had not yet been devoured by the armour, I decided to try and remove it from you. Without getting technical, suffice to say: once again, I used warpstone; once again, I succeeded."

"I was trapped inside Chaos armour," said Konrad, slowly, not liking the direction in which his thoughts were leading him. "That must mean I am tainted by Chaos!"

"Yes," agreed Litzenreich, "but it was not merely the armour which infected you. There was also the warpstone needed to extricate you from the bronze."

"You should have let me die."

"Die?" Litzenreich blinked rapidly, seemingly perplexed. "Why?"

"Because I am evil."

The wizard scratched his head. "What is this *evil*?" He emphasized the word, as though it were foreign and he was unsure how to pronounce it.

"The northern hordes, the mutants, the beastmen, Chaos! Evil." Konrad spat out the word as if it were poison—and it was, a poison which flowed freely through his veins, corrupting his entire body.

He knew evil. He had been fighting it for five years, defending the mine and trying to hold back the forces of darkness on the borders of Kislev.

"Chaos and evil are not synonyms, I assure you," said Litzenreich. "Evil is a creation of men, of humans—and inhumans. Chaos simply is. It exists, it is neither good nor evil. Only the way we are affected by it leads to our interpretation of it as either 'good' or 'bad'."

Konrad neither spoke nor reacted. He had halted his pacing and was busy contemplating what must be happening to himself.

"Is water good or evil?" asked Litzenreich. "It is neither, it is simply there. If we drink water to quench our thirsts, we may say that it is good. If someone drowns in it, we could say that it is evil—unless the one who drowns is our enemy. But the words 'good' and 'bad' have no absolute meaning. A fire is good if it warms us in winter, but bad if it burns down our homes. Fire is not good, fire is not bad. It is neither—or it is both."

Konrad was staring at his hands, watching for any signs of hairs on his palms, of his nails growing into claws. Litzenreich could not fool him with clever words. He had been infected by Chaos, and his body must have begun to change even though he could not yet see the traces of mutation. Wherever he looked, however, he could only find new skin. New skin covered with old wounds.

"I have been working with warpstone for years," said Litzenreich. "Once it has been refined, it is quite harmless. Unless one happens to swallow it!" He laughed. "And even then the chances of mutation are very small. When I have a large enough sample of experimental subjects, I intend to find out precisely how small. I do have a certain group in mind." He nodded slyly.

"Where was I? Warpstone. Yes, in its powdered state it is harmless. Admittedly, I do have occasion to use some of the raw stuff occasionally, but I always take the necessary precautions. I am as human as you are, Konrad."

"You're a wizard."

"Wizards are human, too, although I like to think of

myself as a man of science." Litzenreich stood up. "Let us go through into my main research chamber." He walked towards the door, beckoning for Konrad to follow.

They made their way along a series of narrow passages, all hewn out of the mountain, until they reached the area where Konrad had been extricated from the armour. A group of women were in the centre of the room, dissolving various powders into numerous containers of liquid, then pouring them into glass bottles of different sizes. Two dwarfs were busy in the far corner, working with tiny pieces of metal. One of them, Konrad noticed, was Ustnar. He glanced at Konrad for several seconds before returning to his intricate task.

"As far as I am concerned," Litzenreich said, "the name 'wizard' has fallen into disrepute, particularly in Middenheim. Ever since the art was legalized, it has become more regimented and more backward. There are no advances in magic these days. The guilds see to that. No one is allowed to try anything new. There are so many rules and regulations, our predecessors achieved far more when they had to operate in secret." He glanced around the cavern. "As, indeed, I do."

Konrad was also gazing around, and he stared up at the metal device which hung from the ceiling: the object whose claws had stripped the bronze armour from his body, and which he had imagined as a spider. Litzenreich kept on speaking, even though his audience was not paying much attention. Konrad was busy studying the doors and searching for possible weapons. He refused to be hypnotized by the wizard's words. It was still his intention to escape as soon as possible.

"The only reason magic was legalized," Litzenreich continued, "was because of its military implications. But there is far more to sorcery than devising new weapons, new defences. Try and find funding for pure research, however, and it is impossible. Yet that is where the greatest advances will be made. I have to finance all my own experiments, you know. And I have to hide away beneath Middenheim, hoping that the colleges of magic will not realize what I am doing. I have to be here because of the guild's library and the various bits and pieces I need from the university. You understand?"

"Er... yes," Konrad agreed.

He knew very little about magic, and he had always been very suspicious of such unnatural powers. On the frontier, Wolf would not employ war wizards; but he was very old-fashioned and did not believe in anything new, such as gunpowder. "Never trust a sorcerer," he had often said. "They trick you, they cheat you—and you don't even know it. Not at the time."

Konrad, however, had good reason to be grateful to sorcery. His arm had been saved by Elven magic, and it seemed that the spell had continued to protect him against Kastring's snake-hilted sword. For all Litzenreich's talk of warpstone, Konrad knew it was magic that had released him from the armour. It was a subject about which he should learn more, although perhaps not now.

"You've always been a magician?" he said, to keep Litzenreich talking.

"Of course. It is my vocation. All my ancestors have been sorcerers. It is rumoured that some were hedge-wizards, although we never mention those. I am basically an elementalist, with a strong dash of alchemist, but I will try my hand at any of the disciplines. Why should they be separated? A master chef can cook many meals, he does not restrict himself to one dish." He shook his head slowly. "I despair of the future. The academies seem content to turn out clever young wizards who have no interest in the ancient arts. They only care about the money they can make, about owning expensive homes and fancy carriages—and expensive and fancy women."

"What happened to the bronze armour?"

"What? Oh, it was all melted down. I needed to extract the warpstone. It took a lot to stop the bronze knight, and a lot to get you out of the armour. Raw warpstone, I mean, as well as the powdered stuff. My supplies need replenishing, which is not easy, because it is illegal even to possess warpstone."

"What is warpstone?" asked Konrad, having seen all that he needed to.

"There is much argument over that. It is a substance that is not of this world, or so it is generally accepted. Some say that Morrslieb is made of warpstone, but how can there be proof? No one has every been there to find out. Or if they have, they have not returned to tell the tale..."

Konrad looked at Litzenreich and saw that he was smiling.

"There are easier sources of warpstone, however. It can be found in quantity in the Chaos Wastes, for example. As I said, current theory is that warpstone even creates the wastes and is responsible for all the mutations which are spawned there. It is fascinating stuff, and I have only begun to explore its uses. And, of course, because of its potential it is regarded as dangerous and therefore illegal. But so what?" Litzenreich shrugged, and continued:

"Magic used to be illegal; now it is legal. Warpstone is illegal; someday it will be legal. At present, it cannot be used unless in imperial service whatever that means. Laws are only used to benefit the law makers. If there is a law preventing something, I always ask myself *Who made that law?* Never confuse law and justice, they are completely different.

"You have heard of the Gods of Law?" the wizard asked. "Theologians believe that they are also the creation of Chaos. And as far as I am concerned, Law and Chaos are both used to the same purpose to breed ignorance and despair and maintain the forces of brute strength over reason and enlightenment. Laws are imposed by our rulers in order to maintain their power. That is why I try to ignore all the rules of the magic colleges."

The wizard had been walking slowly around the cavern as he spoke, his eyes taking in everything that was happening. Now he had halted, and he was looking at Konrad.

"It cost me quite a lot of warpstone to liberate you," he said.

"You already said that."

"I need more in order to continue my researches."

Konrad knew what was coming next.

"I want you bring me more warpstone," said Litzenreich.

"Where do I get it from?"

"You may have heard of them. They are called skaven..."

CHAPTER TEN

Konrad had indeed heard of the skaven.

It was three of the ratmen who had prevented him escaping from his native valley the day it had been attacked by the feral hordes. They had forced him to turn back, to join in the assault on the village, to witness all the foul atrocities that had been committed by the army of beastmen and their allies. Possibly this was why he had always hated skaven so much more than any other Chaos creatures. Or maybe it was because they were so much like humans, yet so different. He had come across very few during his time on the frontier. Whenever he had, they died.

Konrad was still unsure of Litzenreich and his motives. It was always the best policy to mistrust everyone, and Konrad remembered Wolf's warnings about sorcerers. If Litzenreich wanted repaying for helping Konrad, and he were allowed to pay that debt, then he would be satisfied with the arrangement. He did not wish to be beholden to the magician for ever. What was the price of his life—a lifetime of slavery?

The dwarfs and humans who worked for Litzenreich did not seem to be slaves, however. The dwarfs were hardly even servants, because they would often argue on equal terms with the wizard, although they all called him 'boss.' Konrad was never sure how many people Litzenreich had working for him, but there were at least six dwarfs. The underground chambers were guarded by a dozen humans; there were also several women engaged in various abstruse tasks; and they were all fed by a halfling cook.

The sorcerer had built up quite an organization, and he must have financed it somehow. Konrad suspected he did so through trading in warpstone. If it was illegal, it was inevitable that money could be made from dealing in the substance. Litzenreich had spoken of needing warpstone for research, but Konrad was well aware that there had to be far more to it than that.

There could be no doubt that Litzenreich had saved his life, and Konrad was not a man prepared to cheat his creditors. He would do as the wizard asked, this one time. A further incentive was that his enemies were skaven, and this could be a chance to kill a number of the ugly rat-things.

"Here," said Varsung, handing Konrad a scabbarded sword. "Don't worry, it isn't like the one you took from me last week!"

A week, was that all it had been? Despite a regular routine of waking and sleeping, he could not get used to measuring the days without seeing the sun rise and set. He had not been allowed on the surface, probably because Litzenreich thought he would take the opportunity to escape. Although no longer locked up, Konrad was still a prisoner. He could not work out the configuration of Litzenreich's base. There were so many different levels and tunnels, and so many strong doors everywhere. But by now Konrad had resolved not to leave until he had settled his debt.

He had kept studying his body, watching for some indication that it had begun to change, for hints of tough skin which might be developing into scales, for evidence that his feet were becoming hooves, for traces of hair which seemed more like fur, for signs of webbing between his fingers. But there was nothing.

Touching a mutant's weapons did not necessarily lead to mutation, he knew. No matter how slender the risk, it was always best to be avoided, which was why such armaments were never taken as trophies. Yet he had been within the bronze for countless days, weeks, and he had almost become a part of the armour...

And if warpstone were as harmless as Litzenreich claimed, why had he worn protective armour while the bronze was being removed from Konrad? Why had the dwarfs been clad in gauntlets and gloves, and been shielded behind a barricade of armour, only watching what they were doing through mirrors?

Konrad understood what Litzenreich had said about Chaos, but he was uncertain as to whether he should believe any of it. Men used the word 'Chaos' to explain all kinds of unexplainable phenomena. If the northern wastes were the lands that bred mutants, and that was the realm of Chaos, then it was only to be expected that Chaos would be considered evil because of the nature of the creatures it spawned.

How else could men describe the malevolent legions who fed on human flesh and drank warm blood, who lived only to torture and ravage, to slaughter and destroy, who were neither animal nor man, but something far less—how else could they be accurately described except as evil?

Whether it was 'law' or 'justice' that was opposed to such malign forces, Konrad did not care. That was the side he was on, the banner beneath which he would fight and, if necessary, die. If Litzenreich's enemies were the skaven, then Konrad was the wizard's sworn ally.

He had spent most of his waking time regaining his strength and muscle tone. Litzenreich had many books for him to choose from, far more volumes than he had imagined ever existed, but their attraction had soon faded. He still did not feel entirely fit, but he craved action, and the sorcerer finally announced that it was time.

Konrad examined the blade closely. It was an excellent weapon, made by a craftsman. He checked its sharpness and flexibility, then tested the balance, practising several sweeps and thrusts. It felt wonderful to hold a sword in his grip again. He slid it back into the oiled sheath. The next time the weapon was drawn, he swore that it would taste skaven blood.

He and four dwarfs were preparing themselves for their expedition deep into the hidden heart of Middenheim. The dwarfs were the same ones who had been with Litzenreich when he had found the bronze rider, and who had removed the armour from Konrad's body. Varsung, Joukelm, Hjornur...and the one known as Ustnar, who was in command.

It was the dwarfs who went on such raiding expeditions, Varsung had told him. The human guards were there to protect Litzenreich's domain against his enemies. It seemed he had many, both in Middenheim and below. Skaven could smell warpstone, and so they would try to retrieve it from the sorcerer—who had probably stolen it from them originally. This was why he kept his stock in various places beneath the city, only taking it from its lead-lined boxes shortly before it was needed.

Litzenreich had other sources of warpstone. The substance was often smuggled into the Empire, but it was a very risky enterprise. The danger did not merely lie in the potential for mutation. The penalty for trading in warpstone was execution, assuming that the skaven did not find the smugglers first. The punishment they inflicted made execution seem very mild in comparison. These factors tended to make the price of warpstone very high, which was why the wizard preferred not to pay. Instead, his dwarfs stole from the skaven.

It felt strange to be wearing armour again, but at least it was armour which he knew he could remove if necessary. His leathers and metal were black, as camouflage in the tunnels, and the four dwarfs were similarly clad. He wore a helmet without a visor and a breastplate, otherwise his torso and arms were protected by a long coat of chainmail. He wore gauntlets and carried a round shield which bore no emblem; and in addition to his sword, a poniard was sheathed at his hip.

The dwarfs were all armed with axes and daggers, protected by mail and armour and hide shields like Konrad's. Middenheim had been constructed by their ancestors, who had dug upwards through the mountain known as Fauschlag. But, dwarfs being dwarfs, they had kept on tunnelling. The whole area beneath the city, and far beyond, had become a maze of passages. Litzenreich had established himself in one such section.

This was below the web of tunnels which the humans had built for their own purposes: the cellars, the sewers, the escape passages for the Graf and the ruling families of the city, the supposedly hidden vaults for the rich, and the burial chambers of the rich and the dead.

In ancient times, the whole of the known world had been linked by Dwarven tunnels; all their centres of habitation had been connected. Half a century before the Empire was founded, Artur, chief of the Teutogens, had enlisted the dwarfs and begun to build the fortress city. Artur was later defeated in single combat by the chief of the Unberogens, and the eight warring human tribes were finally united by the victor—Sigmar.

Because of its relatively recent construction, it seemed unlikely that the dwarfs had made Middenheim a part of their subterranean network. They would not reveal this information to any human, just as they maintained the secret of their own clandestine entrances into the city.

It appeared that Middenheim was, however, part of another series of passages that joined every region of the Old World. Many of these tunnels had originally been built by the dwarfs, but they had been taken over and expanded. Few even knew of the shadowy creatures who now dwelled beneath almost every town and city in the Empire, perhaps even in the world: the sinister breed called skaven.

Litzenreich had told Konrad far more than he had ever known about the rat beings. They were believed to be hybrids of humans and rats, as he had suspected, and their mutation had been caused by warpstone. Unlike most mutants, however, the skaven were clever. They possessed the animal cunning of their rodent ancestors combined with the intelligence of their human forebears. They were like a new race, just as humans and elves and dwarfs were.

They had their own benighted city, Skavenblight, which was reputed to be hidden deep in the marshlands of Tilea. Once a human town, now it was but ruins. Because of their extensive web of warrens, nowhere was safe from the skaven. They had originally lived beneath towns that had fallen into decay, and it was their intention that every centre of habitation should similarly become abandoned and left for their own diseased purposes. For this, they needed more and more warpstone.

"So, by taking warpstone from the skaven," Litzenreich had said, "I am helping to preserve Middenheim."

Konrad was unsure who the wizard was trying to persuade by this argument—himself or Konrad. He was sure that Litzenreich felt no loyalty to the city. But Konrad needed no convincing. He was content to do anything that would harm the skaven, although he was not really sure why he was needed on the mission. Even if he had not been here, the dwarfs would have ventured deep into the subworld in search of precious warpstone. But an extra blade was always useful, and the magician knew that Konrad had been a professional soldier.

It had been a dwarf who taught Konrad the skills of tunnel fighting. He had been his axe instructor on the frontier, and he swore that such a weapon was all that was needed below ground. In such a confined space, a two handed axe could be swung back and forth with devastating effect; it could also be thrust forward, and its hooked blade could snare an enemy, shredding him apart.

Konrad, however, preferred a sword. In a narrow passage, one man could hold back a dozen enemies, because only one foe could attack at a time. Often, the one would be at an advantage over the dozen, because his first opponent would be unwillingly pushed forward by those behind—pushed towards his death. It was hard to fight when there was no room to make a tactical retreat, no space to lean back and avoid a blow.

The tunnels almost seemed the dwarfs' natural habitat. They were the right size, because the passages had been constructed for their race. They could also see better in the dark than humans. So could skaven, thought Konrad, and they also tended to be of a similar size to dwarfs. He had never considered this connection before. Maybe that was why dwarfs hated the ratmen so much. But dwarfs seemed to hate everything, from elves to goblins...

The only other race tolerated by dwarfs were humans. This alliance had originally be forged by Sigmar, and now Konrad was continuing this military tradition. Their mission was to find the skaven that lived beneath Middenheim, and to take their warpstone. The dwarfs had accomplished similar tasks previously, or so Varsung had said, and they had claimed great quantities of the stuff. The skaven had not expected to be attacked on their own territory, and were at first easily overwhelmed. Assaults upon the rodent domain had become more dangerous, less rewarding, as time went by. The lairs where they hid their warpstone were both better hidden and better defended.

The plan now was to raid quickly, grab whatever could be carried, then retreat with equal alacrity. This was to be a swift surprise attack, which was why there were only five of them.

Konrad needed no instructions in fighting, that had been his life for the five years he had lived in Kislev. But how could he find the warpstone?

"What do I look for?" he had asked.

"The dwarfs know," Litzenreich had replied—and so Konrad had asked Varsung.

There were two forms of warpstone, he discovered. Its origins were supposedly unearthly, and most of it was found in fist-sized pieces. This was raw warpstone, and it was black, more than black; it was deeper than absolute darkness because it seemed to absorb all light.

Konrad realized that this was the stuff which had been used to extricate him from the bronze armour; he remembered the ultimate black at the centre of the implements that the dwarfs had manipulated. Raw warpstone could not be properly resolved by the human eye because of the way it drew in light; its edges could not be properly defined except by touch.

The skaven could also transmute warpstone from its raw state into a refined form, a powder known as grey warpstone. This served the giant rats in many ways. It could be consumed to give them strength, or swallowed in a potion before they went into battle in order to enhance their combat skills. It was used in their weaponry and magic and worship. Warpstone was indispensable to the skaven—and Konrad and the dwarfs were going to steal it from them...

Grey warpstone presented no danger to humans, or so he had been told. But he had been told so much, he was unsure what to believe. The only thing in which he placed any trust was the sword Varsung had given him. As he anticipated the battle ahead, he could feel his heart pounding and the blood pulsing through his veins, and he felt truly alive once more.

The five checked each other's black armour, making sure all the straps and buckles were secure and tight. Each shield had been constructed with an oil lantern built into it. The lamps were recessed into the layers of leather to protect them during combat. They were partly obscured in order not to give off too much light, and they cast an eerie glow ahead of them.

Konrad noticed Ustnar watching him. "I hope you were worth it," said the dwarf, slinging his double-headed axe across his shoulder.

They were on the lowest level of Litzenreich's haunt that Konrad had yet visited, but there was no sign of the wizard. Two guards stood by the heavy wooden door at the end of the passage, otherwise there were just the five of them. The tunnel itself was much narrower and smaller than the others in the complex, and Konrad had to duck to avoid the roughly hewn ceiling.

The two human guards drew the wedges from the door, yanked it open, then sprang back, their halberds pointing into the darkness as they stood side by side. The lanterns revealed nothing except the tunnel. It continued straight ahead, vanishing into the shadows beyond the light. The soldiers stepped aside.

Varsung was the first one through; Konrad was the second.

Time passed slowly, and Konrad grew more tense, all his senses totally on edge. He had drawn his sword to give his clammy right hand something to do. They seemed to be descending towards the centre of the world, following a maze of passages which endlessly spiralled down.

Sometimes there would be a series of steps carved out of the mountain, sometimes they had to climb down an almost vertical wall of rock.

Varsung led the way, never hesitating despite all the junctions and alternate routes they passed. Konrad soon realized that he would never find his way back alone, but there was very little chance he would have to: if the dwarfs were all killed, then he would probably have met the same fate.

Most of the tunnels had been hewn from the rock, and the walls were still pitted with the ancient tool marks of the forgotten excavators, and the occasional runic name could be seen carved in the stone. Other passages seemed to be natural fissures, underground fractures in the strata. The original tunnellers had adapted these flaws in the solid rock as part of their construction.

There were occasional rockfalls, where the passages had become partially blocked. But there was always room to squeeze by, because earlier explorers had come this way and removed most of the obstruction. There was no way of telling when the route had been cleared, whether it was a year ago, a hundred, or a thousand.

Here and there, the roof had sunk, as though the whole weight of the mountain had pressed down upon it. Even the dwarfs had to bend double to pass through such places. Elsewhere, the floor had buckled, or the sides had been compressed; but there was always enough space to wriggle through.

It was not only rocks and stones that littered the floor, the dust and debris of millennia. There were also bones. They could have been as old as the tunnels, or they could have been very recent, picked clean by the predators which Konrad imagined lurked around every bend.

Then the shafts began to change. The difference was very subtle, and at first Konrad hardly noticed. He gradually became aware that the passages were not so even, not as well finished, not so regular. These were the tunnels that must have been constructed by the skaven.

He and the four dwarfs spoke not a word throughout the whole journey. There was nothing to say, they all knew what must be done, and any sound would carry along the empty shafts, echoing and magnifying. Such noise would serve as a warning of their presence, just as the reflected light from their shaded lanterns must inevitably do.

On and on they went, further, deeper, down and down.

They were still moving in the same order; there had been few chances to change places, and no reason to do so. Varsung was the pathfinder, leading the way, and Konrad followed. Ustnar was behind him, the other two dwarfs took up the rear.

Then Varsung halted, glancing back. For the first time, he looked past Konrad towards Ustnar. The location appeared no different from any of the other passages through which they had come, but evidently the dwarfs recognized this part of the tunnel. Konrad also glanced around, and he saw Ustnar nod. He turned back, and Varsung gestured for him to continue. He did so, but after a few seconds he looked around again. There was no sign of the other three. Konrad and Varsung were alone. For a moment, he wondered where the others had gone. Were they waiting to see what would happen, or had they taken another route? There were so few of them, it seemed a mistake to split their forces.

He licked at his dry lips, wiping the sweat from his forehead with the back of his wrist. His heart was beating faster than ever, his whole body poised for action. He knew something must happen soon, and he felt he would burst if the tension that was building up within him could not find a swift release.

A few minutes later Varsung suddenly stopped again. He was two yards ahead, and Konrad also paused, wondering why the dwarf had halted. The tunnel was very narrow, and he could not see past him. He glanced back briefly, looking for a glimmer of light. There was none.

When he turned again, he noticed that the dwarf was slowly falling backwards towards him. As he toppled over, Konrad glimpsed the crossbow bolt through his throat...

He was dead, Konrad knew that instantly. Without a moment's hesitation, he leapt forward, threw aside his shield and grabbed hold of the dwarf, pushing him upright. A body was usually a far better defence than a shield. He held the dwarf vertical with his left hand and shoulder, ducking down so that he could see ahead by the light from Varsung's lantern.

There was nothing to see, nothing except another narrow twisting passage. He was tempted to smash the lamp, because it was like a beacon signalling his position. But without it, he would be blind—yet the skaven would still be able to see him.

He heard a sound from ahead, like a sigh of breath, and he felt the impact as Varsung's body jerked back. Another crossbow bolt, he realized.

What should he do? He could have retreated, dragging the dwarf's corpse backwards, but he was aware there could be no escape. He had come too far, and he did not know where he should go to get back. Even sprinting away on his own would be futile; he would simply become lost more quickly. Remaining here was pointless. He was pinned down. If he stayed, he would certainly die. That left one alternative, the only alternative for a warrior: to go on.

He could not go on with Varsung. The corpse would have been heavy enough to drag back as protection; it was far too weighty to push forward. He reached behind, picked up his shield and its lantern, which was still lit, held it in front of him and allowed Varsung to fall. By bending double, the shield completely covered him. He grabbed the dwarf's axe, wedging it into his belt. Then he moved forward, very slowly, very cautiously, peering past his shield every few seconds. An arrow bounced off it, but the next one missed his right ear by an inch.

Judging by the time it took to load a crossbow, there was only one archer ahead; and the passage was also too narrow to allow more than one bowman—or bowrat. If there were but one isolated guard ahead, maybe he could take him before he could sound the alarm. Having counted the seconds between the arrows, he knew that for a brief while he could dash forward without fear of a crossbow bolt halting his progress. He waited for another shaft to hit his shield, then sprang upright and ran.

He heard voices, inhuman voices, skaven voices, dozens of footsteps echoing in the passage. A whole pack of them were rushing at him. The archer could have held him back, but it seemed that all the others were anxious to get to him first.

That was fine by Konrad. He halted, ducking beneath his shield, remaining absolutely still and waiting while the rat things came nearer. Then he leapt up, slamming the first one aside with his shield. The lamp smashed with the impact, but the oil from within splashed across the skaven's fur, and the flames set the rodent alight. It screamed hideously as it burned alive, but the tunnel was now brighter than ever.

The second creature ran straight onto Konrad's sword, impaling itself. "That's for Varsung!" he yelled, and he spat into its ugly, tortured face.

The death cries of the first two beasts mingled, an unholy duet of death. Konrad's earlier vow had been fulfilled: drawing his sword had meant spilling skaven blood.

A second later, the next skaven's throat was torn out with a single sword sweep. It gurgled, blood bubbling from its mouth and pouring from its neck as it died. He wrenched his blade free, then plunged it into the chest of the next creature. Its hot blood spurted over him, and he laughed in triumph. Four down, a hundred more to come!

Konrad's sword ripped out the guts of the fifth ratman, and it went down screeching as the blade decapitated the next giant rodent. The bodies piled up in front of him, a furry rampart. They had their own weapons, and he felt himself cut and stabbed, but it was of little consequence. His injuries were not enough to slow him down; he seldom felt battle wounds until later.

He advanced across the corpses of his enemies, trampling upon the bodies of the dead and the dying, deflecting their weapons with his shield, dealing death with his sword. They were vermin, he was their exterminator. Their lives were nothing, and he annihilated them as simply as if he had been squashing insects. He did not need to think, his reactions were automatic.

Then suddenly there were no more, the way ahead was clear.

The flames from the burning rat had died, but the shaft was not totally black. There was light coming from ahead, a ghostly green radiance from what must have been the skaven nest.

Breathing heavily, Konrad paused, wiping the foul blood from his face. Then he walked slowly on, and after a time the passage widened. The roof receded, the ground sank and he found himself on a gallery over a huge pit, above a scene from damnation. His own level seemed to be lit with tiny red lights which encircled him, but then he realized that every pair of lights was a red-eyed skaven. They were all watching him, lined up around the walls of a cavernous amphitheatre. High above, stalactites hung from the domed roof like threatening weapons.

There could be no retreat. This was where he would make his stand. Konrad leaned on his bloody sword, breathing heavily, and he gazed at all his enemies. There were hundreds of rat beings, all clad in various pieces of armour and bearing their jagged knives and swords and spears. Their dark garments were decorated with runes, their fur branded with their clan insignia, and the same emblems were on the tattered banners their standard bearers carried.

The skaven were not the only ones in the vast cave, he noticed. Far below, there were humans—or creatures who had once been human. They carried on with their arduous tasks, slaves to the rat-things, performing their unknown functions amongst the huge fiery furnaces.

The reflection of the green flames had illuminated the tunnel. The sound was deafening, the heat overpowering, and it was difficult to see what was happening because of all the thick choking smoke that rose from the abominable processes. The whole place seemed to be a bizarre amalgam of a sorcerer's lair and a blacksmith's forge, but magnified a hundredfold, a daemon's workshop.

Here was where raw warpstone underwent the process of refinement. The transformation was so dangerous that they employed slave labour for the lethal operations. But not all the slaves were human, Konrad observed; amongst the labourers below there were a number of skaven.

As he glanced around, Konrad remembered the last time he had been underground like this. He had also been up against hundreds of enemies, but now the odds were far less in his favour. Varsung's axe was no substitute for the massive double-bladed weapon with which he had wreaked such carnage amongst the troglodyte goblins.

Time had seemed frozen as he surveyed the scene which confronted him, but now the immobile seconds melted and it was again the time for fighting—and for death. That must inevitably include his own death, Konrad knew, but not until he had claimed a few more enemies...

He saw an armoured figure moving rapidly towards him along the high rocky ledge where he stood. It was armed with a sword, defended by a shield. He could tell it was human, and he raised his own shield in defence and lifted his sword. His blade clashed with that of his enemy, the sound lost in the cacophony from below. They fought.

Konrad and his opponent were evenly matched. They were both the same height, of equal weight and strength, bearing identical armament, and their combat techniques were very similar. For every stroke that Konrad made, his enemy offered an appropriate counter-stroke, bringing up his shield in response, or else blocking the blow with his own sword. Whenever his antagonist made a strike, Konrad could anticipate and repel the attack.

He had never fought such an enemy. It seemed that they both knew the same techniques, were masters of identical tactics; it was as though they had been instructed by exactly the same tutors. As their swords rang together, metal sliding down against metal, hilts touching, Konrad found himself staring directly into his enemy's face. In the gloom and beneath the shaded figure's helmet, he could not see much—except that the man's eyes were different.

His left was green, his right was gold. It was like looking into a mirror....

And Konrad realized that he was fighting his double, his own image!

Somehow, the skaven had created his doppelganger. That was why every sword stroke was matched and returned—because he and his reflection were so equally balanced. The duel could last forever. They were not exact opposites, because his antagonist carried his blade in his right hand, bore his shield in the left. Yet that seemed a minor detail and in any case, Konrad was ambidextrous with weapons.

He could have fought himself until all that defeated him was exhaustion. It seemed that his twin was stronger; his energies had not been depleted and drained by a prison of bronze. He could not win by strength, because he had less, nor by skill, because that was evenly apportioned. The only route to victory was to do something he had never done before, to adopt a completely different technique. He had no other chance.

"Who are you?" he demanded. He already knew the answer, but he needed more time, any time.

But his opponent gave him nothing. Neither time nor an answer. As Konrad parried like a fencer, then bludgeoned like a barbarian warrior, he wondered what tactic he could adopt that he had never used. He had learned so much, been taught by so many masters. What could he do that was completely against all his training, against all his double's expectations? This was a time for thought in the midst of a deadly duel, but he could think of nothing—except nothing.

He swung his left arm out, releasing his grip and letting his shield fly off. That distracted his foe for an instant, who watched it vanish into the gloom. Then Konrad threw his sword away.

His enemy became still momentarily, sword and shield immobile, and Konrad lashed out with his right foot, catching him in the stomach and unbalancing him. He flung out his arms to try and keep himself upright. A moment later Konrad used his head as a battering ram, the helmet taking his duplicate in the midriff. Down went his twin, and he was instantly on top, kneeling above him, the poniard in his hand, plunging the blade deep into his neck.

There should have been blood. Instead, maggots poured from the wound...

He had been fighting a dead man. But the dead could die again, and this one became still—except for the hundreds of white wriggling worms that crawled from the gaping wound in the neck.

Konrad was suddenly seized from behind and dragged to his feet by two huge skaven warriors. His dagger was knocked away, his helmet torn off, Varsung's axe wrenched from his belt. He kicked at his captors' legs and tried to elbow himself free.

Then he felt cold steel at his throat. The weapon was held by a third figure, and Konrad leaned back so that the point of the blade would not bite into his flesh. As he did so, he recognized the weapon: it was the stiletto he had given Krysten.

A voice hissed: "Surrender..."

The sibilant syllables sounded familiar. The shape with the knife was in shadow, and Konrad could only just make out its outline, but he almost recognized the size and the way creature stood.

"...Konrad."

Its fur was grey, and it held the stiletto in its left paw because it had no right one.

It was Heinler.

CHAPTER ELEVEN

There had seemed something odd about Heinler, but now all was explained: he had not been human, he was skaven.

When Konrad had first encountered him in the mine compound, Heinler had seemed to be a man. In retrospect, his features had certain rodent traits; but now he was a true skaven, a giant rat that walked like a man. Originally, he must have transformed his appearance, or else he had used sorcery to convince Konrad that he looked human. A spell of illusion would have been simple enough, because Heinler was one of the most powerful of all skaven: he was a grey seer.

Konrad had learned of these creatures from Litzenreich. The wizard had made a point of knowing everything he could about his enemies. Grey seers were skaven who were able to transform warpstone, and the process gave them increased power. They were great magicians, the direct servants of the Thirteen Lords of Decay.

The Thirteen were the high priests and leaders of the

monstrous rats. Many were rulers in their own right, governing the main centres of skaven infestation, their underground cities of corruption; others were far more reclusive, supreme sorcerers and experts in entropy. Only twelve of these lords were skaven. The thirteenth and final place in the circle of ultimate command was reserved for their lord of lords: the Horned Rat, one of the mightiest of the Chaos pantheon. The Horned Rat was a close ally of yet another of the most powerful lords of Chaos: Nurgle, the god of plague and pestilence.

Heinler had hissed his commands at the two burly skaven who held Konrad in their grip, and he was dragged helplessly backwards through a long dark passage, down into a dank cave where a metal collar was clamped around his neck. The collar was chained to the rock wall. It was as if he were a wild animal that they had caught and tethered; that it was he who was a beast, not them.

The two warrior rats were taller than Konrad, both brown, their fur covered in leather armour and chainmail. They were armed with short swords, and they held the serrated blades at the ready. Both were veterans, their limbs and ugly faces marked with ancient scars. One had an eye missing, and a silver coin was embedded in the empty left socket; the other had both its ears torn away. Each wore the same emblem branded on their foreheads: a circle, with four lines from the circumference meeting in the centre, like an inverted "Y" with a fourth radius to the base of the circle.

There was very little light in the cave, because the skaven needed neither lantern nor candle, but Konrad could see that he and his three captors were not alone. There were more chained figures in the cavern. None of them moved. Human and inhuman, they were all dead, their corpses rotten and festering, or long turned to dried carcasses, or skeletons, or just a pile of bones...

The place stank of disease and decay. The miasma of

putrefaction made Konrad choke and almost throw up.

In the gloom, Konrad saw Heinler bare his teeth in what may have been a skaven grin. He was dressed in a black velvet robe. The hood had been pulled back to show a purple silk lining. The neck of the garment was held by a golden clasp which was in the shape of a horned rat, the skaven deity.

"When I took on human form," he said, "I wished that I could have had your eyes." The sibilant whisper was completely different from the voice he used when he had pretended to be a miner, a convicted criminal—a human. He touched the point of the stiletto to Konrad's lower eyelid, the left one.

"And now I can."

Konrad drew back instantly, and he lashed out with his right leg in an attempt to crush the grey seer's ribcage. But Heinler sprang out of range, and Konrad was dragged back by the chain. The two guards pounced, pummelling him with the hilts of their swords. Konrad fought back, punching one of the creatures in the jaw, but it had no effect. He was forced down beneath a hail of blows. All he could do was sink to the ground and try to protect his head.

"No, no!" they yelled at him, in urgently whispering parodies of human voices. "Stop! Stop!"

Heinler issued a command, and the two skaven moved back.

"It was a joke," said Heinler. "Probably. I learned that kind of humour from humans."

He tapped the handle of the stiletto against the wall, and Konrad wondered what had made him keep the blade.

"Don't give them any excuse," Heinler warned. "These are my personal bodyguard, but they may not be able to restrain themselves if provoked. They can smell you—and they want to know what you taste like..."

"Smell me?" Konrad managed to say.

Why should he smell different from any other human?

And he had no doubt that the skaven warriors must have tasted human flesh before. They were like the creatures from which they had evolved; rats were scavengers who would devour any kind of flesh—whether alive or dead, fresh or decayed.

"They can smell the warpstone," explained Heinler.

There was a shout from beyond the cavern, and Heinler turned away as another skaven rushed in through the roughly hewn entrance. The newcomer was smaller, piebald, unarmed and wore no armour. It had two tails, Konrad noticed. Skaven were highly resistant to warpstone mutation, but they could still be affected by various physical changes. The two-tailed rodent bowed to Heinler, then spoke very rapidly. Before it had completed what it was saying, Heinler began to scurry from the cave. The two soldier rats started to follow, but Heinler shouted a command and one of the two remained.

The guard stood in the entrance, staring back along the shaft. After a minute, he returned to where his captive sat, and he loomed over him. Konrad tried to lean back, but he was already wedged against the fetid rock. The deformed snout moved closer to him, and he could smell the skaven's disgusting breath. He noticed its teeth; the two front fangs had been replaced by metal spikes. The creature's long tongue rolled from its jaw, and it licked at one of the wounds on Konrad's cheek, lapping up the blood.

It stepped back. "Good, good," it hissed, gazing down at him with its single eye. "We be friends, friends." It made an awful sound, a coughing noise which Konrad realized must have been laughter.

He rubbed his cheek with his hand, wiping away the sticky skaven saliva, and hoped that Heinler would soon return from the shadows. What had drawn him away? There must have been some kind of emergency, judging by the all the inhuman yelling that was going in the distance.

Konrad had been wounded during his battle with the

ratmen in the tunnel, although not seriously. He felt sore, and his body was bruised. The chainmail had been severed by one or two severe blows, and his right arm was bleeding where the metal links had broken and sliced through the protective leather jacket beneath. His arm was in pain and he folded it behind him, tugging at the chainmail which had penetrated his flesh. He hoped that the one-eyed rat would not notice; but he realized that the creature did not need to see the blood to know of the wounds.

Recalling the rough feel of the skaven's kiss, Konrad kept touching his face. He moved his fingers up to his eyes, thinking of what Heinler had said.

His left eye had given him no warning of impending danger; he had been unaware that he and Varsung were about to be attacked in the tunnel. This could have been example of his erratic talent abandoning him at the crucial moment, but he knew it was of far more significance: it was confirmation that the gift of foresight had truly deserted him.

He kept watching his guard. Having tasted blood, the creature was even more dangerous that the rest of his dark breed. Konrad knew there was no way that he could escape, but he had to stay totally alert in order to defend himself from the predator. The guard's tongue snaked from its mouth, between its pointed teeth, and it licked at its lips.

"Taste good, good," the guard assured him, in rapid Old Worlder. "Later more, more."

Konrad covered his facial wound with his left hand and tried to ignore the skaven.

Warpstone, he thought; skaven could smell warpstone; and Litzenreich had used warpstone to extract him from the bronze armour.

As he sat on the cold damp stone, surrounded by bodies and bones, a hungry giant rodent standing two paces away, Konrad's mind went back over the events which had brought him here—and he did not like his line of reasoning and where it led him.

Heinler finally returned, the other guard with him. Konrad rose to his feet, ready for anything.

"Litzenreich!" the skaven snarled.

Konrad remained silent, showed no reaction.

"I wondered what had brought you here, but now I know some of it. Several pounds of warpstone have been stolen, both raw and refined material. It was taken by dwarfs, it seems, but they must have been working for Litzenreich. You were a diversion while the raid took place."

Konrad still said nothing, but the grey seer's words confirmed his own conclusion. Litzenreich had sent him here in full knowledge that the skaven would detect the warpstone which he had absorbed, knowing that he would be captured or killed—or worse. The magician did not care what happened to Konrad, or even to Varsung. They were both expendable. Their only purpose had been to distract the attention of the rat-things while the other three dwarfs stole the warpstone.

"Litzenreich amused me once," Heinler continued. "The idea of a human working with warpstone! Maybe I felt too much sympathy, regarding him as a fellow sorcerer despite his race. I paid the price then. I can no longer tolerate such interference with my vital work. He must die!"

Heinler held the stiletto beneath the human's throat, and for a moment Konrad believed that his own moment of death had arrived.

"I can help you," Konrad said quickly. As he moved his lower jaw, he felt the point of the dagger prick his flesh.

"Help me?" Heinler repeated, and he made the coughing sound of skaven laughter, but he lowered the knife.

"Yes," said Konrad quickly, and he wiped the drops of blood from his chin.

His first thought was to save his own life; but he owed Litzenreich nothing. The wizard had not cared about Konrad's fate. To him, Konrad he had been a sacrificial offering, the price paid for acquiring warpstone.

"Never trust a human," whispered Heinler. "That's the first thing young skaven learn."

His gaze shifted from Konrad's green eye to his golden one. Konrad remembered the threat to take his eyes—and he also recalled his double, whose eyes were a mirror image of his own.

Heinler must have been responsible for his twin opponent. But had the grey seer managed to create an identical likeness of Konrad, or had he been under the skaven's spell, deluded into believing that he was fighting against himself?

"Who did I fight out there?" he asked. "Was it me? Was it myself? Or was I just...just trying to fight my own shadow?"

Heinler gazed at him for several seconds, and Konrad thought that he would not reply, but he eventually said: "It was you, Konrad. Or almost you. More than your reflection, less than your analogue. It could have been an interesting contest, perhaps an infinite duel, if only I'd known you were coming."

"But..?" Konrad shook his head. He had so many questions that he did not know where to begin, and he was unsure whether the skaven wizard would answer any of them.

When Heinler sighed, it seemed a very human sound. "I refine warpstone," he said, "that is my task. I've organized the process so that the system can function almost without me, which means I need a hobby to keep myself occupied. I began further experiments with reincarnation for my own amusement." He glanced at the bodies in various stages of decomposition which surrounded Konrad. "Here below Middenheim is an ideal location, and I will be recruiting again very soon." He raised his head, as though he could see the city far above him. "We had some problems here several years ago, but production is increasing once more, and again my pastime is becoming more than that."

Konrad realized that the humans he had seen at work in the inferno were were all dead. Transmuting warpstone must have been so hazardous that only the resurrected corpses could survive. The creature with whom Konrad had fought had also been a zombie, a life without life, that had been given his own appearance.

Yet Heinler seemed to be saying that he had not known Konrad would be here, although he had his twin ready to do combat with him.

"Are you under Litzenreich's spell?" said the grey seer, and it seemed that he was asking himself the question. "Who *are* you, Konrad?"

Their eyes locked, and Konrad said nothing for several seconds, partly because he did not have an answer; but he did not look away.

"Why did you build a likeness of me?" he asked.

"Chance."

There is no such thing as chance—Wolf had told him that so many times, and over the years Konrad had come to believe it was true. Fate, coincidence, they did not exist. They were all part of a larger, although incomprehensible, pattern.

"I was transforming life," Heinler continued, "taking one of the undead and refining their image into that of someone else. One of them happened to be you. Before we parted, I took a sample of your blood and a piece of your flesh. That was enough to build a semblance of your life. An excellent semblance, in fact."

Blood, flesh. When Konrad had regained consciousness, discovering himself a prisoner of Kastring's marauders, he had lost plenty of both.

"The eyes were wrong," he said, "the colours switched

from left to right."

"Perhaps. Or perhaps it's your eyes that are wrong."

To distract Heinler from his eyes, Konrad said: "You must have known it was me in the tunnel. That was why you sent my double to fight me."

"I had made a simulacrum of a human warrior. I wanted to see how it would fare against a human combatant. That human warrior happened to be you, Konrad. Chance," Heinler said again.

And again Konrad did not believe it could be chance. The rat wizard must have been lying; everything he said had probably been a lie. Heinler's long sleeve covered the end of his right arm, and the missing paw. If he were such a great sorcerer, if he could create an imitation of life, why could he not replace his own missing limb?

The grey seer spoke to each of the skaven warriors, they both replied, and then the one without any ears left the cave. The guard with the single eye remained by his master's side.

"I don't know what to do with you, Konrad," Heinler said. "I sense that..." He shook his head, which seemed such an unreal gesture from such an inhuman, but he did not finish the sentence.

Konrad waited, hoping that he would conclude what he was saying and that he might provide some clue to the enigma that was Konrad's life.

"What were you doing at the mine?" Konrad asked. "Waiting to kill me?"

"The knife I threw? If I'd wanted you dead, you would have been dead." He glanced at the stiletto and threw it into the air. It spun around and around, but he caught the handle easily in his one paw. "Good with a knife, aren't I?" he said, in the voice of a Kislevite mine slave. "I was a miner. For a day. Until I caused a dark mist to envelop the watchtowers so that the raiders could attack without warning."

"Why did you join me when I followed the beastmen?"

Heinler said nothing.

"Were you obeying Skullface's orders?"

The grey seer still did not reply, but there was something strange about his expression. Was it doubt? Could it be that he did not know the real answer? Perhaps he knew almost as little as Konrad. Heinler stared at him for a long while, and Konrad did not glance away. He met the skaven's red gaze without flinching.

"Why didn't you kill me?" he asked. "It was you that hit me, wasn't it? You called out a warning, I turned, then you knocked me out."

It took a while for the grey seer to reply. "I took your blood, I took your flesh," he insisted, "that was all I wanted. This time I will take more, far more."

He spun around and left the cave, and Konrad was left alone with one of the giant warrior rats.

Time passed, and it was almost like being locked in Litzenreich's chamber. But that was several miles away, both horizontally and vertically, and there were a number of other differences. He was chained up, it was dark, he had to lie on the hard rock, and he was given no food. He managed to keep his tongue and throat moist by sucking on the moisture which oozed from the damp walls.

There was no locked door, but there was no door. Instead, there was always a guard nearby. It was often one of the first two warrior rats, who he came to think of as No Ears and Silver Eye. If not, they were members of the same clan and branded with an identical circular emblem. There was never any sign of the grey skaven. Konrad shouted out his name many a time, hoping that the sentries would call their leader, but to no avail. Perhaps Heinler was not even the grey seer's name, just one he had invented when he had transformed himself into human form.

He began picking up the nearest bones. There were plenty lying loose, and he did not have to prise them from the nearby corpses. He smashed the bones against each other, or rubbed them upon the wall, until they became splintered and pointed. He used most of these to pound into the rock, as if hoping to dig his way free. The skaven seemed very amused, and he often saw a few of them in the entrance, coughing their rodent laughter. They did not even seem concerned when he tried to lever the metal collar from his throat or dig the chain out of the wall. He soon gave up on the former, because the only damage he did was to his own neck.

After he had snapped several femurs, the rusty securing bolt was still securely embedded into the stone. It had remained in place for centuries, and hundreds of prisoners must have been chained to it and died in this very cell carved from the strata. But when he was not apparently attempting to lever away the solid metal, or to chisel into the solid rock, Konrad collected a few sharpened bones which would serve as weapons if ever one of the rat-things approached within range. They seldom came close enough for him to reach with his bare hands.

Without day or night, there was no telling how long he had been chained up. He had slept a few times, but never properly, and it had been impossible to calculate the passing days.

He thought of Heinler, and how he had first met him at the mine. It was because of Heinler that he had become a prisoner of Kastring's band. Kastring was Elyssa's brother, and Konrad had been with Elyssa when he first saw the bronze warrior. Then Konrad had become the bronze warrior, and it was Litzenreich who had saved him from the armour which imprisoned him. Now he was Heinler's prisoner, and Heinler seemed to know Litzenreich.

Everything seemed connected, each separate occurrence like the link in a chain—an invisible chain which had always held Konrad captive without him ever being aware of his confinement. All he could do was contemplate the situation into which his unseen slavemaster had now driven him, and try to work out his place in the larger pattern. There seemed no solution because as a forgotten hostage of the skaven, his role in the greater scheme must be over. He was lost beneath the world, where all true events occurred, and he must surely die and rot like every previous inhabitant of the fetid cavern.

As always, he was leaning against the damp wall, gazing through the darkness towards the slightly less dark entrance opposite, when he thought he heard a sound behind him. But the only thing behind was rock, and he realized he must be hallucinating. He was delirious through hunger.

He was almost beginning to hope that Heinler would return, to carry out his threat of taking more blood and flesh. That would be a much swifter way to die, although Konrad did not like the idea of his unliving double continuing to exist after his own death.

Then he heard the noise again, a distant echoing which seemed to be coming through the very rock. He leaned back against the cavern wall, pressing his ear to the moist surface. It sounded like a hammer hitting a chisel, as though someone were tunnelling through. There must have been other caves nearby, where more prisoners were incarcerated. One of them was hitting the wall with a stone or a piece of bone, doing what Konrad did. That was the only possible explanation.

Konrad stood up and walked as far towards the centre of the cave as the chain around his neck allowed. He kept moving as much as he could, although he realized that it depleted his energy. Any kind of activity kept his senses alert, however, and he exercised his muscles regularly. He paced two yards to the left, two yards to the right, because that was as far as his tether allowed. He saw the red eyes of No Ears watching him.

Suddenly, Konrad was flung across to the other side of the cavern, near the entrance. He lay on his back, gazing up at the low ceiling. The cave was full of swirling black smoke, and he could not work out what was going on.

A squat shape loomed above him. He seemed to recognize the figure, but could not identify him. He saw the mouth moving, but he heard no words. Just as the smoky clouds had obscured most of his vision, so he seemed to have become deaf. The shape pulled him to his feet. A dwarf; it was a dwarf.

He felt dizzy, saw the dwarf mouthing a word, and he shook his head again. Another squat and bearded figure emerged from the jagged hole that they must have blasted into the cave. The dwarfs had blown their way into the cavern where he was held prisoner. The explosion had freed the end of the chain that held him, but it had also stunned and deafened him for a while.

"Varsung?" yelled a voice. It was Ustnar, he realized. That was who was supporting him.

"Dead," he whispered. "Dead!" he shouted.

The other dwarf closed his eyes for a second, shook his head, then said: "Let's get out of here!"

But before Konrad and the two dwarfs could escape through the passage they had created, the cavern was invaded by a pack of skaven.

Ustnar leapt forward, his axe swinging. Furry limbs were severed, and rodent bodies tumbled, sliced and screaming. Konrad joined the fray, swinging the freed end of his chain as though it were a weapon. He caught one of the rat-things around one of its upper limbs, dragging it closer to him. It was No Ears.

The skaven's jagged blade arced towards Konrad, but he ducked away and evaded the blow. As he did so, he picked up one of the bones that lay scattered on the ground—and thrust it into the rodent's mouth, down its throat.

The creature fell, dropping its weapon. Konrad raised

yet another bone, one of those he had sharpened, and drove it into the skaven's chest. Foul blood spurted from its writhing body, but he kept on stabbing the beast with more and more bones until it had been totally impaled. And still it kept twitching, refusing to accept that it was dead.

"Come on!" yelled a voice. It was Hjornur, the other dwarf.

Ustnar was busy slaying skaven, and the cave was a mass of bodies. It seemed that he would have preferred to venture out into the warren beyond, to find more of the enemy and keep on killing rather than retreat. Konrad knew the way he felt.

Hjornur beckoned to Konrad, and he gathered up the chain, then bent down into the tunnel. Hjornur pushed him through. He saw another figure ahead, lit by a lantern. As the shape gestured for him to hurry, he recognized Joukelm. He obeyed, moving as fast as he could, following the dwarf as he turned and made his way along the passage. He heard more sounds behind him. Hjornur and Ustnar were bringing up the rear, although he paid little attention. He was too busy trying keep up with the dim figure of the distant dwarf clambering through the narrow tunnel.

There was a sudden thunderous roar, and a blast of turbulent air knocked him forward. Blood trickled from both nostrils, another cloud of dust enveloped him, and he coughed. Choking and deafened again, he realized that the dwarfs had used more gunpowder to block off the passage behind in order to prevent pursuit.

Konrad kept on scrambling through the gloom, but with each step he was climbing, heading back the way he had come an unknown number of days ago, back towards Middenheim, back towards Litzenreich's subterranean workshop.

CHAPTER TWELVE

"Thanks for coming for me," said Konrad.

"We didn't come for you," said Joukelm.

"We came for Varsung," said Hjornur.

Konrad already knew that, but he said nothing else; the first five words had been difficult enough. He drank some more water. The dwarfs had taken no such luxury item into the skaven domain, being laden down with tunnelling equipment, weapons and gunpowder.

After a long and arduous journey, they had at last reached the labyrinthine levels beneath Middenheim. Several times Konrad thought he could not go on, he was too exhausted, but the dwarfs had half-dragged, half-carried him over the worst obstacles. It was as if they had to get him back or else their whole mission would have been wasted. He was covered in sweat and dirt and blood, his body was cut and gashed and bruised; but he was alive, he was free, and that was worth any pain and deprivation.

He stripped naked and used more water to bathe his

fresh wounds and wash away the dried blood, to rinse off the dust and the sweat. But he was not completely naked, because the iron collar was still around his neck, as was the length of rusty chain which had fettered him to the wall of the cave. Konrad remembered the black links that Wolf wore around his neck. He had said it was part of a chain which had once held him captive, that he kept it in order to remember how bad incarceration had been and to remind him that he would rather die than ever be taken prisoner again. But Konrad needed no such reminder, and Joukelm removed the iron necklace with a few accurate blows from his hammer and cold chisel.

"How did it happen?" Ustnar asked, finally.

"It was all over in a moment," Konrad replied, knowing exactly what the dwarf meant. "An arrow from a crossbow. Varsung never knew what hit him. There was no pain. He died instantly. I killed his killer."

Only the last sentence was untrue, although Konrad had slaughtered so many skaven in the tunnel that he might even have slain the one with the crossbow.

Ustnar stared at him, and Konrad returned his gaze. "That's what happened," he affirmed.

Ustnar nodded, and he walked off into the gloom of the cavern. The other three watched him go.

"Varsung was his brother," said Joukelm.

"But that's not why we returned," said Hjornur. "We went back because Varsung was a comrade."

Konrad drank some more water, then chewed on a piece of dried bread. It had taken them long enough to return, he thought, or maybe that was only the way it appeared. After the warpstone raid, the skaven would have been on full alert, and the dwarfs must have taken a different course into the rat warren, even carving a new route part way through the rock.

He was certain Litzenreich had nothing to do with their expedition. The wizard had sent Konrad to his death, and also anyone who was with him. It was Varsung's bad luck that he was the one. Or had it been Litzenreich's suggestion that it should be Varsung who accompanied Konrad while the other three took a different path?

Konrad thought of when they had first ventured into the skaven domain, and he asked: "You got the warpstone?"

"Yes," replied Joukelm.

"Why?"

"Why?" repeated Joukelm.

"Why did you do it? Why work for Litzenreich?"

"We work *with* him," said Hjornur.

"But you call him *boss*," Konrad said.

"Only to keep him happy," said Joukelm.

"But he's the one who gives the orders. He *is* the boss. He wants the warpstone, not you." Konrad looked at the two dwarfs.

"We are allies," Hjornur said. "We get the warpstone. Litzenreich uses it."

"No, he uses you."

"Maybe. But it is the result that matters."

"The death of Varsung? Isn't that the result?"

"No," said Joukelm, joining in. "No one lives forever."

"Varsung didn't have much chance to, did he?" said Konrad.

"There are always casualties."

Now that he was beginning to recover, Konrad was becoming irritated at the way the dwarfs seemed to consider Litzenreich. Did they not realize that he manipulated them for his own dubious purposes?

"Litzenreich wanted the skaven to know I was there. They could smell the warpstone you used to get me out of the bronze armour. Varsung and I were a diversion, so that you could steal the warpstone. Because of that, Varsung died. You didn't want that, did you? That's why you came back, hoping he was alive."

"We hoped," Joukelm shrugged, "but..."

"We're fighting a war," said Hjornur, "just as you were in Kislev." The dwarf must have heard of Konrad's years on the frontier from Litzenreich. "You were defending a gold mine, which meant battling against beastmen. Each one you killed slowed the advance of Chaos by a fraction, although that may not have been your motive. And we are part of that same conflict here."

Konrad stared at the two of them, hardly believing what he was hearing. Had the magician enchanted them?

The reaction of Joukelm and Hjornur was completely contrary to what he had expected. Dwarfs were notoriously short-tempered, and he had thought they would be absolutely incensed at the idea of Litzenreich deliberately using Varsung to bait a trap. Ustnar seemed naturally upset at the death of his brother, yet that was all. The other two appeared totally unconcerned, as though the wizard's behaviour had been entirely reasonable.

They had not even seemed surprised when Konrad revealed that the skaven must have been warned of their approach by the smell of warpstone. The reason, he suddenly understood, was obvious: the dwarfs knew. They knew all about warpstone and its effects; they knew warpstone had permeated throughout Konrad; they knew that the skaven could detect the scent of warpstone.

What of Ustnar? Had he also known that his own brother might die as a result of Litzenreich's scheme? He must have done—and Varsung must also have known...

The only member of the mission who had been unaware that the skaven would smell the odour of warpstone on Konrad had been Konrad himself.

Would he always be affected? Or would the taint fade over the years? He needed to ask Litzenreich. He hoped never to encounter another skaven; but if they could smell him, they would seek him out for the warpstone that they craved.

Although relieved to be free, Konrad still resented the

way Litzenreich had used him. He had used the dwarfs, too. They knew it, yet they remained loyal. It made no sense, but Konrad was used to the defeat of logic in the face of unreason.

After he had slept for an uncounted number of hours and eaten his first proper meal, the dwarfs took Konrad higher up through the network of tunnels, returning him to the area where the magician dwelled. The guards allowed them through, and they made their way to the central chamber. When Litzenreich saw Konrad and the other three, he hardly spared them a glance. He continued about his work of assembling a weird copper contraption.

"Hold this," he said to Joukelm, and the dwarf hurried to do as he was requested.

Konrad walked towards the wizard and stood in front of him. Litzenreich must have known he had been captured by the skaven, but even when he had finished his immediate task he ignored Konrad. This was also the first time he had seen the dwarfs since their recent expedition to the rodent underworld. Even if he did not know of their mission, he must have observed that they had been absent for a while; but he paid no attention and behaved as though nothing had happened.

While chained up a few miles below, Konrad had frequently passed the time by considering all the possible slow and painful ways that he could kill Litzenreich if ever he encountered him again. Now, however, the idea of such vengeance seemed hollow. In the fury of combat, when the blood was hot, revenge was an ideal motivation, an incentive to action. If a comrade had been killed or badly wounded, a warrior would seek out and slay the opponent that had been responsible.

Thoughts of vengeance had helped Konrad to survive, yet the flames of anger had died down, and he no longer felt much hostility towards Litzenreich. Perhaps he had been influenced by the dwarfs, the manner in which they had treated the whole episode so calmly. There was no way that Konrad would have sought to avenge himself in cold blood. The past was over and done. He had been liberated, and that was the most important thing. Nothing he did to Litzenreich could make things any different. Neither would he be saving himself from any future threat by dispatching the wizard, because he had no intention of having any further dealings with Litzenreich.

Within the hour, he planned to be away from here. First, he needed a new outfit, weapons, a horse and money. And that was what he told Litzenreich as soon as the magician quit the central chamber, leaving the three dwarfs to finish constructing a complex web of copper tubes that seemed almost to be a model of the tunnel network through which they had so recently travelled.

"Money?" said the wizard. "Money?" He frowned as though it were an unknown word. "I do not have money." He attempted to move past Konrad, but found his way blocked. "You are free to leave whenever you wish."

"Armour, clothes, a helmet, a shield, a sword, a horse," repeated Konrad.

"I owe you nothing."

"You tried to kill me."

"I did not."

"You sent me into the skaven tunnels knowing that they would smell the warpstone."

"Yes."

"You tried to kill me," Konrad repeated.

"No. I do not understand why you are complaining. You are not dead. If you were, you would not be able to complain."

"The only reason I'm not dead is because the dwarfs rescued me. And they didn't come for me. They came for Varsung, who is dead."

"I thought he must be."

"Did you know he was Ustnar's brother?"

"All dwarfs are brothers."

"His real brother."

"What of it?"

Litzenreich had saved his life, and Litzenreich had nearly cost him his life. These two balanced out. Originally, the wizard claimed he had wanted Konrad to bring back the warpstone as payment for resurrecting him from the bronze armour—and so, by such reckoning, Konrad was still owed for the role he had played in the mission to the skaven lair.

"I'm leaving as soon as you pay what I'm due for bringing back the warpstone," he said.

"But you did not bring any back. You did not come back."

"I've come back now. And if I hadn't gone, if Varsung hadn't died, the other three would have captured no warpstone."

"Not necessarily," said Litzenreich, and he made to pass by Konrad again.

Konrad touched him for the first time, holding his palm against Litzenreich's chest to prevent him moving.

"I do not think it would be wise for you to threaten me," said Litzenreich.

And Konrad remembered who he was dealing with: a sorcerer...

Even without a weapon, he could have slain Litzenreich in under a second if necessary. A dead magician could not cast a spell. Konrad lowered his hand, but he wondered how fast Litzenreich could have protected himself. Was it possible to conjure a defence faster than the reflexes of a trained warrior? Would the wizard have died before he could even utter a death curse?

"You do not have to leave," said Litzenreich. "I can give you everything that you need here."

"Ha! Are you offering me a job? You want me to go back and let the skaven smell my scent again, so that the dwarfs can loot more warpstone? I may be a soldier, Litzenreich, I may live by the sword, but I'm not stupid. I'm leaving before the skaven get here."

"Before the skaven get here?" echoed the wizard, and for the first time he looked at Konrad instead of through him. "What do you mean?"

"They're coming for you. They're fed up with you stealing the warpstone. They plan to kill you."

"You are guessing." It was a statement, not a question.

"They know who you are, Litzenreich, and they probably know where you are. They are going to kill you. I don't intend to be here when they arrive."

For the first time, the wizard looked confused. He appeared never to have considered that the skaven might take action against him; he seemed to believe that he could keep on stealing from them for ever and they would do nothing to prevent it.

"You are guessing?" This time there was doubt, and it was a question.

"No. Heinler told me."

"And who is Heinler?"

"Their leader. A grey seer."

Litzenreich stared at him with undisguised incredulity. "A grey seer told you? Do not be so ridiculous."

Konrad shrugged. "He does not seem to like you, Litzenreich, he said something about already having paid a price for what you had done to him. Since then, your dwarfs have been back down there, killed several more skaven and blown up a tunnel. Heinler will be even less pleased with you, I imagine."

"This grey seer, he really spoke to you?"

Konrad nodded. "He can do all sorts of things. He's one of their sorcerers, he's like you."

"Nothing like me!" He became totally still for a few

seconds, his eyes unfocused, then suddenly he held up his right hand. "His paw was missing?"

"Yes. You know him?"

"*Gaxar*. That was the name by which I knew him. It was I who removed the paw. So he is back, that one?"

"You 'removed' the paw? By sorcery?"

"With a—" Litzenreich paused, as if trying to remember the word "—a sword."

"If he is a wizard," said Konrad, bringing up a subject that had earlier intrigued him, "why can't he do something about his hand? His paw, I mean. He can give life to the dead, so why not life to his missing paw?"

"There is an old saying, *Magician, heal thyself*. It is a paradox, but what wizards can do for others they often cannot do for themselves." Litzenreich shook his head slowly as he contemplated the mystery. "But you say he is restoring the dead?"

Konrad told the sorcerer what he had seen in the skaven nest and what Heinler—or Gaxar, if that was his real name—had told him of his necromancy.

"Creating simulacra once more, is he?" said Litzenreich, when he heard of the duel Konrad had fought with his double. He stood without moving, his unblinking eyes staring past Konrad

But this was not what Konrad wanted to discuss. He was wasting his time trying to talk to the wizard, he realized. He would get nothing from him; he would have to take what he needed. There would be weapons in the guardroom, armour and a change of clothing; and there must be something of value that he could sell or exchange for a horse once he reached the surface of Middenheim.

He turned away from the wizard. He had no real idea of the topography of the tunnels. All he could do was search through the various passages until he found what he required. His progress was soon blocked by a solid wooden door. He drew back the heavy bolts and passed through, but there seemed no more chambers off the shaft ahead. All he could see was another door.

When he reached it there were no locks, no bolts. The door was secured by more than mere locks and bolts, he discovered. He could not get out of Litzenreich's domain until the sorcerer allowed him to. He turned and headed back the way he had come. He had left the first door open, and he could see the magician still standing at the end of the passage, illuminated in a halo of light from the lantern hung from the bracket next to him.

As reached the doorway, Konrad heard a loud detonation behind him. It was like a sudden clap of thunder, and he spun around in time to see the lightning strike...

The heavy wooden door at the end of the tunnel shattered into a thousand pieces, and he was hit by a number of splinters and blinded by a flare of luminescence. He knew what a gunpowder explosion sounded and smelled like, but this was something different. It was no physical force that had demolished the solid door with such ease.

He was still wearing his chainmail and leather armour, which protected him from the wooden darts, and he had instinctively thrown up his hands to shield his eyes. As he blinked, beginning to recover from the brilliant glare, he saw the outline of a shadowy figure appear through the dust and smoke. The creature was covered in fur and carried a sword—a skaven!

Although still half-dazzled, Konrad sprang, armed only with the weapons of his primitive ancestors—his hands, his feet. The creature could not have expected an opponent to be so close, and the advantage lay with Konrad. He lunged forward, using the techniques taught by his eastern tutors on the frontier, chopping with the edge of his hand against the intruder's neck.

Down went the creature, and Konrad's boot followed it

down, crushing its throat. He retrieved his victim's sword and noticed that it was not the usual kind of jagged skaven blade; he also realized that the creature had seemed to be wearing armour beneath its fur...

But by then, a second combatant was facing him in the tunnel. The two swords clashed, and as Konrad's eyes finally adjusted he observed that he was not fighting a skaven. His opponent was human, wearing a wolf skin over his helmet and armour. He could not be a true human, Konrad knew, he must have been one of the undead resurrected by Gaxar. Yet when he fell, mortally wounded, he bled red blood, not white maggots.

Wolf fur, thought Konrad, as he tackled the third intruder. And this was the city of the white wolf. They must have been Middenheim troops, he realized. No longer did he attack so ferociously, instead concentrating on defending himself. He did not want any trouble with the city authorities; he hoped to leave Litzenreich's domain via Middenheim. But, having killed two of their troops, the military command were unlikely to take kindly to him.

"Litzenreich!" yelled a voice from behind Konrad's opponent. "You are under arrest for illegal use of warpstone! Order your men to surrender!"

Surrender was not a word in Konrad's vocabulary. He had just slain two of his opponent's comrades, it would be sheer madness to give up his sword. In many circumstances, surrender meant summary execution. Here, he would be regarded as an ally of Litzenreich's, and the punishment for handling warpstone was death.

He heard footsteps racing up behind him, and he recognized the sound of the strides. Only dwarfs ran like that. A second later, he was joined by Ustnar. Dissatisfied by Konrad's evident reluctance to finish off his opponent, the dwarf pushed past. His axe swung twice, and the trooper dropped, both his legs severed at the knee.

Joukelm and Hjornur also arrived, and the three of them

trampled the wounded trooper underfoot as they advanced along the passage, cutting a swathe through the ranks of attackers. They were the experts, born tunnel fighters. Konrad gazed down at the third warrior who was screaming and writhing in agony. All he could do was put an end to him as swiftly as possible. This was the first lesson that Wolf had ever taught him, when the mercenary had finished off the second of the woodsmen who had ambushed Konrad in the Ferlangen stables. He placed the tip of his sword against the trooper's throat, then leaned down with all his weight. The soldier jerked and screeched one final time, then became both still and silent as twin streams of blood spurted from his throat and mouth, joining the rivers of red that flooded from his amputated limbs.

Konrad went back in search of Litzenreich. He found the sorcerer in his central chamber. The place was an inferno, and he wondered how the invaders could have reached here so soon. Then he realized that the destruction was the magician's own work. Litzenreich stood in an untouched part of the cavern, while the blaze raged around him. He was destroying all the evidence of what he had done, all his books and notes, all his equipment and machinery and apparatus.

Forced to step back from the blast of heat, Konrad sheltered away from the arched entrance, and yet the wizard stood untouched by the devastation he had wrought. He could have used his powers to throw back the assault. Instead he chose to annihilate every trace of what he had done in his secret lair beneath the city. That would not save him, Konrad knew. The very fact of immolating his work would be sufficient proof. It would be the death penalty for Litzenreich—and for Konrad.

Then the wizard stepped calmly out of the furnace he had created, and he noticed Konrad watching him. "They shall not have the benefit of my genius," he said calmly. "My years of research are mine alone. And I still have the most important thing of all." He tapped his forehead.

Four of the human guards pushed past them, to join in the battle.

"Back to your posts!" Litzenreich commanded. "They will be breaking through elsewhere!"

"At least it's not the skaven," said Konrad.

"I think I would have preferred the skaven," said Litzenreich. "You saw how that door was disintegrated? The so-called sorcerers of Middenheim are afraid to face me, so they send in their mercenaries, the city's troops."

If the whole of the fortress city, the military and the magicians, were in alliance, Konrad realized they stood very little chance.

"What about your magic?" said Konrad.

"My rivals have combined to restrict my talents. I can sense the constraints. It is as though they have put a shell between me and Middenheim. I cannot summon any enchantments against our attackers."

"Then all we can do is fight."

"Fight? No, no. Perhaps I ought to try and explain, tell them about the skaven, that it is all happening again."

Konrad stopped listening. Talking was no use to him. That would only lead to surrender, which meant exchanging one form of imprisonment for another. He needed to escape, and he knew that the dwarfs had their secret routes out of Middenheim.

"The skaven," he said. "That's it! We're trapped between two enemies. We must bring them together, let them fight each other, not us."

"How?"

The skaven were a secretive breed. Few even knew of their existence. Perhaps even the Graf of Middenheim was unaware of the rival domain far beneath his own territory. The foul beings that lurked in the deepest shadows were a much greater threat than Litzenreich, and somehow Konrad had to bring the city marshals' attention to the danger. The garrison would then divert all its energies to defeating the giant rats—while he took his leave.

The Middenheim troops had to be led towards the skaven. The rodent lair was too far away, and the soldiers would be unwilling to pursue Litzenreich's band down into the deepest darkness. If, however, they learned of the existence of the subterranean skaven city, a whole army would be despatched to eradicate the hidden menace.

"Heinler... I mean, Gaxar... said something about new recruits," Konrad remembered. "That means dead bodies. The skaven were going to take them soon. Where would they find them?"

"Morrspark," said Litzenreich. "The catacombs."

"That's where we're going," said Konrad. "And we've got to make sure that we're followed. Understand?"

"I may not be a soldier," said Litzenreich, "but I am not stupid."

There was no way that Middenheim could grow larger; its boundaries were the edges of the mountain. The plateau was not much more than a mile square, which meant that land was at a premium. There was not enough room for the living, and very little for the dead. The poor simply threw the bodies of their relatives over the Cliff of Sighs. Those with more respect and money paid for cremation or burial at the foot of the slopes. Only the very rich could afford a place in the vaults beneath Morrspark.

This was the point where the clan of dwarfs who had tunnelled up through the granite originally reached the surface. It was the oldest part of the city, and there were more shafts radiating from here than anywhere else in Middenheim. With the passing years, many of these passages had collapsed. This made the room available for burial even more restricted, and the price of entombment had increased accordingly.

Funerals took place on the surface, but that was not the only access to the cemetery. The dwarfs knew how to reach the area via the crumbling maze of tunnels, a long and winding route which involved travelling via some of the sewers. The city troops were to be held back for a short while, then allowed to follow the defenders; but they had to be unaware that they were being deliberately led.

Joukelm and Ustnar were at the head of the fugitives, who were composed of another dwarf, a number of Litzenreich's guards, the women who included Gertraut and Rita, the cook—and also the sorcerer and Konrad. It was still impossible to discover how many dwarfs worked for the wizard, because some of them must have stayed behind with Joukelm and the other sentries in order to delay pursuit. Finally, that pursuit came. In the distance, reverberating through the web of tunnels could be heard the sounds of combat, the ring of clashing weapons and the cries of the wounded and dying.

Joukelm and Ustnar had halted the group within the passage, waiting while the last of the defenders caught up with them. The Middenheim troops must enter the catacombs only seconds behind, so that they would also see the skaven scavengers—if there were any...

Konrad had planned to escape from Middenheim, and that was still an option. But if the alternative to fleeing the city was to kill skaven before he disappeared, then his choice was not in doubt for an instant.

The rest of the desperate band arrived, and there were very few of them left. Three humans and one dwarf; it was not Hjornur. The footsteps of the pursuers came closer. The reflected light from their lanterns could been seen around the next twist in the tunnel, and Konrad feared that the body stealers might already have been warned away by all the sounds. But they were there!

As Konrad sprang out into the cavern of the dead, he saw several of the skaven in the distance. They were disinterring fresh bodies from the stone coffins which lay in the recesses carved from the rock. They froze, trapped in the sudden glare of lamplight.

There was no need for a command. The guards and dwarfs sprinted forward, while the skaven dropped the corpses and tried to scuttle back into the passages from which they had emerged. Konrad's fighting instincts urged him to join them, but instead he spun around, waiting to encounter the first of the Middenheim troops. An armoured shape loomed out of the darkness of the tunnel.

"Beastmen!" Konrad yelled, guessing that the word 'skaven' might have no meaning. "Truce! A truce in the name of Ulric!"

Middenheim was Ulric's city, the city of the white wolf. That was why the troops wore wolfskins over their armour. The leading warrior slowed as he emerged from the passage, his sword raised ready to cut down Konrad. Konrad stood his ground, his own blade lowered. An officer appeared from behind the first trooper. He stared past Konrad, and gazed at the scene of desecration where a pack of beastmen had infested the sacred ground beneath his own city.

"Forward!" ordered the captain, and his troops rushed from the passage to battle with the rat creatures, joining in combat with the other humans and the dwarfs who were already fighting the verminous breed. "Stay there," he warned, his gaze encompassing both Litzenreich and Konrad.

He hurried to join his command. Several of his men remained, and they encircled Konrad and the wizard. Konrad could have evaded them, could have tried to escape, but there seemed nowhere to go; he could have fought, could have slain a number of the troops, but there seemed no reason to do so.

A short plump man emerged from the shaft. He was not in uniform, but wore dark garments decorated with runic symbols. He carried a carved wooden staff, its head tipped with a golden orb. Konrad suspected that he was a sorcerer, the staff his wand. He halted and looked at Litzenreich, who returned his gaze.

The skaven, meanwhile, were slaughtered. There had been relatively few of them, and they were all swiftly butchered. When the massacre was over, Litzenreich's group surrendered their weapons to the Middenheim forces.

"The sword," the captain said to Konrad when he returned, and he held out his hand. He was no older than Konrad, and his face bore a single neat scar on his cleanly shaven left cheek. It was a duelling wound, which he wore as proudly as a medal of valour. He had probably never met a real enemy in combat. Even now there was no trace of skaven blood on his uniform, and his blade was untainted with rat gore.

Konrad had met his type before. Their commissions had been purchased by their families, and their arrogance and inexperience frequently led to more casualties amongst their own troops than was ever caused by enemy action. The possibility of losing the sword was of more importance to him than the loss of the soldier who had borne the blade.

"I need it," Konrad replied, exaggerating his rural accent, but he made no move to bring up the weapon. "Those creatures are called skaven, and the tunnels below Middenheim are infested by them. Extend the truce and we can lead you to their nest and you can destroy them all. Take us captive, and instead the skaven will destroy the city."

"That is true," said Litzenreich, addressing the other magician.

"That is true," repeated the wizard, speaking to the captain. He moved closer to Litzenreich, and they began conversing.

"I want to speak to your commanding general," Konrad

said, not even bothering to look at the officer. "We must act now. One or two of the skaven will have escaped and be carrying word back to the rest of their legion."

"I know about skaven," said the captain, biting back his anger. He gazed around the necropolis, at the distant corpses, both human and inhuman. He summoned a messenger.

"The dwarfs know the fastest way to the surface," Konrad told him.

With evident reluctance, the officer gave his consent, and Ustnar led the ensign back through the tunnel. Two other troops accompanied them, to guard the dwarf.

"No matter what happens," the captain said to Konrad, lowering his voice, "whenever the truce ends, you are dead. That sword belongs to my regiment."

Konrad glanced at the blade in his hand. He had no scabbard for the weapon, that was still on the body of the first trooper he had killed.

"No," he said, "it belongs to me."

CHAPTER THIRTEEN

The military command of Middenheim had sent as many troops as it could spare to join the underground expedition: part of the garrison, members of the watch, a group of mercenaries, a number of Templars of the White Wolf and also a handful of Knights Panther. Even without their horses, the elite cavalry were anxious to be part of the mission to protect their native city.

Litzenreich's men were at the head of the long column, the dwarfs leading the way. They would bear the brunt of the action and take the most casualties, shielding the Middenheim warriors during the initial assault.

Konrad had half-intended to slip away during the descent. He had done more than enough, and the city troops could take care of the skaven without him. He was sure that Litzenreich would wish to avoid becoming involved in any military action. One of the dwarfs could escort them both safely through the twisting tunnels and out of the mountain. But it seemed that the wizard wanted to investigate the skaven warrens, and his only possible motive could be the hope of discovering how raw warpstone was refined into grey powder.

In order to prevent any of Litzenreich's column from deserting, there was a city soldier behind each one—and the captain was immediately behind Konrad. Konrad was unconcerned. Had he wished, he could easily have evaded the arrogant officer and got away. As he had nowhere to go, he kept on descending the spiralling shafts. He was becoming almost used to it by now. Only the dwarfs and their guards were ahead of him; Litzenreich was immediately behind the captain.

Neither did the officer's threat concern Konrad, although he had been glad of the warning. For the captain to reveal his intention had been stupid; equally stupid was for him to have had such an intention. Konrad had fought and killed one of the captain's men, taking his sword. What of it? He had also slain a second Middenheim trooper and given merciful release to the one whose legs Ustnar had severed. It had all occurred during combat, yet the captain seemed to consider that murder had been committed. Why had he taken it so personally?

One of the captain's men must have killed Hjornur. The dwarf had helped save Konrad's life, but he had no reason to seek out Hjornur's killer and slay him. He remembered what he had been thinking recently, of revenge. During a battle, a warrior might hunt down a comrade's killer. But that would not happen after hostilities had ceased—probably because two opposing sides seldom become allies so immediately.

As he clambered down another steep incline, Konrad realized that he might soon have an opportunity for his own vengeance. He would never have gone out of his way to search for Gaxar, but it seemed that they might soon come into close proximity again. In that case, he would do his best to avenge himself against the grey seer.

He recalled what Litzenreich had once told him about the difference between justice and law. Perhaps that was what he really sought, not revenge but justice. Gaxar was not only responsible for his incarceration in the dark damp grotto for an unknown number of days. Konrad had been knocked senseless by the treacherous inhuman, and when he regained consciousness he was a prisoner of Kastring's outlaw band of beastmen.

Konrad did not simply wish to kill Gaxar. He wanted to interrogate him first. The more he considered the idea, the more he anticipated another encounter with the grey skaven. He hoped that the rodents had not all fled. They must have been aware of the strike force being sent into their domain. Would they make a fight of it, or would they turn tail and flee into the deepest tunnels of their shadowy realm?

If the rodents had gone, Konrad knew that the truce with the Middenheim soldiers would be instantly over. Only then would he have to worry about the death threat. Until that time, he had a stay of execution. The captain would not stab him in the back. He clearly regarded himself as a gentleman, and for him honour was as important as his own life. He had obviously never served on the frontier. He would not make his move until the subterranean battle was over. With luck, he would be killed by the skaven; with luck, Konrad would not be killed by the skaven.

His new sword was thrust into his belt, and he had to be careful that he did not cut or stab himself on the naked blade as he climbed down the most difficult of passages. Konrad was still clad in the same leathers and chainmail he had worn on his first underground venture; but he had neither helmet nor shield, all he had was the sword. It was quite a fancy weapon, with elaborate quillons and a wolf's head emblem etched into the guard. The blade itself was decorated with fancy hieroglyphs; it was probably a motto inscribed in an ancient language. Perhaps it meant *Death before dishonour.* Konrad smiled at the idea, because there was nothing else to smile about.

He began wishing for a return of his future vision. Erratic though it might have been, it was better than nothing. In the narrow tunnel, in the darkness between two Middenheim soldiers, there was nothing to be seen with his normal sight.

It was Joukelm who led the descent, but he was not the first to die. The first screams came from further back, higher up, echoing down the narrow shafts and magnifying as they bounced from wall to wall.

The skaven knew that their regions were being invaded, and they had reacted accordingly, defending themselves with an outer ring of suicide squads. These lurked in side passages, then sprang out, killing and maiming many of the humans before they were themselves slaughtered.

They had also prepared traps, but they allowed the first group of the enemy past, cutting them off, before the floor of a chamber suddenly dropped away and a dozen troops tumbled into a pit lined with barbed spikes. The next rat beasts' victims were those crushed beneath tons of rock when the roof above them collapsed. The Middenheim brigade had their own dwarfs, who were able to bridge the gap and to unblock the tunnel within a few minutes. The forward section waited for them to catch up, and by then it was their turn to be attacked.

Joukelm was the first in line, and now it was his turn to die. He was slain as Varsung had been, with an arrow from a crossbow. Most of the others ahead of Konrad took the precaution of ducking down, and so it was the trooper immediately in front of him who died next. The bolt took him in one eye, its point penetrating the back of his skull and his helmet.

Konrad's head had been directly behind. He leaned

down as he advanced, and he picked up the shield dropped by the crossbow victim. The captain would not like that, he presumed, but it was of no use to the dead man at arms. The embossed crest on the shield was that of the white wolf.

In the flickering lantern light, Konrad thought he recognized where he was. All tunnels should have appeared the same, dark passages hewn from the solid granite, but this seemed to be the place where Varsung had died. If so, the huge central cavern was not much further. He strained his eyes for a glimmer of the weird illumination that had come from the warpstone furnace.

"Ustnar!"

"What?"

"We nearly there?"

"Yeah."

"Next arrow, then we sprint."

"Right."

The next shaft hissed past Konrad. There was a slight bend in the passage, and it splintered against the rock face, otherwise it would have finished off the captain.

"Go!" yelled Konrad, and he dashed forward, after Ustnar, after the two dwarfs whose names he did not know, after the three Middenheim troopers. Soon, it was only two troopers, as one of them became the next victim of the unseen archer.

Last time, after the first arrows, Konrad had been attacked in this tunnel by a pack of skaven, and he expected to hear the sounds of another mob rushing towards them. Instead, there was a sudden glare of light and they were out in the open—and the skaven were all waiting...

He had been wrong about the tunnel, this was a different passage. Instead of coming out on a gallery, they emerged on the floor of the massive central cavern.

By the time Konrad reached the end of the passage, the other two soldiers and one of the dwarfs were dead. Ustnar

and the other dwarf were defending themselves from a
furious skaven onslaught, their axes swinging. Already
there were several dead rat things, Konrad noticed, as he
killed another. But there were more, far too many more still
alive. He thrust his sword forward again, and another
skaven died, the blade deep into its heart. Then the captain
was by Konrad's side, claiming his own first kill; perhaps
he was not as inexperienced as Konrad had presumed.

Litzenreich was the next out. He had no weapon, and
Ustnar was immediately in front of him, defending the
wizard. One of the skaven evaded him, lunging toward the
human. Litzenreich threw out his right arm as though he
were armed with a sword. Without even being touched, the
rat thing became absolutely still, frozen in the act of
stabbing with its spear. Ustnar's axe severed its head, and
head and body both fell.

More of the invaders poured from the tunnel. Most of
them made it alive, and they began to push the brown
swarm back. But they were retreating too willingly, Konrad
realized. The humans were deliberately being drawn
forward. He hung back, gazing up, wondering where Gaxar
could be and how to reach him.

The huge chamber was like a vast unholy temple, in the
centre of which Gaxar's monstrous metallic mechanism
was an effigy of an evil god, belching fire and smoke; but
the acolytes were missing, the undead slaves of the
warpstone cult who worshipped at this huge altar.
Constructed upon a stone dais, the great idol did not accept
its votive offerings in quiescent silence. The huge
interlocking wheels and linked levers with which it was
ornamented were forever in furious motion, rotating and
thrusting, around and around, up and down and in and out.

Konrad had grown used to the perpetual pounding noise
while he was a prisoner here. But now the sound was much
reduced, the heat no longer so fierce, the glare more
bearable; the cogs and pulleys no longer spun so fast. The

deity seemed to be slumbering. Knowing the attack would come, operations in hell's foundry must have been suspended.

Then the dead attacked.

The unliving who were slaves to the skaven had become a battalion. They did not need weapons, because there were so many of them. They emerged from the tunnels opposite, fat flies buzzing around them as they slowly shambled forward, confining the invaders by sheer weight of numbers. Most of the undead were easily destroyed, but there were always more to take their place. Konrad hoped that he would not see himself amongst the dead, but there was no sign of his double in the necromantic legion.

The resurrected were not the only ones who had processed warpstone for their rodent masters. The rat things had made many of their own number into slaves, and these also joined the assault against the human invaders. These were armed with a variety of weapons, but they were also chained to one another. They were suicide squads, their deaths as inevitable as the annihilation of the unliving. With iron collars and heavy rusting chains around their necks, Konrad could not but help think of his own incarceration. They were as much prisoners as he had been—but that did not stop him from slaying as many of them as he could.

The enslaved skaven died, joining the festering zombies and decayed skeletons, rotting carcasses and mummified corpses, putrefying ghouls and embalmed cadavers, which dropped to the ground and formed a rampart that held back the human warriors, trapping them.

And that was when the trap was sprung. A hail of arrows lashed down from above, and many of the humans fell victim before they could raise their shields to form a huge protective canopy.

But this was no protection from the skaven's next appalling weapon. A sudden thunderbolt of yellow flame shot from one of the upper levels, pouring a cascade of molten lava down onto the warriors below. Shields dissolved and metal melted. More than half of the troops were killed almost instantly, cremated within their armour coffins. Others took longer to perish, shrieking hideously as they burned alive.

The Middenheim troops had raised their shields in unison, as they were trained to do. Konrad had not added his own shield, and that was what saved his life. The fluid flames had not flowed across him, and he had avoided being caught in the conflagration.

Many of the chained skaven and the undead also fell victim to the fireball. Some burst into flames, others disintegrated in the blast of heat. A number of the dead kept on with their parody of life, advancing through the mayhem despite being ablaze, as though drawn by the nauseating scent of cooked human flesh. They had no voices, they felt no pain, they could not scream and did not need to.

Litzenreich stared up towards the skaven with the incendiary weapon. There seemed to be two of them standing on an upper gallery. One carried a wooden barrel on its back, and the other held some kind of brass device. It was like a musical instrument, an ornate trumpet. And the skaven was aiming the thing downwards, ready for another silent solo of fiery death.

The wizard raised both his hands, pointing up at the rocky ledge, and lightning flew from his fingertips. An instant later, the lethal barrel exploded, splashing both the rats with the incandescent liquid. They were afire as they dropped into the abyss, already charred bones by the time they smashed to the ground.

Litzenreich staggered back, and Konrad thought he had been wounded, but he leaned against the cavern wall as if resting from some great exertion.

Konrad's face had been burned and blistered by the

terrible heat of the skaven flame machine, and the blade of his sword had become red hot. The heat was transferred up to the hilt, through his gauntlet, and he had been forced to drop the weapon. He searched for another, loosened one from the grip of a corpse.

The corpse was that of the captain. Death and dishonour were all that was left to him now. He had been eviscerated, and his spilled guts mingled with those of the disembowelled skaven with which he was entwined. They lay together like loathsome lovers, mating in some obscene fashion.

"Thanks," Konrad said.

The sword was identical with the other, and with it Konrad continued to slay more of the undead. Maggots and all kinds of carrion-eating insects spilled from his new blade. The cemetery stench of ancient leprous flesh mixed with the odour of roasted bodies, a daemon's emetic perfume.

Konrad saw that Litzenreich had recovered and was making his way through the necromantic legion. The animated corpses which were still upright seemed to move aside for him. Ustnar was with him, his blade hacking at the few surviving skaven slaves. The wizard gazed up at the bizarre apparatus where the warpstone was transformed, which seemed as if it could be a much larger version of some of his own convoluted equipment.

No more human troops emerged from the tunnel. Could these who surrounded him be the only ones who had survived? Were reinforcements sheltering in the passage? Where were the skaven? Even the archers who had such easy targets had only fired one volley. Konrad glanced all around. There were no ratmen in sight. They had withdrawn between the arrows being unleashed and the eruption of the volcanic torrent of fiery destruction, and they had not returned.

The skaven could surely not have retreated, they must

have been preparing another devious tactic. Konrad felt very vulnerable, and slaying the undead was pointless. He wanted to go up, but the walls were far too sheer. There had to be steps leading from some of the passages at the foot of the cavern. He began to investigate.

The third archway led to a spiralling stairway carved from the rock. Cautiously, he climbed. There was still no sign of any skaven. But even if they could not see him, they could smell him...

He reached the next level, paused and listened, then climbed again and kept doing so. At the fourth level he seemed to be at the same height as the tunnel from which he had originally entered the skaven hub. If he ventured all around the ledge within the chamber, he ought to find that tunnel, and also the passage down which he had been dragged.

He did—but before he discovered the latter, Silver Eye was waiting for him. They stared at each other, and this was the first time Konrad had seen the huge skaven in so much light. It was not a silver coin in his eye, he observed, but something that appeared to move like quicksilver: a piece of warpstone. Silver Eye's tongue emerged from beneath his metal fangs, and he licked his scarred jowls.

Konrad shuddered, remembering the rasping touch of the skaven tongue on his cheek. He thrust his sword forward, the ratman brought up his shield, metal clashed on metal—and Konrad gazed in utter astonishment at the emblem on the shield.

The shield was long, triangular, black, with a golden crest. And the crest showed a mailed fist between two crossed arrows. It was the same heraldic device that had been on the bow and arrows that Elyssa had given him!

He was so totally amazed that he was almost gutted by Silver Eye's sudden sword strike. The point of the jagged blade hacked through his chainmail and leather tunic, and he felt blood flow as his skin was sliced. He swung his own sword, raised his guard, and they fought. He was the better fighter, faster, more skilled. The skaven's only advantage was its size, but Konrad could turn that to his own benefit. He knew that he could win the duel and kill Silver Eye. But, as with Gaxar, he did not want to kill him—not yet.

He wanted to question him, to ask where he had got the shield. It was battered and rusty, made of metal instead of layers of tough hide, and it had seen much combat; but had that been while defending the giant rat? Skaven were scavengers, their armour fabricated from various pieces of leather and metal that they had looted from battlefields and corpses. The same must be true of the shield. Silver Eye could only have stolen it somewhere, from someone. But where, from who?

Konrad fought defensively, and the creature pressed its advantage, pushing him back. There was no way that Konrad could talk to him. They were of different races, and Silver Eye could speak only a few human words. Konrad needed the grey rat as translator. His only hope was to capture both skaven, force them to answer him. But even if such impossible circumstances could be satisfied, he knew they would lie.

It was hopeless. He might as well kill Silver Eye now. If nothing else, he could take the shield as his prize.

A skaven voice shouted. It came from behind Silver Eye, who pushed Konrad even harder, his sword thrusting, the black and gold shield pressed against the human's shield, forcing him back towards the edge of the cavern. From the corner of his eye, Konrad glimpsed a figure reaching the top of the stone steps. It was Litzenreich.

Then the other skaven shouted again, and Silver Eye barked a reply. Beyond him was a passage, wider than most but equally as dark. There was a movement in the gloom. The second skaven was coming nearer, emerging from the shadows. It was Gaxar.

The grey seer was not alone. There was a human with

him, a hunched figure, naked and pale. Gaxar held a chain around the human's neck, as a man would leash a hound.

The hostage would not remain so for long, Konrad vowed. The two skaven would die, their captive be liberated.

Gaxar spoke again, and Silver Eye drew back a pace. Konrad lunged towards him, but the blow was deflected by the strange shield.

Litzenreich arrived, standing a few feet from Konrad, and he gazed at Gaxar. The skaven sorcerer stared back at the human magician.

Konrad was distracted for a moment by this, and Silver Eye struck. Konrad stepped back to avoid the sword stroke, but then the skaven pulled his blade away and instead swung his shield. Caught unawares, Konrad was hit on the shoulder and sent flying. He teetered backwards, flinging out his arms for balance, unsure how far he was from the lip of the chasm.

A strong hand caught him in the small of his back, pushing him upright. Ustnar stood behind him.

"Shall we go, boss?" he said to Litzenreich.

In a moment, Gaxar and his prisoner had vanished into the dark, and now Silver Eye was disappearing after them. Konrad started to follow.

"No," said Litzenreich.

Konrad ignored him, taking several steps towards the blackness.

"I know where they are going," the wizard added.

Konrad slowed, reluctant to allow Gaxar to escape. But an impenetrable maze of tunnels must lie ahead, and he had no idea how many skaven lurked within. He had no lantern, he was wounded. If he went on, it would only cost him his life. The price was too high to pay for vengeance—or even justice.

"Where?" he asked.

"Altdorf," Litzenreich told him, then he asked Ustnar:

"Is there anyone else?"

"None of us," said the dwarf.

Konrad walked back, glancing down to the bottom of the huge pit. It was like a mass grave, full of the dead and the again dead, human and skaven and Gaxar's death spawn. There could have been no more than a dozen of the Middenheim troops left alive below.

"Why Altdorf?" he asked.

"That's where the Emperor lives," said Litzenreich.

Konrad waited.

"Did you see who that was?" the wizard added, gesturing in the direction the skaven had fled.

"That was Gaxar," Konrad told him.

"No, not the skaven. The man with them. That was the Emperor..."

Konrad gazed up at what could be seen of the sky. It was grey and very overcast, with heavy dark clouds. Rain threatened and a cold wind blew icy blasts through the tears in his clothing, but to Konrad it was a beautiful day.

This was the first time he had been outside in countless weeks, the first time his horizon had not been the nearest granite wall. And it was the first time he had been free for far longer. He was free of the labyrinth of tunnels within and below Fauschlag, free of the bronze armour, free of Kastring's Khorne worshipping band of bestial marauders.

He stretched out his arms and did not touch stone; he leapt as high as he could; he roared out his appreciation, long and loud, a mixture of unfettered joy and sheer boundless exuberance.

He gazed back at Middenheim, which seemed to grow out of the pinnacle of rock, and he realized that he had never seen the city. He had glimpsed the outside walls and a few streets through the bronze visor, but then he had found himself covered up and carried underground. Until a minute ago, he had been underground ever since.

He had emerged from a cave on the side of a rocky crag some three miles from the city of the white wolf. Seeing the distant point of beckoning daylight growing larger, he had hurried ahead, unwilling to stay a prisoner of the underworld a second longer than necessary.

Hearing a sound behind him, he turned and watched as Litzenreich and Ustnar stepped out into the open and clambered the few yards down to ground level. The dwarf had led them up through a series of tunnels, away from the subterranean battleground. It was hard to judge who had been the victor. Most of the Middenheim troops had been massacred, but they seemed to have accomplished their mission: the skaven had been driven out from their dark domain, for a time at least.

Only one skaven was of any interest to Konrad: Silver Eye, because he carried the shield with the mysterious heraldic device that had fascinated Konrad for so very long. It was over a decade since Elyssa had given him the black bow, the ten matching arrows, the quiver made from rippled hide. The gift was a reward for saving her from a beastman. It was the first such creature he had slain. In the years since, he had destroyed countless mutants of every size and description—all, he now knew, servants of Chaos.

The shield with the golden emblem was the only link Konrad had with his past, of life in his native village. Even if he could not find out anything about the shield, he wanted it. Such an artefact should not be possessed by a skaven.

There had been little chance for conversation during their long and arduous ascent from the skaven city, and now Konrad said: "That was not the Emperor."

"Not the Emperor himself," replied Litzenreich, leaning back against the side of the peak, breathing heavily, "but certainly his double. Gaxar can resurrect corpses, and he can also give them a different appearance."

Konrad knew that. He had been forced to duel with his twin, a creation of Gaxar's. But the Emperor? He found that hard to believe, although Gaxar must have considered his prisoner very important; he had taken none of his other resurrections with him, so perhaps Litzenreich was telling the truth.

"I have seen the Emperor when I was in Altdorf," added the magician.

"You said they must be heading for Altdorf, but why? It's the capital of the Empire; it's where the real Emperor lives. But..?"

"I can think of only one reason why the skaven have constructed a replica of the Emperor: in order to replace him with a duplicate—a creation of Chaos. They have tried something like it before."

It took a while for Konrad to comprehend the enormity of Litzenreich's claim. Finally, he nodded. It sounded extremely cunning and devious, the very tactics that the skaven would adopt.

"How far to Altdorf?" he asked.

"About three hundred miles, as the skaven crawls," said Ustnar, speaking for the first time.

Could there really be an underground route all the way to another rodent city beneath Altdorf? Was that the direction which Gaxar was taking at this very minute?

"I suggest we travel together," said Litzenreich. "We can all be of service to one another."

Konrad did not like the idea of accompanying the magician. Now that he was free, he wanted to be totally free. He had previously resolved to have no more to do with Litzenreich. Nothing had happened to alter his decision.

"I don't plan to go to Altdorf."

"You do. That is why you asked how far it was."

He wondered what the sorcerer considered his motive in making Altdorf his destination. Revenge..?

Konrad shrugged. "I've never been there." He would not tell Litzenreich of the arrows and fist emblem. "Why do you want to go there?"

"I have to begin my researches somewhere new. I have lived in Altdorf previously, and it would be suitable for my purposes. As I know there are skaven below the city, I will have a fresh source of warpstone. And, as I do not believe it would be very beneficial if the Emperor were a skaven puppet, perhaps I can also foil Gaxar's plot..."

That might be the only way in which Konrad could find the grey seer again, he realized. And wherever Gaxar was, Silver Eye would be close—and so would the enigmatic shield.

"Which way?" asked Konrad.

"South-west," said Litzenreich, and he pointed.

"Three hundred miles? How do we get there? We have no money, no horses."

"You forget my chosen profession, Konrad," said Litzenreich. "A dwarf, a warrior, a wizard. We make a fine team. Agreed?"

"Yes, boss," agreed the dwarf.

The warrior nodded, but only repeated half the dwarf's reply.

CHAPTER FOURTEEN

The road between Middenheim and Altdorf was one of the major highways of the Empire, and they travelled upon it by stagecoach. Konrad had never ridden in such a vehicle, and at first he felt sick because the coach was so well-sprung; but by the end of the initial day's journey, he had become used to the swaying motion.

Every evening, he and Litzenreich and Ustnar dined in the coaching inn where the vehicle had halted for the hours of darkness. They would feast on the best food available, then retire to their soft beds. After the first sleepless night, Konrad preferred to sleep on the floor. Each morning, they would break their fast before climbing into the coach once more for the next stage of their journey to the capital.

The wizard proved to be a useful travelling companion, arranging all the details of their journey. The normal procedure, it seemed, was for passengers to pay the innkeeper for each night's hospitality; meals and board were not included in the coach fare. Litzenreich neither paid for the meals, the rooms, nor their passage; but he used his magical talents to convince everyone that he had done so.

Fresh clothing was also acquired for each of them in a similar manner, and Konrad was able to discard his stained battle outfit. He had worn the same garments ever since first venturing into the tunnels which led to the skaven nest. It was a relief to bathe, to change into different clothes; and his wounds and burns gradually healed, the injuries to his right arm much more swiftly.

He could well understand why the wizard had no need for money, not when he could obtain everything he required at no expense. Everything except warpstone...

During the long days that passed, Konrad found himself wondering again about the purpose of his own visit to Altdorf. Having had very little to do except consider his motives for undertaking the journey, his reasons for heading to the city had begun to seem very tenuous. Even if Gaxar and Silver Eye really were making for the capital of the Empire, how could he ever find them and the mysterious shield again? And if he succeeded, then captured and questioned the two skaven, they would never reveal the true history of the shield.

Did he really care about the shield? It was merely an old piece of metal. The only thing that meant anything to him was the gold emblem and what it represented: his past, his life before he left the village. And there was only one part of his early existence which he wished to remember: Elyssa. But he did not need a rusty and dented shield to remind him of the girl, she was always in his memory.

Where had the weapons she gave him come from? Why did Wilhelm Kastring have them? Or some of them. The bow, the quiver and the arrows had been in his keeping. Someone else must have had the shield. And, Konrad realized, there must also have been other weapons and accoutrements bearing the same pattern. There would be a sword with its scabbard, probably a dagger and sheath, and a belt made from the same black rippled hide as the quiver. Could there also be a helmet and breastplate, perhaps even a full suit of armour?

The arrows Elyssa had given Konrad were not the shafts that an ordinary bowman would have carried to war. They were perfect arrows, all identical, each the product of a craftsman. They had belonged to someone of wealth and significance. The very fact that two crossed arrows were part of the heraldic device proved the importance of archery to their owner, while the mailed gauntlet that composed the rest of the emblem would certainly not be worn by a bowman. One possible explanation was that the crest might be the insignia of some prince or warlord, and worn by all those under his command.

Yet Konrad *knew* that the shield and his bow and arrows belonged together, once had the same owner. The feeling was not so absolute as *seeing*, and there was probably no way that it could ever be proved, yet when he had first seen the shield he sensed that it was part of a greater whole. He had tried to hold on to that conviction, although over the days he had lost his initial certainty.

One thing he knew he had definitely lost, however, was his gift of foresight. Perhaps it had been the warpstone that had deprived him of the extra sense. In freeing him from the bronze armour, the substance had restricted him to normal vision. By now, he was sure that the talent had left him, but he had no regrets. In future, he must rely upon his five normal senses like every other human. Or like most humans...

He had allowed Wolf to throw away the black quiver, to drop it in the ashes and dust of the manor house where Elyssa had lived—and died. Looking back, it seemed as though Wolf had been familiar with the emblem, yet for some reason Konrad had never later questioned him on the subject. Neither had he ever asked about the bronze knight, who Wolf said had been his twin brother. Both of these seemed so important now, although they had appeared of little significance at the time. They were matters which belonged to Konrad's past, which he had wanted to forget—yet suddenly they had become a part of his life once more.

What had happened to Wolf? Had he left the frontier and returned to the Empire? Altdorf was his native city, and so perhaps he was back in the capital. A town might suit him for a few days, but he soon became restless with nothing to do. Wherever there was action and danger, that was where Wolf could be found.

After the beastmen had destroyed the mine, they had headed south. There had been relatively few of them, compared to the number of troops that Kislev could muster. But many more marauders could have swept down from the frozen wastes since then. Kastring's brutal band had penetrated deep into the Empire, and his could not have been the only bestial pack that had crossed the border. Was Wolf now fighting on the new frontier?

There was no chance of ever recovering the rippled leather quiver that Wolf had casually cast aside. The bow had snapped years ago, and all the arrows were long gone—the final shaft fired into Skullface's chest, only to be pulled aside and snapped. But not, Konrad remembered, until the bald inhuman had studied the crest.

Skullface had stood in the blazing entrance to the Kastring house, and five years later Konrad had encountered one of the Kastring brothers. When he had asked him about the arrows and fist design, Kastring answered that he thought the heraldic pattern was something to do with an elf—but he could have been lying.

Whether the first owner had been elf or human, the shield should not now be possessed by a skaven. Konrad ought to have it, yet he was aware that the chances of doing so were very slim. Having survived two recent encounters with the giant rodents, he should do his best to avoid all future contact. He had killed enough of the ratmen to settle old scores.

Was Litzenreich serious when he claimed that he intended to stop the skaven from replacing the Emperor with a double? Konrad was all in favour of so doing, but surely all that was necessary was to issue a warning to the imperial bodyguard. It appeared that the wizard personally planned to foil Gaxar's scheme, that they were old enemies.

Konrad was still not convinced that the pathetic figure he had seen deep in the skaven domain had really been an incarnation of the Emperor. Gaxar had fabricated a replica of Konrad from a corpse, using some of his flesh and blood in the necromantic recipe. Would it have been so simple to obtain the necessary ingredients from the Emperor? Konrad only had Litzenreich's word for what Gaxar was planning, and the sorcerer was almost as untrustworthy as the grey seer.

The stories that he told their fellow coach passengers were complete lies; but the more improbable his tales, the more he was believed. Konrad said very little during the journey, and Ustnar contributed even less to the various conversations.

Litzenreich had stood in front of the stagecoach a few miles beyond Middenheim, halting it so that he and his two companions could board. Neither the driver, the two guards, nor the five other passengers ever commented upon this. Even the two who were displaced from their seats within the vehicle and forced to ride outside made no objection. It was apparent that the magician had blocked the event from their minds, just as he was able to persuade all the tavern owners that he had paid for each night's lodgings.

Observing Litzenreich's talent in operation, Konrad wondered if his own will was similarly held in thrall. Had Litzenreich mesmerized him? Was that why he was going to Altdorf? If such was the case, what did the magician want with him?

Konrad resolved that as soon as they reached the capital, he would slip away from Litzenreich. There was no point in doing so now, not when they were so close to the capital. And if he were unable to break free, it would prove that he was indeed under Litzenreich's spell. He wondered, however, if the very fact that he was capable of considering whether his mind had been enslaved meant that it could not have been...

He would soon find out. They spent the night at the Seven Spokes inn, the last stop on the route to the capital. The driver and the two guards were looking more relaxed now that the journey was almost over. Although the coach may have been travelling from one side of the Grand Duchy of Middenland to the other, over roads that were regularly patrolled, even the heart of the Empire was not safe from the Chaos predators.

The capital of Sigmar's Empire had been Reikdorf, which was later renamed Altdorf; but in the two and a half millennia since then, the focus of central government had moved several times. The location of the capital depended upon the balance of power and political alignments amongst the different states that composed the Empire. Now, however, Altdorf was once more the imperial capital and as the stagecoach rounded a curve in the road and finally emerged from the Drakwald Forest, it was revealed to Konrad for the first time.

Surrounded by massive white walls topped with red tiles, the city lay at the confluence of the rivers Reik and Talabec, built upon the islands between these rivers and their tributaries. The Reik was navigable all the way to Marienburg and the Sea of Claws, and the harbour was full of ocean-going vessels as well as river boats. But their tall masts and furled sails were dwarfed by the two great buildings which dominated the city, two of the most magnificent constructions in the known world: the Imperial Palace and the Cathedral to Sigmar.

As the coach passed through the northern gates and entered the capital, Konrad stared at all the buildings, all the people. Excluding his brief sighting of Middenheim, the largest town he had ever seen until now was Praag, but it was as nothing compared to Altdorf. The largest city in the Empire was a place of untold wonders.

The vehicle halted and Konrad was the first to jump out. As he did, he gazed down at the cobbles beneath his feet, wondering if there were another city far below the human capital, a skaven lair deep underground. Then he noticed that the central square was deserted. Or almost deserted: a line of troops encircled the coach. Most of them were halberdiers, clad in red caps, long ochre tunics, red leggings, brown boots. They held their weapons horizontally, pointed at the stagecoach—at Konrad, Litzenreich, Ustnar.

No blades longer than a certain length were permitted to be worn within the city walls, except by the military, and Konrad's sword was wrapped up in a bundle. He cast aside the material, gripping his weapon by the hilt. He no longer had a shield, having abandoned it during the ascent from the skaven warren. Ustnar was clutching his axe. Konrad glanced at Litzenreich, expecting him to use his powers to reduce the odds to more favourable proportions. But the wizard studied the array of troops, and his attention focused on the only two figures amongst them who were not clad in uniform. Altdorf had its own wizards. Litzenreich shrugged. Taking this as a signal, Ustnar lowered his weapon.

The halberdiers advanced, closing up around the coach. Konrad knew it was hopeless, although that had never stopped him before.

"It's them we want," said a voice. "Not you."

Turning, Konrad looked at the soldier who had spoken.

He was a sergeant, thick set, clad in a brass helmet which was topped by a cobalt plume, wearing a scarlet uniform and polished brass armour. His breastplate was embossed with a twin-tailed comet, one of the insignia of Sigmar. His sword hung at his hip; amongst so many armed men, he had no need to draw his weapon.

Konrad wondered how many of the Altdorf soldiers he could kill before they could overpower him, but he lowered his blade.

There were various ways that a message from Middenheim could have arrived in Altdorf before the travellers had done. The authorities in the city of the white wolf could have sent couriers to neighbouring towns, or used the Empire's network of semaphore towers to deliver a warning of the fugitives. Signals must have gone out to every town and city, because there could have been no way of knowing which direction Litzenreich had taken. The wizard had most likely been identified at one of the coaching inns, and a message forwarded to the capital.

Unable to find Litzenreich's corpse, the survivors from the attack on the skaven lair would have known that the wizard had escaped. The signal sent from Middenheim must have been to arrest him and any dwarfs in his company. It was known that the dwarfs assisted Litzenreich with his warpstone experiments. There had been no warrant issued for Konrad. No one in Middenheim was aware of his existence, no one still alive.

Litzenreich and Ustnar were chained and manacled, loaded into a cart and driven away. The sergeant and two other troopers escorted Konrad away from Konigplatz and through the crowded city. Once it had been wrapped again, he was allowed to carry his own sword. He was not a prisoner, but it was clear that neither was he a free man, and he tried not march in step with his escort.

Although concerned about where he was being taken, but determined not to ask, Konrad was overwhelmed by the sight of the city's two great buildings that lay ahead of him. Alone, they would have been very impressive. Together, they were absolutely spectacular, each so different in shape and construction yet perfectly complementing the other.

Sigmar's Cathedral stood to the left, its huge central gilded cupola gleaming in the early winter sunlight. Close by was the Imperial Palace, its pinnacle built from granite blocks brought back from Black Fire Pass, the scene of Sigmar's greatest triumph. The apex of each imposing edifice was exactly the same height, so that neither could be said to dominate the other.

Altdorf was Sigmar's city, and tribute was paid to him throughout the capital. The palace spire was topped by a huge replica of Ghal-maraz, the immortal hero's great warhammer. The massive cupola of the cathedral was etched with a pattern of eight-pointed stars, symbolic of the eight divided human tribes that Sigmar had united as one.

The long shadow of the palace blocked out the low sun as Konrad was led into the courtyard below, through a doorway into a building that formed part of the defensive walls. He found himself in a guardhouse, and a number of troops sat near the fire which blazed in the hearth. They talked and laughed together, paying little attention as Konrad and his escort entered. The other two soldiers shrugged out of their armour and joined their comrades.

"Sit down," said the sergeant, as he took a seat on one side of a roughly hewn table. He removed his helmet and set it down in front of him. He was a grey-haired veteran, and the wounds on his face were true battle scars. "Let's take a proper look at that sword."

Konrad sat down opposite, laid his blade on the table, then unwrapped it. The sergeant studied the wolf's head embossed on the guard.

"Those other two," he said, "have broken imperial law.

David Ferring

You, however, seem to have broken Middenheim law. It appears that you've stolen a sword."

It was evident that he recognized the weapon as belonging to a Middenheim regiment, and the imperial law to which he was referring must have been the one about using warpstone. Perhaps, however, the sergeant did not know the precise nature of Litzenreich's crime. He may never have heard of warpstone. Konrad had only recently learned of the substance.

"I bought it off that dwarf," Konrad said, "the one you arrested. He and his companion were dangerous criminals? They broke imperial law? I thought there was something suspicious about them. I lost my previous sword when a beastman ran off with it; it was wedged in the thing's skull."

The sergeant nodded slowly. He seemed amused. "Possession, they say, is nine-tenths of the law. Possession of a stolen weapon is therefore nine-tenths as bad as having stolen it."

"It's a Middenheim sword. You said it came under Middenheim law. What does it have to do with Altdorf?"

"We like to oblige our allies. The sword will be returned to them, but the question is: do we also return you?"

"What for? I bought it from the dwarf, ask him."

Konrad had no doubt that they would not ask Ustnar about the blade. Wherever he and Litzenreich were, there would be far more important questions for them to answer. Altdorf had a reputation for the excellence of its judicial system. During their interrogation, the two prisoners would be tortured less than anywhere else in the Empire. There would also be a trial before they were executed.

He did not expect that the sergeant would really believe his story about the sword, but the most important thing was that he should not think there was any connection between Konrad and Litzenreich. So far as Altdorf was concerned, it was chance that he and the sorcerer had been on board the same stagecoach.

"Evidence from a criminal is no evidence," said the sergeant. "And if I send the sword back, there'll be so many queries, so much paperwork."

"Then don't send it back."

"No, we must do that. If they found an imperial guard sword in Middenheim, I would hope they would return it to us. If you went back with the sword, you could answer all their questions personally. That would seem to be the most prudent course of action. What do you say?"

Konrad said nothing. If he were sent back to Middenheim, even under armed escort, he had no doubt that he could escape before ever reaching the city. But he did not wish to leave Altdorf, not yet.

The sergeant was watching him strangely, and he kept smiling. It seemed that he was not taking the interrogation very seriously, and Konrad did not understand the joke.

"If," the sergeant added, after a while, "this sword had happened to come into the possession of, say, an imperial guard, then naturally he would be above suspicion."

Konrad finally understood, but he said nothing.

"It's a good job, good hours, good—" the sergeant slapped a golden crown on the table— "pay."

"The imperial guard?" said Konrad, and he studied the soldier's immaculate uniform: the polished brass, the plumed helmet, the pearl buttons, the decorative braid, the elaborate insignia. "I don't know if I want to be a toy soldier—marching up and down, standing in a sentry box, holding a flag instead of a sword, all neat and tidy like some ornament."

"We are not toy soldiers, Konrad! We are the Empire's best, the Emperor's loyal bodyguard!"

Konrad stared at him, wondering how he knew his name.

"I was in Praag that winter," came the unbidden answer. "Remember? My name is Taungar."

Konrad nodded. He remembered Praag. How could he forget that siege? But there was no reason why he should have recognized an Altdorf sergeant, although Taungar knew him.

"Whatever your reason for coming here," Taungar said, "you can't do better than enlist in the guard. It's the best opportunity for any fighting man. And I mean 'fighting'—not marching, not parading. I know you're the kind of man we need."

"Or..?"

Taungar shrugged and looked at the sword with the wolf emblem.

"Do I get another sword?"

"We've discovered that guards can perform their functions best if they are armed." Taungar reached behind him, taking down a belt and scabbarded blade from a peg on the wall. He put it on the table, next to the Middenheim sword, next to the gold coin.

Konrad drew the blade from its oiled sheath, gripping it by the handle of white bone. The guard was embossed with the imperial crown. He glanced at the crown on the sword, the golden crown on the table, and he picked up the latter with his left hand.

"You've accepted the Emperor's coin, Konrad. Now you must swear allegiance. Stand up."

Konrad did so, and he pledged the oath of blood loyalty, swearing by Sigmar that he would faithfully and obediently serve the Emperor, laying down his life if necessary in the service of the Empire.

"Welcome," said Taungar, offering his hand.

Konrad transferred the sword to his left hand, held out his right. The two men gripped each other's wrists.

There had been many questions in Konrad's mind, but he did not ask them. He would soon be able to discover what he needed to know. For the rest, he did not intend to stay around long enough to require the answers.

Konrad's hair was cropped so that it did not hang below his helmet. He also had to shave, for the first time since leaving Kislev, because only officers were permitted beards. Then he was fitted out with his uniform. The outfit was the same for every infantryman, whether a raw recruit or senior officer. The only difference was in the colour of the long helmet plume. The higher the rank, the deeper the blue, from aquamarine through to indigo.

There was no need for to Konrad stand in one of the imperial sentry posts. Taungar had plenty of identical troops to do that. But even ornamental sentries had to learn more than parade drill and standing straight and immobile, and Konrad was enlisted as a combat instructor. That did not mean he was able to avoid his share of dressing up, of polishing armour so that he could see his face—his scarred face—in the burnished brass. And, as always whenever he saw his reflection, he remembered the first time he had seen his own image, in Elyssa's mirror.

He almost became used to wearing clean outfits, of hearing his boot heels click on the marble floors of the palace. There was something very reassuring in being one of so many others, all doing precisely the same task, of having regular hours and knowing exactly when he would next be able to eat, to rest, to sleep. There was no need to think, because everything was so organized; all he needed to do was react.

Even his own training sessions had a regular routine, although during those hours Konrad tried to introduce the unexpected. It was the only time when he was on duty and out of dress uniform, as were the trainees. Combat practice was dirty and sweaty, and uniforms could never be allowed to become soiled either on the outside or the inside.

It was not only others that Konrad trained. He had encountered most kinds of weapons during his career on the frontier, but there was always something else to be found, and the armoury provided a different armament with which to practice.

On a few occasions, Konrad went into the palace to serve as a member of the honour guard when the imperial banners were furled and unfurled at dusk and dawn. From the ramparts, two hundred feet above the ground, the entire city, the roads, the docks, the rivers, the canal to Weissbruck, the surrounding forests, nearby villages, distant mountains, were all clearly visible. Even higher up, from the observation turret in the spire, the view would be even more extensive—which was why there were always guards on duty up there.

Everything within the building was on as large a scale as the exterior. Halls were vast, doors enormous, stairways and corridors wider than roads, ceilings as high as most other buildings. It was as if the palace had been built for giants.

The statues of all the previous Emperors were three times life size, their titanic figures lining the first hallway from the steps beyond the main entrance. Further within, different chambers were dedicated to each successive ruler. The history of their reign was chronicled by separate paintings commemorating each significant event, making up a frieze which encircled the entire room. Above this would be richly embroidered tapestries depicting the Emperor in triumph, upon his coronation, showing him as a great warrior, hunting the most ferocious of creatures, achieving famous victories. From what Konrad had read in Litzenreich's volumes, the majority these magnificent works owed more to their artists' exaggerated imaginations than to the annals of history.

Every hall contained effigies of each Emperor defeating hordes of hideous beastmen in single combat, fighting duels with deadly rivals, and held trophies of every kind from all across the Empire, from the known world—and the unknown: golden ornaments and jewelled treasures, bizarre animals, strange weapons, relics of forgotten wars and campaigns. Many of these objects had disintegrated over the centuries and were no longer recognizable. Some were little more than piles of dust, although still venerated by their very antiquity.

In the centre of each room, resting on a simple stone plinth and illuminated by the natural light shining through the circular stained glass windows in each ceiling, was all that remained of each Emperor. There were coffins of base metal and of gold, of granite and of marble. There were even glass sarcophagi in which gilded skeletons were visible. Many pedestals were empty, because those Emperors had reigned when the capital had not been in Altdorf, and they were buried elsewhere. The very last plinth was also almost empty, because no one knew Sigmar's final resting place. According to legend, at the end of his days the founder of the Empire had ridden alone into the Dwarven realms, to return Ghal-maraz to its original owners. No human ever saw him again.

The only known relic of Sigmar's reign lay upon a black velvet cushion in this position of honour: the ivory handle of the dagger he had carried at the Battle of Black Fire Pass. The blade of the knife had rusted away over the millennia.

By each pillar, every hour of the day and night, stood a member of the imperial guard. They were not merely the Emperor's bodyguard, they were literally the guards of every Emperor's body. Konrad seldom saw anyone within the palace except for these guards. The building was so large it could have hidden a whole army. Occasionally, he would glimpse a liveried servant going about his duties.

One reason why it may have been so quiet and empty within the imperial palace was that the Emperor was absent. It took a week for Konrad to discover this. The Emperor, his retinue and most of his guards were on a state visit to Talabheim. He had sailed in the imperial yacht, voyaging some three hundred miles east up the River

Talabec.

Konrad wondered if Gaxar had somehow known this, and, instead of making Altdorf his destination, had taken the underground skaven route to the city state.

Twelve days had passed since Konrad had arrived in the capital, and he had done much in the course of that time. But twelve days was a very brief span in the legal calendar, and he knew that Litzenreich and Ustnar were still languishing in a cell beneath the Altdorf barracks.

They had been arrested under imperial law, but they were being held by the city militia. The Altdorf army and the Emperor's guard were two distinct forces, very jealous of their responsibilities. The city's standing army was recruited mainly from the capital itself, although inhabitants of the nearby villages in Reikland were also eligible to enlist; but the imperial guard was comprised of troops from every province and city state in the Empire, including Altdorf itself.

Technically, because Litzenreich and Ustnar were accused of breaking imperial law, they had been arrested by the imperial forces. This was why Taungar and a few of his men had been amongst the troops waiting for the stagecoach to arrive. The fugitives, however, had been taken into custody by the city militia.

Having discovered the whereabouts of the captives it was time for Konrad to get them out of there. He owed them that much. Had it been only Litzenreich, he may have left him to his fate; he had already done more than enough for the wizard. Ustnar and the other three dwarfs, however, had saved him from the skaven cave. The others were dead, but Konrad could now repay his debt to the surviving dwarf.

It was dusk when he went off duty, and he walked straight out of the main gateway of the fort. The sentries watched him go, assuming he had permission to leave. He headed north, across the wide bridge over which he had arrived, each parapet of which was lined with painted statues of warriors and gods and mythical creatures, and made for the army quarters. The days were growing shorter as winter began to bite, and he was glad of the warmth afforded by his long cloak.

He entered a dark and narrow alley, where he removed his brass helmet. When he emerged a few seconds later, a purple plume hung from the helmet. Konrad had become an officer in the imperial guard.

CHAPTER FIFTEEN

The first sentries looked on idly as Konrad strode confidently past them into the courtyard. He made his way to the guardhouse, which he knew was directly ahead.

"I want to see the officer of the watch," he told the soldier who stood by the entrance.

"Officer!" yelled the guard. "Stranger at the gate!"

Konrad waited, and a few seconds later an officer stepped out into the evening, buckling on his sword belt. He looked at Konrad and pulled himself up to his full height, clicking his heels together and saluting crisply. Konrad returned the salute, although more casually. The imperial guard considered themselves superior to the Altdorf army; but although he was of apparently equal rank, Konrad had no authority here.

"What can I do for you?" asked the officer. "The imperial guard run out of polish?"

"I have a warrant here," said Konrad, pulling a parchment from his tunic, "requesting that I am granted admission to see one of your prisoners, a dwarf you are holding in custody under imperial edict."

He unrolled the parchment, which was stamped with an impressive official seal. He hoped that the officer could not read, because it was the quartermaster's inventory for the imperial garrison's armament store.

"You do hold such a prisoner?" he asked.

The officer appeared to study the document and he nodded. "Yes. But what's this about?"

"It's on another matter, not the reason he is being held. The dwarf is believed to have stolen a sword from one of the Middenheim regiments."

"I heard something about a sword."

He gazed at Konrad's face, but Konrad knew how different he must look without the beard and in imperial uniform. Only imperial officers were permitted beards, but that did not mean they were compulsory. Word of the stolen sword must have spread from the guards to the army. The two forces were rivals, but a few individual soldiers were friends.

"We have to make sure that the blade is returned."

"Of course," agreed the officer.

"I need to question the prisoner about how the weapon came into his possession."

"We can do that."

"Fine. I'll leave you to make a full transcription of the interrogation, with copies for myself and for the Middenheim authorities. You'll also have to handle every other detail, all the documentation, arrange to have the sword transported to Middenheim, a full acknowledgement of receipt. Is that all right by you?"

"Er..."

"You know what these things are like. The more simple something seems, the more complex it really is."

The officer glanced up at the sky, as if seeking inspiration in the heavens. "How long will it take?" he asked.

Konrad punched his right fist into his left gauntlet. "Not long," he said.

The officer grinned. "I'll need to be with you. He's my responsibility."

"Of course."

"And I don't want any visible marks left on him."

He led Konrad into the brick building, picked up a huge bunch of keys and called for another guard to accompany them.

The guard carried a lantern in one hand, the keys in the other, and he led the way through a series of narrow passages. The brick walls became stone as they began to descend, passing through several heavy doors all of which were locked behind them. There was a guard at each door.

The sequence of doors reminded Konrad of Litzenreich's domain. Once again he was underground, deep below the surface. This time the tunnels were wide and high; this time there were steps cut into the rock, worn away by the footsteps of countless generations of warders; and this time his destination was not miles away.

He would not be able to talk himself back through the guards and the doors, but he did not intend to return this way.

The warder opened each door in turn, and the officer followed Konrad. They had passed many other doors, doors recessed into the tunnels, doors with barred windows. It seemed that the most important prisoners were kept on the lowest level, as Konrad had hoped.

Another door was unlocked and pulled open—and the guard on the other side fell through the doorway. Konrad drew his sword, hearing the officer do the same. The warder knelt over the dead man. Konrad also bent down. There was no mark on the body. It was still warm; he had died not long ago.

"Are they here?" asked Konrad.

"Those two doors at the end."

Konrad advanced into the shadows, and the officer followed. Another heavy door blocked off the tunnel, but there were two more doors before it, one on either side of the passage. They were both closed—and they were both locked. He peered in through the bars of the first door, lowering his voice so that the officer could not hear what he said.

"Litzenreich?" he whispered. "Ustnar?"

There was no response from either of the cells.

"Keys!" shouted the officer, and the guard hurried forward. "Open the door!" The guard did so. "Inside!"

Drawing his own blade, holding the lantern in front of him, the guard stepped into the first cell. Konrad and the officer also entered. The place was empty. So was the one opposite.

"They can't have got out that way," said Konrad, gesturing in the direction of the corpse. "They must have gone through here." He pointed with his sword towards the end door.

"How did they get out of the cells?" asked the officer, his voice low. "How did they kill that soldier?"

"I don't know. I don't care. But get that door open, before they have more time to escape."

"We can't go through there."

"Why not?"

"It's locked. We don't have a key. It's never been opened while I've served here."

So far, the subterranean jail had been as Konrad expected. He had learned of it from one of the imperial guard who knew the layout from a warder. It had been Konrad's intention to get this far, dispose of his escort, break Ustnar and Litzenreich out of their cells, then let the wizard open this final door. But it seemed that Litzenreich had already used his abilities to free himself, annulling the spell that the Altdorf sorcerers would have cast in an attempt to make their prisoner's cell resistant to his magic.

Konrad pushed at the heavy door the officer claimed had never been opened, and it creaked on its rusty hinges, swinging back. It was a much thicker door than the others, far older, its ancient wood held together by heavy bands of metal. He looked at the officer, who nodded and took the lantern from the guard.

"We're going through," said the officer. "Bring as many men as you can, and as fast as you can. Send out a warning to block off all the sewer exits."

The warder turned and ran back, the keys jingling as he vanished in the gloom, while Konrad peered ahead. The tunnel continued as far as could be seen in the flickering lantern light, but it became narrower, steeper.

"There's an underground river somewhere," said the Altdorf officer. "The sewers and drains empty into it, and then it joins up with the Reik downstream, beyond the city walls."

Konrad knew this, and the subterranean stream had been his proposed escape route. Had the wizard and the dwarf headed this way? They must have done; there was nowhere else they could have gone.

The officer entered the passage, and Konrad followed. It was cold and damp within, and the lamplight seemed to be absorbed by the absolute blackness. They advanced cautiously, the sound of their boots echoing in the silence. After a time, Konrad noticed that they were no longer descending. The tunnel had become level. He felt a breath of air on his face. Somewhere ahead of them, there must have been a route to the open.

Not only that, but there was a distant glimmer of light and some kind of sound...

Konrad had expected to hear the rush of water across rocks as the hidden river cascaded beneath the city. But it was not that kind of natural sound; it seemed unlike any natural sound. He shivered, and not because he was cold.

The officer paused and glanced back. "What is it?" he breathed.

Konrad shook his head. He removed his gauntlets, tucking them into his belt.

"I don't like it," whispered the officer. "Maybe we should wait for reinforcements."

Konrad said nothing, but he tried to push past the officer; the officer began moving again, keeping ahead of him. As they continued, the light ahead grew brighter, the noises louder. It was some kind of animal sound, almost like babies crying, hundreds and hundreds of them, whining and screaming in their hungry infant voices.

But the sounds were not human, Konrad knew. His mouth was dry, but his body soaked in sweat, and he gripped his sword with a clammy hand.

The officer suddenly halted, and Konrad almost bumped into him. He was staring straight ahead, gazing into the cavern which had opened up ahead of them. Konrad also stopped, watching the bizarre tableau with which they were confronted. The chamber was hung with stalactites speckled with phosphorescence, its spectral light illuminating the whole hideous scene.

"Konrad!" hissed a familiar voice. "We've been waiting for you."

It was Gaxar, but the skaven had taken on his human form, and he stood only a dozen yards from the end of the shaft. The cave was much smaller than the area where he had refined warpstone; a natural grotto, its walls and floor uneven, the river flowing through a channel at its centre.

Litzenreich and Ustnar lay stretched out on the ground. They were naked and had been crucified, their ankles and palms nailed to the rock

But those were not their only wounds: their bodies had been lacerated, and rivulets of red coursed over their tortured bodies. They had been gagged so they could not scream.

There was a space between them, Konrad realized—a space waiting for him, with four heavy nails lying on the rocks, ready for his impalement.

All around the two prone figures crowded more naked shapes, small, sexless, humanoid, hairless. They were almost like the babies that Konrad had imagined he could hear crying—but they resembled infants in no other way.

There were scores of them, with massive deformed skulls, huge pink eyes, their bodies white like maggots. They were some breed of troglodyte beastmen, with long tongues, sharp fangs, bloated torsos, stunted tails, scaled skin, three claws at the end of each limb. They pushed and grabbed at each other in their eagerness to lap at the blood from the wizard's and the dwarf's wounds. It was they who made the awful wailing sound, the sound of craving for living flesh.

It seemed their helpless victims' weeping wounds were caused by teeth bites. The creatures had already begun their feral feast.

Silver Eye was there, standing close to Gaxar, the metal shield with its enigmatic golden emblem held in front of him. He thrust his tongue from his jaws, and Konrad remembered the skaven kiss when the rodent had lapped at his blood. A few other creatures were also present, but Konrad could not make them out properly. They stood on a high ledge on the far side of the cavern, like spectators waiting to be entertained.

Konrad noticed all this in less than a second—the same second in which he transferred his sword to his left hand, while his right reached behind his back for the holster hidden beneath his cloak, from which he pulled his new weapon, aimed, fired.

The device was a one-handed crossbow, a precision tooled mechanism of brass wheels and steel cogs. The six inch bolt had already been in place, the taut wire drawn back. It was the armament Konrad had been practising with for the past week.

Gaxar may have been a grey seer, but he was not swift enough to save himself. The projectile took him in the right eye, jerking him back. He tried to clutch at the missile with his right hand—but he had no right hand. Without a sound, he slowly collapsed and became still.

There was a terrible anguished scream, a howl so chilling that Konrad froze for a moment. The cry came from Silver Eye, a cry of despair that his master was dead. The ratman rushed towards Konrad, but the Altdorf officer intercepted him. Their swords rang as they fought.

Konrad cast the bow aside and leapt forward, his sword swinging at the first of the pygmy predators who rushed at him. Its head was lopped off and keep screeching as it flew across the chamber.

Konrad slew more of the ugly pale things as they swarmed through the cavern. They sprang at him from rocks, clawing at his face. Others tugged at his legs, tearing at his flesh, trying to bring him down by sheer weight of numbers. He kicked them aside, pulled them off, stabbed at them, sliced them, squashed them underfoot. The noise they made as they died was more horrendous than the sounds of their feeding.

He reached Litzenreich, and leaned down, tearing the gag away from his mouth. While he was distracted, a few of the shrunken mutants leapt on him, and this time he almost lost his footing. Once he was down on their level, he would stand no chance against so many.

"Magic!" he yelled. "A spell!"

"Free my hand," he heard the wizard say, weakly.

Konrad threw his painful burdens aside. His sword whirled through the air. Several corrupted heads were severed, spraying blood everywhere. He leaned down again, vainly trying to drag the nail from the magician's right hand with his fingers.

"Pull the hand, pull the hand!"

Konrad obeyed—and splinters of shattered bone and shreds of gory flesh from Litzenreich's palm remained attached to the nail as his hand came up. The wizard screamed, then threw out his right arm, the scream lowering in pitch and becoming transformed into a spell. A bolt of lighting flashed from his blood-stained index finger.

His chant was answered by a demented shriek as the first of his torturers erupted in a ball of incandescence. Then another monstrosity began to burn, and another, and the cave filled with the stench of roasting flesh.

Slaying several more of the hunched troglodytes as he did so, Konrad moved across to where Ustnar lay. He slid his blade below the head of one of the wrist nails, rested the sword point on the ground, and levered the nail free. Ustnar reached up and grabbed one of his assailants by the neck, crushing its throat, while Konrad freed his other hand.

There were fewer of the misbegotten brutes now, fewer of them still alive, yet they still attacked with the same maniacal fury. By the time Konrad was releasing Ustnar's second ankle, Litzenreich was on his feet, having freed himself. Konrad's sword snapped in two as the final nail slid from the rock.

He glanced around. The Altdorf officer was down, and from the twisted angle of his body he must have been dead. There was no sign of Silver Eye, nor of Gaxar. The skaven must have escaped and taken his master's human corpse with him. The figures on the ledge beyond the stream seemed to have gone. All the pygmy deformities were now dead or dying in flames, victim's of Litzenreich's incendiary revenge, and the air stank of charred flesh.

Konrad and Litzenreich and Ustnar stood and looked at each other, blood dripping from all of their wounds. They were alone within an arena of death and destruction. The only sound was their own heavy breathing and the infantile wailing of the fatally maimed blood beasts.

But then there came another noise, from deep within one of the tunnels that led off from the chamber. It was a noise that Konrad could not fail to recognize: the distant warcries of Chaos marauders. These beastmen would not be undersized, they would not be unarmed, and there would be more of them than could be counted.

"The river!" ordered Konrad. "It's our only chance of getting out!"

They hurried to the edge of the river. In appearance, it was like any other swift stream, its foam-flecked waters rushing through a channel worn away in the rock. It vanished into a low arch at the edge of the cavern.

"I hate water!" said Ustnar—and he jumped in.

He vanished beneath the surface, then reappeared after a few seconds, already halfway out of the chamber. Litzenreich seemed hesitant, and so Konrad shouldered him. The wizard dropped, splashing under the water, bobbing up again before disappearing down the tunnel.

Konrad threw his helmet aside, tore his cloak free, pulled his cuirass off, kicked his first boot away, started to remove his second, but there was no time. He caught a glimpse of gleaming red eyes approaching through one of the passages, then another pair, and another. That was enough. He sprang into the cold river, staying beneath the surface as he allowed the fast flow to carry him towards the tunnel.

A second before he was swept into the culvert, his head broke the surface, and he gazed up. There were still two figures on the ledge above. He could see them properly now.

And the first of them was Skullface!

There could be no mistake this time. Even after five years, he could remember the creature as clearly as if it were yesterday. The same thin body, the same bald head which seemed to have no flesh on the bone.

By his side stood someone else Konrad had not seen for

half a decade, someone else who he could never forget, although for different reasons. She was older now, but she was instantly recognizable.

For a brief moment their eyes met, his green and gold, hers jet black.

Elyssa...

KONRAD

by David Ferring

The beginning of Konrad's epic quest across the Chaos-haunted Warhammer world.

The Beastman was not much taller than Konrad, but it seemed far bigger because of its width. Covered in thick reddish fur, it was also clad in pieces of rusty armour which were worn seemingly at random, and around its fat belly was a belt from which hung a variety of knives, saws, cleavers – the tools of a butcher.

They both froze, staring at each other. The moment stretched into eternity, then the being rapidly raised its right arm, in which it held a massive axe. It roared out a blood-curdling war cry and hurtled towards Konrad.

His home destroyed, his true love slain by daemonic forces, Konrad sets out on a perilous quest for vengeance and the secret of his destiny; a quest that will take him to the dark edge of the world where Chaos waits.

Konrad's search for the secret of his destiny is concluded in
WARBLADE.

WARBLADE

by David Ferring

*Concluding the epic quest begun in KONRAD
and SHADOWBREED*

*"Konrad!" hissed the skaven. "We've been waiting for
you..."*

Gaxar had adopted his human guise, and he stood in the cave into
which the narrow tunnel opened. The cavern was illuminated by
phosphorescence from the subterranean rocks, a ghostly light
which cast no shadows.

Konrad and the Altdorf officer gazed at the terrible scene which
confronted them.

Litzenreich and Ustnar were nailed by their hands and feet to the
ground, their limbs outspread ... They writhed in agony, but were
unable to voice their pain because they had been gagged.

Human and dwarf lay eight feet apart. Between them was room for
another crucifixion, and four iron nails marked where the third
victim's palms and ankles would be hammered to the rock – and
Konrad was the intended sacrifice ...

DRACHENFELS
by Jack Yeovil

Above them, the fortress of Drachenfels stood against the crimson sky, its seven turrets thrust skyward like the taloned fingers of a deformed hand.

This was where their adventure would end, in a fortress older than the Empire, and darker than Death. The lair of the Great Enchanter – Drachenfels.

With the help of Genevieve the vampire, Detlef Sierck, greatest playwright and impresario in the Warhammer world, attempts to recreate on stage the death of Drachenfels, the Great Enchanter. But the dead do not sleep so easily...

Other Boxtree books in association with Games Workshop:

*In the war-torn universe of the 41st millennium, all is whelmed in
darkness, and the Emperor is the only light . . .*

WARHAMMER®
40,000

INQUISITOR
BY
IAN WATSON

SPACE MARINE
BY
IAN WATSON